AN EXPLICIT NATURE

VIVIAN MASON-HUNT

Ladera House
PUBLISHING

AN EXPLICIT NATURE
ISBN: 979-8-9871712-1-9
© 2022 Vivian Mason-Hunt

Disclaimer

This book is a work of fiction. The names, characters and incidents are the products of the author's imagination, and are not to be construed as real. While the author was inspired in part by actual events, none of the characters in the book are based on an actual person. Any resemblance to persons living or dead is entirely coincidental and unintentional.

® and ™ are trademarks owned and used by the trademark owner and/or its licensee. Trademarks indicated with ® are registered in the United States Patent and Trademark Office, the Canadian Trade Marks Office and/or other countries.

www.laderahousepublishing.com
Cover Designed by Amir Nebic
Printed in U.S.A.

To my dad, Kenneth,
Thanks for encouraging me to explore my hidden talent.
Apparently, you were right.

AN EXPLICIT NATURE

One
basic truth
can be used as
a foundation for a
mountain of lies, and if
we dig down deep enough
in the mountain of lies, and bring
out that truth, to set it on top of the
mountain of lies; the entire mountain of
lies will crumble under the weight of that one
truth, and there is nothing more devastating to a
structure of lies than the revelation of the truth upon
which the structure of lies was built, because the shock waves of
the revelation of the truth reverberate, and continue to reverberate
throughout the earth for generations to follow, awakening even those
people who had no desire to be awakened to the truth—Delamer Duverus

.

ACKNOWLEDGEMENTS

It wasn't until I made a serious effort to head out on this journey of creative writing that I realized that writing a book is a team effort. Now that I have achieved my goal, I'd like to thank those of you who were instrumental in helping me get there.

First and foremost, I must give thanks to my Heavenly Father who, for so many years, has been gently nudging me to write, not just this book, but any book. Thank you for anointing me with the blessing of the gift and the courage with which to share it.

To my husband Charles, thanks to you for putting up with my countless endeavors. It's been a true test of wills on your part, but you've passed with flying colors.

My heartfelt thanks to you, Mom, for your enduring love and your unyielding support of everything I do. I appreciate so greatly your insistence that I maintain a pure and giving heart in a world where cold, hardened hearts surround us. You are the force that grounds me.

Dad, you are my inspiration for testing my writing skills. If not for your urging, this book probably never would've been conceived. Thank you for having the foresight to be able to see in me the God-given talent that I, otherwise, may never have seen in myself. Maybe someday we will write that book together.

Brandon and Tianne, my dear children, you both are the pride of my life, and as your mother I will continually strive to make you as proud of me as I am of you.

My cherished friend Synthia Lewis-Lee, thanks for taking part in following my progress by reading and providing feedback at the beginning of this journey. You don't have any idea how vital a role you played in making this book possible.

Maria Gonzalez-Pitchford, my dear friend and most unique person

I know. Your creativity and imagination helped to inspire me to investigate my creative inner-person. I now understand, because of you, the power of creative energy.

To another dear friend who wishes to remain nameless, you know who you are. Despite your request to remain in the shadows, there was no way that I could allow you to go unrecognized. I can't thank you enough for your willingness to take time out of your busy schedule to show some interest in something that means so very much to me. I've always had nothing but the highest regard for you, but I have even greater respect for you now for being so selfless as to not want any credit for your greatly appreciated contribution to the making of this book.

Pamela Samuels-Young, as a successful attorney and published author several times over I can't tell you how valuable your willingness to share with me your recipe for success has been. In light of the fact that I've only recently met you, you've taught me that in this business there are hard lessons to be learned. Despite that, I've learned that it's the most unlikely sources that God places in our lives at specific times that are the most gracious, the most encouraging, the most supportive and the most caring enough to want to see others succeed at reaching their goals. I'm one of your biggest fans and you can always count on me and my big mouth to spread the word about your next novel.

Clearly, it takes a village to get a book from concept to published; therefore, I want to thank you all, and I pray that God continues to shed his grace upon you.

PROLOGUE

The sun's rays filtered through a wooded stretch just west of the Garden State Parkway in the Pine Barrens of South Jersey. Her 600-horsepower sports car handled the hairpin curves like a champ. She couldn't have chosen a more perfect day for a one and a half hour drive down a scenic country road.

The engine revved as she pressed down harder on the accelerator in anticipation of a steep uphill climb. Earth, Wind, and Fire's *"That's the Way of the World"* bellowed through the speakers of the car's state-of-the-art sound system.

It was three o'clock and her girlfriend Tracy and her husband Darryl were having a backyard barbecue. It would be a long-anticipated house-warming to christen their lovely new home. Although she was already an hour late, she wouldn't miss the celebration for anything in the world.

Her husband was supposed to go with her, but the argument they had the night before carried over into the morning. Rather than talk things over, he simply left the house in a huff, giving her no indication when he would return. As a result, she simply left without him.

On the drive to Tracy and Darryl's she thought it curious that hers was the only car on the road. It was strange for a Saturday afternoon. Although it was a rural area, several new residential subdivisions and commercial developments had gone up over the past five to seven years. Certainly, with the increased population there should've been more traffic.

As her car reached the crest of the steep hill, she noticed, in the distance, a large tree limb had fallen, making passage impossible. The closer she came to the fallen limb, she realized that she had no other option but to find another route.

A dirt road off to the right ran through a cluster of trees, but unsure if that would take her back to a main road, she slowed down to look for a detour. As though fewer decibels would somehow sharpen her judgment, she turned the volume down on her car stereo.

With no other visible detour, she turned down the dirt road. She was forced to close her windows and sunroof to keep from breathing in the billowing clouds of dust that formed due to driving off-road. As she drove further, the landscape became more and more wooded and the sun barely permeated the dense foliage.

Up ahead, there was something red in the brush. She could hardly make it out, but it looked like a car. As she came closer, she saw that it was most certainly a car. Slowly, she approached and shifted the gear selector into park and let down the passenger side window to ask the driver if they needed her help. She could barely see inside, as the car's windows were tinted very dark, however, there did appear to be two occupants inside. The driver seemed to be a woman and it looked as though the passenger was a male.

She sat parallel with the car for a moment, but the occupants would neither let down the window nor get out of the car. Getting an eerie feeling about the situation, she put her car back in drive and slowly began to pull off.

As she pulled away, she looked in her rearview mirror and noticed the red sports car backing out of the brush. Still, she thought it strange that the occupants didn't even as much as acknowledge her presence.

As she continued down the dusty path, she again looked in her rearview mirror and noticed that the red car was picking up speed. Afraid and confused, she did the same. Within seconds, the red car was directly behind her, and within a blink of an eye, it rammed into the back of her car and began pushing her forward.

Through the thick cloud of dust that had engulfed her car, she could see about twenty-five feet ahead. There was an embankment, beyond which was about a fifty-foot drop into the swampy wetlands.

She wondered who her assailants were and why they were trying to harm her? The idea of jumping out of the car entered her mind, but a row of trees was too close to the driver's side door to allow her escape.

The maniacal driver continued forcing her closer toward the embankment. It became increasingly obvious that the intent was to actually force her over the edge. Terrified, she prayed for her life.

As she was pushed closer and closer to the road's edge and just before plunging over, she awoke to the shrieking sound of her own screaming.

After composing herself and getting her bearings, she realized that the hellish drive was just another nightmare. It had to be a nightmare, because she had all along been tucked safely away in her own bed.

Of all the night terrors that she'd had in the past, this one seemed the most real. The dream was so incredibly vivid, it was as if she was actually there....or *maybe she was!*

An Explicit Nature

Chapter One

It was happening more and more frequently now. It was to the point where she could no longer control it. She couldn't talk about it with her husband, as he'd only say it was all in her mind. She was unable to tell her parents about it because they were up in age and she would rather not upset them. Her doctor didn't even have a name for it. If he didn't know, then she definitely didn't know what it was. Since a medically trained professional was unable to give it a name, she gave it one, the curse.

What she did know was that she had to tell someone that would understand and help her figure out what to do. There was only one person whom she felt she could trust to help her without judging, and that person was on the phone with her at that very moment. "See, there it goes again! Oh my God, why does this keep happening?" Sharelle cried out.

"What? What are you talking about? Why does what keep happening? Shar, what the hell is the matter with you?"

"Whew! Alright, good, it stopped. Don't worry, it's okay now," She gasped as she attempted to speak words of assurance between labored breaths.

"I'm sorry Joy. I didn't mean to scare you like that, but it just happened again. This is precisely what I was trying to tell you about. I don't know what's going on, but occasionally my arm starts thrashing around as if it has a mind of its own. It just seems to happen for no apparent reason."

"Girl, don't you ever do that again. You almost scared me to death! There's not a thing wrong with you. It's probably just nerves. You know how stressed out you've been lately," ranted Sharelle's best friend Joy, wiping her eyes of the excess moisture that would've soon formed tears.

It had been fifteen years since she suffered a tragic car accident which left her with little to no recall of the events that led up to it. Without a doubt, her recovery from her sustained injuries was nothing short of a miracle. However, this recent onset of seizures had her concerned and completely baffled. Nevertheless, she was determined to get on with the business of living her life, despite her recent physical challenges.

She could hear the frustration in Joy's voice as it transmitted through the speakerphone function of her cell.

"Yeah, you know Joy, you're probably right. I really have been pushing myself lately trying to stay on top of my writing, and God knows Eric has definitely been getting on my nerves!"

"See what I mean? Girl, you just need some time to chill out. Why don't we go and have a nice brunch at Guytano's at about twelve o'clock, then head for the day spa, and later on, we'll go and have an off-the-chain girl's night out. What do you think?"

Sharelle thought that it just wasn't the right time to tell Joy about the doctor's preliminary findings. She decided the best thing to do was to take his advice and try to keep a positive attitude. The last thing she wanted to do was to draw any doom and gloom conclusions. So, she would simply wait. She would just hold her tongue at least until after her appointment with the neurologist.

While contemplating Joy's proposal, she looked down disapprovingly at the dulled nail polish on her toenails, then conceded.

"Alright Joy, you're right. I'll meet you at the restaurant at noon. I'm about to take Maya to school, so I'll talk to you later, okay?"

"Alright girl, see ya later."

On this unusually chilly fall morning, after dropping her daughter off at school, Sharelle returned to her custom-built Mediterranean-styled suburban home. She immediately lit a fire in the fireplace and headed straight to the master bathroom to turn on the shower. She made herself a cup of coffee to take the chill off. Although there was an international coffee café down the street from Maya's school, she never could decide on just what exotic coffee concoction to order. So, she opted for what she knew she'd enjoy…a freshly home-brewed cup of java. Once ready, she poured herself a steaming mug and went into her home office to check her morning e-mail.

Sitting down at her computer desk, she stared blankly at the P.C. It was as though she were in a trance. She stared so intently; it was as if she believed the computer had face-recognition capability and would boot itself up simply because it recognized that she was sitting there. As she honed in on the sound of the shower running, it reminded her that she had turned it on a while ago. She first sifted through a ton of e-mails and sipped the last drop of her French vanilla flavored coffee, then headed for the bathroom.

By now, the shower was steaming hot. The water had been running the entire time. There was no reflection in the bathroom mirrors, as they were clouded by the room's humidity. Slowly, she slid her fleece jumpsuit down over her ample hips while imagining being in his arms. The condensation enveloped her body and glistened like the tiniest of precious gems against her café aù lait colored skin.

The collected droplets began to drip, making tiny puddles on the floor. As Sharelle stepped into the shower, she quivered as the warmth of the water streamed down her curvaceous body from head to toe. A smile came over her face as she remembered when he would sneak in and join her. The tingling sensation of his strong hands gently smoothing her favorite lavender-scented body wash all over her, then her doing the same to him, brought a smile to her face.

Then reality came back into focus. That type of intimacy was a thing of the past. Sharelle was alone. She wasn't alone, simply because she was the only one there. She was alone in a much broader sense.

4

Once out of the shower, she turned on the exhaust, grabbed her fluffy white Egyptian cotton bath sheet, and toweled herself dry. Catching her reflection in the mirror, she imagined herself as the woman she was when she first met her husband, Eric.

Raised in California, she was a fitness guru with a tiny waist and a pretty face that was bronze kissed by the warm rays of the California sun. She had the most alluring dark brown, almond-shaped eyes and curly sandy brown hair that wouldn't conform to any particular style. Hers was just a head full of bountiful curls that she would twirl around her fingers whenever she became anxious or nervous.

As an accomplished editorial writer turned published novelist, she had stopped writing for years primarily due to her husband's ambivalence toward her craft. As a result, she spiraled into a state of self-denial. For the last thirteen years, she discontentedly brokered a small real estate office in New York City. Sharelle decided to sell the business six months prior, only to join Eric after his employer relocated him to Charlotte, North Carolina, where they currently live.

As the 47-year-old reflection in the mirror gazed back at her, she realized that the woman she used to be was lost. She disappeared many years ago. She thought perhaps she had died in that car accident. But of course, she wasn't thinking literally, as in physical death, but death of the spirit, as it were. Just like Alice, when she stepped into that looking glass to explore what was on the other side, she knew that the real Sharelle Langford-Hughes was somewhere in that reflection. She was determined to find her again. Like Alice, she, too, would step into the looking glass and emerge the heralded writer she once was.

She had already been working on her current novel for six months. She had vowed that once she began writing again, she wouldn't allow anything or anyone to stop her. Suddenly, her attention is diverted to the phone ringing. She ran to answer it before it went to voicemail.

"Hello?"

"Hey, baby, whatcha doin'?"

It was Eric calling from the office.

"Oh, hey, Eric. I just got out of the shower and was about to get dressed."

"Oh, yeah? So you're naked, then?

"Uh, no, I do own a robe, you know."

"Well, I know that…never mind, I was just trying to get a visual, that's all…"

Since the move, Eric had changed. Sharelle couldn't quite put her finger on what it was, but there was a definite change in him. He didn't use to call her from work during the day, and she couldn't help but wonder…why now? Although it all sounded good, she thought it to be a little suspicious.

"…Anyway, you say you're getting dressed? You have plans?" He asked.

"Well, ye-a-h. Joy and I are going to brunch, and then we're going to the day spa."

"Oh really? Who's the bustah you're getting all gussied up for?"

Perturbed at the inference that she was plotting some sort of unsavory scheme, she replied,

"Is this why you called, just to start something?"

"Whoa, don't get all mad. I was just teasing you. Listen, just tell Joy I said hi and have fun and I'll see you later."

"Okay, I'll…."

Suddenly, remembering his reason for calling wasn't simply to prove what a jerk he was, he interrupted.

"Oh, hey, wait a minute, I almost forgot why I was calling. I was wondering if you wanted to go out for dinner tonight?"

"Tonight? Actually, Joy and I also planned to go out for drinks tonight."

"Oh, so what do I need to do, make an appointment to spend time with you?"

"No, Eric, you know that Joy and I haven't had much time together lately, so I thought we'd get together for a change."

Sharelle was looking forward to learning her way around Charlotte and discovering new things. Even more anticipated was to reunite with her long-time close friend. Eric really didn't mind her hooking up with her girl, his feelings of guilt made him think that his wife might be on the prowl.

"Alrighty then, I guess I'll see you when I see you! Have a good time," he said in a sarcastic tone.

"Eric, don't be like that. I'll see you later on tonight, okay?"

"Oh, everything's cool. I'll see you later, baby. Have a good time."

"Okay, bye."

Eric was on the fast track up the corporate ladder. He was recently promoted to Regional V.P. of Quality Standards for ΩMEGA SENTRY SYSTEMS, an international home and business security and surveillance systems corporation. But, although his career had soared to great heights, Sharelle sensed that something within his soul wasn't at peace.

As she propped a pillow under her head and kicked back on her bed, she reflected on the good ol' days at the beginning of her relationship with Eric. She recounted how he won her heart when they met in college at the end of freshman year.

From day one, he passed the monkey fingers test with flying colors. Monkey fingers were what she described as raggedy, chewed-up fingernails that looked like little stubs, resulting from years of excessive nail-biting. Her belief was if the eyes are supposed to be the windows to the soul, monkey fingers must be the windows to poor grooming habits! But, much to her satisfaction, Eric's nails were always neat and clean. It wasn't very long before they were in love. They did everything together.

Not only did he have an uncanny ability to make her laugh until it hurt, but he also showed her places and things she had never seen before. He opened a whole new world for her by introducing her to what she referred to as the land where time stood still, the rural deep south. Then, he took her on a whirlwind adventure into the larger-than-life sights and sounds of the Big Apple. It was there that he introduced her to her first porn flick. Not that she had a burning desire to see one, but knowing that she had never seen one before, he felt obliged to be the first to introduce her to the experience.

She recalled him taking her to a seedy triple X theater in Manhattan with sticky floors. The place was so sleazy that she remembered she felt nauseous just imagining what was on that floor. Though she could've thought of a million better things to do on a date, she just enjoyed being with Eric and was somewhat curious about triple X in her own right. As disgusting as she found the movie, her naiveté convinced her that this is just what guys do. So, rather than seem like a prude, she played along. She cherished the memory of their in-depth and heated discussions about the validity of the American penal system and the death penalty. He was in favor of it, and she was categorically against it. He knew, without fail, that he could get her riled up by saying that the death penalty was an effective deterrent against crime.

Her position was that the powers that be within the U.S. penal system were nothing but modern-day lynch mobs. She would argue that they were nothing more than executioners who did their dirty work under the veil of a flawed white sheet known as the judicial system. He would crack up laughing and say, *"you're so cute when you're angry."* Of course, that would just piss her off even more.

Back in those days, she glowed with so much spirit and determination. Now, she saw that the aura surrounding her appeared dim, almost entirely devoid of light.

Suddenly, she sprang up off the bed and looked at the clock.

"Oh, wow! It's almost eleven o'clock. I need to get up and finish getting dressed!"

Sharelle hurriedly finger-combed her hair and applied enough lip gloss to get that just-licked-wet shine to her full, voluptuous lips. Next, she grabbed her chocolate-brown velour jogging suit from the closet and slipped it on. Lastly, she slipped on her comfy python and suede flip-flops and brown suede jacket. Finally, she quickly threw her wallet, cell phone, and lip gloss into her sienna velvet handbag and flew out the door.

An Explicit Nature

Chapter Two

When she arrived at the restaurant, Joy was already seated in a booth. She motioned to get Sharelle's attention just as the hostess greeted her. When she reached Joy, she removed her jacket and said,

"Hey, what's up, girl?"

"What's up? What's up? I'll tell you what's up. It's now twelve-fifteen, and your butt was supposed to be here at twelve o'clock sharp. So, I should be asking you *wassup?"*

Joy was so obsessed with promptness that it bordered on the ridiculous. Although she felt that Joy's angst seemed a bit over the top about her slight tardiness, she thought it best not to get under her skin even more by making some smart-mouthed remark.

She was working on mastering the skill of diplomacy, something her mother, Arlene, had been urging her to practice for years. Sharelle had been an adult for many years, with children of her own. However, Arlene still felt obliged to impart her infinite wisdom whenever possible. Instead of snapping back at Joy, she diplomatically replied,

"I'm sorry, Joy; I didn't mean to leave you hanging."

Eric called while I was getting dressed and threw me off schedule. Besides, I had a lot on my mind, and it slowed me down.

"Yeah, I've noticed that you haven't been yourself lately. What's wrong?"

"Well, I told you I've been having this problem with my arm and...."

Suddenly the waitress appeared at the table and interrupted.

"Good afternoon, ladies. My name is Lisa, and I'll be your server today. Are you ladies ready to order, or do you need more time to decide?"

"Umm, I think we'd both like more time, please," replied Sharelle, presumptuously answering for the both of them.

"That's fine, if you'd like, I can get your drinks now and come back to take your meal order in a few minutes."

"Okay, I'll have a mimosa," answered Sharelle.

"And I'll have a diet Pepsi…."

"Now, what were we talking about?" Joy continued.

Sharelle answered as she twirled one of her curly locks around her index finger and said,

"Oh yeah, I was just saying that I submitted my latest manuscript to my publisher, and they hated it. They hated it so much that they wanted me to start over and rewrite it. Joy, you know I don't write no junk, but for some reason, I just haven't been able to focus lately and…."

She was close to telling her friend what the doctor had told her, but she lost her nerve and quickly segued to another subject.

"…hey, we're here to have a nice brunch and just chat. We can talk about all that other stuff some other time! Why ruin a perfectly good brunch?"

The waitress returned with the drinks, and while perusing the menu, Joy asked,

"Well, Shar, I know I'm just a lowly investment banker with a measly bachelor's degree in finance, but maybe I can help. So, what's the book about?"

"It's entitled "The Bella Donna Boss," and it's about a mafia crime family that…."

"Oooh, that sounds interesting. I love juicy stories about the mob!"

"…Joy, the head of the family is a woman!"

"A woman? I don't think I've ever heard of a woman being the figurehead of La Cosa Nostra. I mean, that just doesn't make any sense."

"Yeah, I know. That's just what my publishing agent said. I thought it was an intriguing premise, but it just didn't work. I don't know what's wrong with me. For some reason, I keep getting distracted, and I'm just not feeling it right now."

The server's timing couldn't have been better as she approached and interrupted the awkwardness of the moment.

"Are you ladies ready to order now?"

"Yes, I think so. I'll have the grilled chicken salad with croutons and bleu cheese dressing," Sharelle answered.

"And you, ma'am?"

"I'll have the patty melt with an order of chili fries."

A health-conscience Sharelle reacted to Joy's meal request with a sense of urgency,

"Dang girl, talk about not making any sense! You order a diet Pepsi, and then you have the nerve to order a high cholesterol platter with a side of coronary artery disease?"

"Well, excuse me, "Doctor" Hughes. When was your graduation from medical school, and why wasn't I invited?" Amused, she said,

"Hey, I'm just looking out for your arteries, seeing as you won't."

Joy quickly changed the subject.

"Oh, and speaking of doctors, when will you see the doctor about that tremor in your arm?"

"Well, I was trying not to talk about it right now, but seeing as you asked, I went to my doctor, and he referred me to a neurologist."

"A neurologist? So-o-o, what does he think is wrong with you, Shar?"

"That's just it. He really doesn't know. He took x-rays and saw something abnormal in the cervical part of my spine, so he referred me to this neurologist, with whom I have an appointment in two weeks. But, hey, I'm sure you didn't come to hang out with Debbie-downer and listen to sob stories. This is supposed to be a day of fun, remember?"

"Well, Shar, the way I see it, there's not going to be any sob story because you're going to be just fine."

"Yeah, I guess you're right."

"C'mon, Shar, you're my girl, and I never want to see anything bad happen to you. Besides, we got some hangin' out to do, so you can't die on me now. I can't wait to take you to this little shop called Veronique's Boutique. They have some serious clothes and jewelry, all top designer labels." Speaking of jewelry, I love that bracelet you're wearing. Where'd you get that?"

"Girl, you won't believe how old this bracelet is. I've had this thing for almost twenty-five years. Eric gave it to me when I first moved to New Jersey."

"You're kidding. That bracelet is gorgeous, and it still looks like new."

"Thanks."

"You know, that reminds me, when you and I first met, I don't remember ever coming over to visit you. Then, of course, you moved soon after we met, but before that, I can't, for the life of me, remember where you lived."

"Probably, because I never invited you over."

"Why not? Oh, I wasn't good enough to come to your house, but you could come to mine?

"No...of course not, Joy. You don't remember me telling you about that apartment that Eric rented for us when I first came to New Jersey?"

"No, what about it?"

"Girl, that apartment was the pits. I mean, it sucked, big time!

Sharelle described a rather drab-looking three-story brick building in the middle of town. As she rolled her eyes, she spoke sarcastically about the deceptive description that listed the units as "garden apartments."

Joy was very familiar with the appeal of garden-style apartment living and appeared quite impressed and chimed in.

"Oh, those are usually very nice."

"Yeah, usually, but this so-called garden consisted of a front lawn full of dandelions and a giant mutant oak tree. That tree would spew some type of bile-colored slime all over your freshly washed car in the springtime."

13

Joy, trying to sift through what she perceived as unwarranted complaining, commented,

"Now, Shar, don't be such a snob. Maybe the landscaping wasn't exactly what you thought it should be, but that had nothing to do with the apartment itself."

"Oh no, girl, you haven't even heard the half of it. Let me finish telling you. They referred to the apartment as an efficiency apartment, meaning that the living room served as a bedroom, a dining room, a den, and just about any other purpose you could think of. So basically, it was one big multi-purpose room."

"Well, okay, I've heard of an efficiency apartment, but Shar, that's how many young couples start their lives together. They move into tiny little apartments until they become more stable and can afford to do better, which is exactly what you did! Of course, I could see if you said that the bathroom didn't have all the essential plumbing or something, but at least you had a decent place to live and...."

"Joy, would you shut up and listen, the damn place had mice!"

"Oh my God, you had RATS?"

"What did I say, rats or mice? They were mice, Joy, mice, although one is just as bad as the other, in my opinion. Anyway, a few days after I moved there, I was at home by myself while Eric was at work, and I saw a mouse in the kitchen coming up through one of the burners on top of the stove in broad daylight. When the little bastard saw me, it just stood there staring at me as if it was waiting for me to serve dinner."

"Girl, you've got to be lyin'!"

"I'm telling you; this place was straight nasty. I could have lived with the mutant oak tree, the cramped conditions, and everything else if it just wasn't for that awful kitchen. That kitchen was an amusement park for rodents, complete with special guest appearances by Icky freakin' Mouse himself! I told Eric when he got home that unless we found another place to live immediately, I was about a rat's ass shy of booking a flight back to Cali. That's when we moved to where you remember me living shortly after you and I met."

14

"Yeah, good thing you didn't invite me over there 'cause that's one thing I definitely don't do…rats, yuck!"

"Joy, Joy, they weren't rats, they…ah, forget it, whatever."

"Okay, we have a grilled chicken salad with bleu cheese dressing for you, and for you, we have a patty melt with a side of chili fries. Enjoy your meal, ladies."

"Thank you," they said in unison.

With eyes bulging, Joy examined her cheese oozing, grease dripping, calorie-laden patty melt. Then, all smiles, she exclaimed, "I don't care what you say; this sandwich is gonna be the bomb and you know it."

"Go right ahead and knock yourself out, Joy," Sharelle replied reticently.

Joy then attempts to steer the conversation away from her unhealthy eating habits.

"Oh, by the way, I've been meaning to ask you, how's Eric doing?"

"Oh, he's doing okay, I guess."

"You guess? Aren't you married to the man?"

"Of course, I am. But as I said, he's okay."

"Alright Shar, you're not fooling me with that "he's okay, I guess" crap. Don't forget, I've been married before. Been there, done that, got the T-shirt and the hat. I know when a woman says, "he's okay, I guess, that usually means I hate the bastard and wish he'd go play hopscotch on the freakin' highway! So, stop trying to play me and tell me what's up with you and Eric."

"Well, it's just that he's never supported my writing, and now that I'm writing again, he's been acting sort of funny."

"Funny? What do you mean funny? Like, funny "ha-ha" or funny gay, or what?"

After dabbing bleu cheese dressing from her lips, Sharelle said defensively.

"Now, Joy, don't you be funny. First of all, he's no comedian, and secondly, I think the LGBTQ community might take offense to that reference. Besides, you know what I mean. He's been acting strange or, not even strange, more like distant. Yeah, that's the word, distant."

"Well, maybe that's why you're having such difficulty writing right now. Don't get me wrong, Shar. I know you love Eric, and I really do believe he loves you, but you're getting bad vibes from him, and that may be what's stopping your flow.

Shar, you're an award-winning editorial writer and an outstanding novelist, and Eric knows it. It's not that he doesn't think you're a good writer. Instead, he's afraid you'll become so successful that you might up and leave him someday. And even worse, he's scared you'll start to open up, begin expressing yourself again and tell something he doesn't want to be told. Don't you see? He's trying to suppress your desire to express yourself, and you're buying into it. As close as we are, you have yet to tell me how your accident happened, and I know that when you're ready, you will, but…."

Sharelle stated bluntly,

"Joy, I wish I could tell you or anybody about how the accident happened, but I just can't remember. From what I was told, I crashed into a tree."

"I'm sorry, Shar. I'm just not buying it. I think you don't want to remember because it's too painful, and I just can't help feeling that there's something suspicious about it. I mean, I just find it strange that Eric wasn't more persistent in demanding a more in-depth investigation.

Then there's the fact that he gets annoyed whenever you bring up the subject. You didn't intentionally crash the car so why does he get so mad at you? I think he's afraid that you might remember something that he doesn't want you to, and then that something might end up in a book. It just doesn't make any sense, Shar, it doesn't. My advice to you, stop letting him get in your head and just write! Find a subject that you're passionate about and go for it."

"Yeah, I'm sure you're right. I guess I have been letting Eric get in my head, and that has to stop!"

Sharelle looked at her watch and was surprised at how much time they'd spent at the restaurant. She abruptly changed the subject,

"Well, Joy, so much for our fun brunch. We've done nothing but talk about all my issues, and now I feel like a total killjoy, pardon the pun."

Jokingly, Joy said,

"You might kill brunch, but you won't kill Joy, heh, heh just kidding."

"Joy, you are so-o-o corny. Come on, girl, let's head to the spa and get beautified!"

Chapter Three

"It's the pearl white convertible over in the second row," Sharelle said, directing the valet as he searched the lot. She flexed her right arm and thought, hmm, maybe that's all I needed was a good massage. She was hopeful that the massage she had at the spa helped relieve her of the curse.

Meanwhile, somewhere in his early thirties, a young dark-skinned man with thick ropes of matted dreadlocks walked past. The thugged-out brotha sporting a gray hoodie, high-top workboots, and sagging jeans looked back at Sharelle and gave her a lengthy stare.

She tried to avoid eye contact, but noticed out of the corner of her eye that his jeans were belted well below his butt cheeks and were big enough to fit a pre-intestinal bypass Al Roker.

The young man shouted out to her with a barely detectable West Indian accent.

"Yo, what up, shawty! Mmm, mmm, mmm, how 'bout you and me go half on a baby?"

Ignoring the young man by rolling her eyes and turning her head in the opposite direction, she silently prayed that her car would quickly arrive. She thought to herself,

No, this Bob Marley wannabe didn't just run down that lame, played-out line on me!

The man, obviously not appreciating being dissed by her, yelled out,

"Bitch, don't try to act like you too good 'cause you ain't even all dat."

Totally disgusted by his rude comments, she fired back,

"Excuse me, but you don't have any right to speak to me like that because, number one, you don't know me. Number two, not only are your pants saggin', but anyone who wears their pants that way is the true definition of saggin', only spelled in reverse.

She found it amusing to watch the young brotha as he tried to figure out what the word saggin' spelled in reverse. Just as he got a clue, her car arrived. Sporting a devious smirk, she hurriedly jumped in and sped off while viewing in her rearview mirror a vulgarly explicit gesture involving a middle finger thrown at her.

On the drive to pick up Maya from school, she replayed the altercation in her mind. She thought, what an idiot! Go half on a baby? Puhleeze, why would anyone want to have his baby? On second thought, he probably already has a few by some poor girl whose self-worth is measured by the number of babies she can produce. Besides, he just doesn't know I would rather shave my head, pierce both nipples and tattoo my tongue rather than have another baby!

Her cell phone rang two miles from Maya's school exit. She was sure that it was Maya calling to inform her that she was already five minutes late. She fit in her wireless earbuds and rifled through the black hole of her handbag, trying to find her phone. While searching frantically, she tried to keep her eyes on the road.

Finally fumbling upon it wedged between her checkbook and her makeup bag, she answered just before the call went into voicemail. It was her girlfriend Tracy in New Jersey.

"Hello?"

"Hey, Sharelle, can you talk?"

"Oh, hey Tracy, yeah, I'm on the move. What's going on?"

"I've got great news! You won't believe this."

Sharelle's demeanor immediately perked up.

"I could use some good news. What's up, girl?"

"You'll never guess who I just talked to?"

"Who?"

Barely able to contain her excitement, Tracy squealed, "Marcus!"

Tracy Logan, age 46, was a fun-loving person with a huge heart and a psychic mind. Although Sharelle never truly understood Tracy's coalescence with the cosmos, she had to admit that there had been quite a few instances where her predictions and sixth sense were on point. Still, Sharelle learned to take her advice with a grain of salt because she couldn't fathom yielding all of her faith and trust to the big dipper.

Married for 22 years to an emotionally detached and inattentive accountant named Darryl, Tracy had a significant crush on Marcus Reynolds for some time. The latter happened to be her boss from previous employment. She and Marcus remained in contact with one another, primarily for business networking purposes. Still, Tracy saw the potential for something more.

Tracy's husband, Darryl, liked to keep up appearances, such as having the perfect wife, the perfect house in the perfect neighborhood, and the perfect kids. But, needless to say, his life with his family was anything but perfect.

One day, a mutual acquaintance of the both of them happened to be at the day spa they frequented. She was a financial advisor who often attended various affairs for professionals. In the conversation, it came out that she knew Tracy's husband, Darryl.

Somehow, Sharelle and the woman wandered into how infidelity among black men in her professional circle was rampant.

She said she wasn't aware of one black male accountant, of those she knew in New Jersey, that wasn't cheating on their spouse, including Mr. Darryl Logan, Tracy's husband. However, the mutual acquaintance made it very clear that she was all too familiar with his roaming eyes.

Most evenings, Darryl had "professional" commitments to attend to and, therefore, was rarely at home. On the unusual occasions that he was at home, Tracy expected an argument to ensue, which normally escalated into him angrily storming out of the house again. As a result, Tracy has immersed herself into what Sharelle saw as a fantasy relationship with Marcus.

Though she wants to be supportive of her girl, she isn't convinced that Marcus was as enthused about having an adulterous affair as Tracy was. She shared a few insignificant details about her phone conversation with Marcus when Sharelle cut in,

"Listen, Tracy, I'm just picking Maya up from school. I'll call you when I get home."

"Okay, wait, I just have to tell you one more thing really quick. I had a dream last night, and you were in it. I don't understand what this means, but in the dream, I kept screaming at the top of my lungs at you. I kept saying remember IRAM! Remember, IRAM!"

Annoyed with what Sharelle deemed an insult to her intellect, she abruptly ended the conversation.

"Okay, Tracy, thanks for the psychic riddle of the day, but I really have to go. I'll call you later, okay? Bye!"

She began to wonder if Tracy might be losing it due to her husband making her feel she had about as much value as a used toothpick.

"Why doesn't she just leave him?" she wondered. But she quickly realized she had some nerve to be judgmental of her friend when her marital situation hadn't been pristine and perfect either. She would never consider telling any woman to leave her husband. Her attitude was that it's a personal decision a woman must make herself. It became apparent to Sharelle that she had some internalized anger about her own issues that needed to be addressed.

Chapter Four

"No, Maya, I'm not taking you to have more holes put in your body."

"Why not?" Sharelle's daughter challenges. "You said I could get my belly button pierced when I turned eighteen, and I'll be eighteen in four days."

"That's not what I said, Maya. I said that when you turned eighteen, you could do whatever you wanted to your body, I didn't then, nor do I now, condone getting your belly button pierced, and I definitely didn't say I would facilitate it. If you insist on becoming a human pincushion, I refuse to have any part in it!"

Maya was a handful. She was the poster child for the defiant, argumentative, selfish, spoiled teenaged divas of the world. Sharelle often commented that her daughter was the black Paris Hilton personified, minus a few hundred million dollars and the jewel-collared Chihuahua, of course. She was the complete and total opposite of her older brother, Darius. He was mild-mannered and so much easier to reason with. In fact, Sharelle and Eric never could understand how it was that they could have parented two extremely different children.

To be fair, there were times when Maya would reveal a soft side of herself. Even though drama was rarely far behind her, she was genuinely a shy, sweet, and sensitive young lady.

Despite endless power struggles between herself and her darling diva of a daughter, Sharelle didn't have to worry about her doing many things teenagers get caught up in. Such as drug use, pregnancy, strolling the corner, or working the pole.

In fact, Maya did well in school and was polite to others. However, it was with her mom and dad that she would morph into the infamous starring role of The Exorcist.

With much divatude, and in her usual *it's all about me* fashion, Maya rudely interrupted Sharelle while she was on the phone with Tracy and preparing dinner,

"Mom, it's only two more months before spring break. When do you plan on getting my plane ticket to New Jersey?"

"Maya, don't stress me out; we'll talk about this later when your father gets home."

"Why do you always have to have daddy's permission? Can't you do anything without him?" Maya asks defiantly with her hands on her hips.

Not believing her daughter's unmitigated gall in challenging her, Sharelle whipped her head around toward her, excused herself from her phone conversation, and then rebuked,

"First of all, young lady, check your attitude, and let's not get it twisted. You're the child, and I'm the parent. The decisions I make may or may not include your father. Still, whichever way it goes, I don't owe you any explanation for how I arrive at those decisions."

Maya stormed out of the kitchen, marching off to her room in a huff, slamming the door behind her. Sharelle was displeased with her daughter's behavior but too exasperated to go after her.

She opened a frozen package of green beans and began feeling that familiarly eerie twitching that signaled the onset of an episode of tremors.

As the sensation intensified, her body stood rigid in the middle of the kitchen floor, motionless. She tried to breathe shallow breaths. She was afraid that normal breathing might somehow fuel more energy to this unknown force that had possessed her body, willing it to reject a part of its own.

"Oh no...not again! Why is this happening? Dear God, make it stop! Please make it stop!" she pleaded.

Her right arm rebelled in spasmodic defiance of her. It was like an out-of-control child in the throes of a tantrum. She attempted to control the involuntary movement in the arm by grasping it with a firm left hand.

After what seemed like an eternity, the trembling gradually subsided until it finally stopped. In shock, Sharelle remained riveted to the floor; her eyes welled into tear-saturated clouds that rained down her frightened, flawless face.

After gathering herself, she sat at the breakfast table and lit a cigarette. She had sworn off of them as her New Year's resolution, but kept an emergency stash around, just in case things got rough. Perspiring profusely and weakened at the knees was emergency enough for her to light up.

Disgusted at the taste and high from the nicotine rush, she extinguished the cigarette while feverishly twirling an unruly lock at the nape of her neck.

A lingering trail of smoke from the expended tobacco drifted through the air just as Eric entered through the garage door. He came into the kitchen, nose wrinkled up and sniffing the air, then questioned,

"Hey, babe. Hmm, what's that smell? Have you been smoking?"

Still twirling her hair, she replied,

"Ye-a-ah, I have."

"Well, what happened? You were doing so good!"

"I don't know. I just had a taste for a cigarette, I guess. I know it was a stupid thing to do."

She decided not to make a big deal about what had happened. She knew it would only prompt Eric to give his dollar store diagnosis as to what he thought the problem might be.

His suggestion was all too predictable. But nevertheless, it was his remedy for everything. His number one panacea, sex! Got a headache? Have sex! Got the flu? Have sex! Cardiac arrest? Have sex! "For whatever ails you, sex is the cure." She knew that would be his mantra.

"What's for dinner?" Eric asked matter-of-factly.

"I'm making a roast with green beans and red potatoes."

"Mmm, sounds good! So, what time are you and Joy going out to get drunk?"

"Why is it that when you go out with your friends, you're going out for drinks, and when I go out, I'm going out to get drunk?"

"Okay, okay, let me rephrase that. At what hour are you going out for cocktails?"

"Very funny! We said we'd meet around eight o'clock."

"Meet where?"

"Some place called The Jazz Café."

"I've never heard of it. Where is this place, and what is it, a bar?"

"Eric, I've never been there, so what do I know? Joy just gave me the address and said it's a nice little jazz club!"

In a predictable attempt at inciting an argument, he quipped,

"A jazz club, huh? We both know you're probably going out to hook up with some old broke joke who thinks he's a player."

She wasted no time walking through the door of retaliation that Eric had just opened.

"Baby, the only player I have is you!"

Though she would have taken great pleasure in wishing him away to a place of eternal damnation, she decided to take the path of least resistance. She thought it best to kill him with kindness instead. Kudos, Arlene! Your infinite wisdom prevails once again, she thought to herself while wearing a malicious grin.

After finishing putting dinner together, she went to take a much-needed soak in the whirlpool bath.

Settling into a swirling cloud of freesia-scented bath bubbles, she steadily reeled over Eric's smug comment and mulled it over once again.

"I like his nerve! How dare he accuse me of cheating when his track record isn't exactly a glowing testimonial of fidelity! Maybe I should take Joy's advice and write about my life with Eric. Yeah, that's exactly what

I'll do. I'll write my memoirs! Perhaps writing about my life would help me work through some things. Duh! Having one's memory intact is a must to effectively write a memoir. The last thing I want to do is to piss Oprah off by ad-libbing what I don't remember and then slipping another embellished memoir into her book club! So, until I regain my memory, I guess, for now, it's au revoir to my memoir!"

As she unwound, her buttocks glided effortlessly along the tub's surface until the soles of her feet braced her and stopped her momentum. Agitated bubbles cleansed her limp body of the stresses of the day as they danced and gently tickled her face, the same as those from a vintage bottle of the finest champagne.

"Aaahh, heaven," she sighed as the weight of her eyelids gradually shut out the ambient light of the candles which burned in the room.

An Explicit Nature

Chapter Five

The Jazz Café was jumpin' this particular Friday night. Ronnie B. and his band were bringing down the house. The place was packed with some of Charlotte, North Carolina's most and least eligible bachelors, all of which were stylin' and profilin' to the max.

There was a small dance floor jam-packed with people getting their boogie on. Everyone was groovin' to the soulful sounds of the saxophone, keyboard, bass guitar, and drums, all synchronized into an orgy of melodic vibrato.

Apparently, this was where single women went to meet men. But, single or not, it was a veritable feast of six-packed, bicep-buffed, testosterone-pumped men up in the house!

There were black men, white men, Hispanic men, Asian men, and various combinations of the above, just swarming the entire place. But, of course, they weren't just your average "Joes" either. There were pro football players, prominent business owners, and all other walks of Charlotte's finest in the house.

Then there were, of course, the women. They were some of the most ghetto fabulous hoochies in all of the southern U.S.

Sharelle wondered why she hadn't received the memo informing her that it was "X-treme Hoochie" night at The Jazz Café. Still, she enjoyed the band, despite all the fronting that was going on.

"Joy, this place is nice, but what's up with all the hoochies?"

"Girl, you know that whenever there are ballers and shot-callers around, the bloodhounds are gonna sniff them out!"

"So, is this where you come to meet men?"

"Oh, what are you trying to say, that I'm one of these hoochies?

"Nope. I just asked a simple question, that's all. So, is it?"

"Is it what? Where I come to meet men?"

"Yes, Joy."

"Not really. I come here for the entertainment and the atmosphere. But, on the other hand, if a nice guy happens to offer me a drink and then engages me in some interesting conversation, then it's all good right?"

"I guess there's no harm in that. Don't get me wrong, Joy, I'm not being judgmental of you. It's just that this whole scene seems so pretentious and phony!"

"Shar, where have you been, under a rock? It's always been this way."

"It has been quite a few years since I've been in the game, you know."

"Well, don't look now, but there's a fine-looking brotha over at two o'clock checking you as we speak."

The waiter approached the table with a tray of drinks and said to Sharelle,

"A Cosmopolitan for you, ma'am. Compliments of the gentleman over at the far-right end of the bar."

"Well, that's pretty presumptuous of him, remarked Sharelle. What makes him think I want him to buy me a drink?"

By this time, Joy was annoyed with her friend's snobbish attitude.

"Shar, the guy is just trying to be friendly. Take the drink!"

She took a quick sip, turned her head in the gentleman's direction, and flashed a quick smile and a gracious nod.

"Joy, remember back in the day when you only accepted a drink from a guy if you welcomed his attention?"

"Yeah, I remember."

"Well, I'm not welcoming!"

"Welcome to the new millennium, Shar. Nothing in the rule book says you have to go home with the guy just because he buys you a drink."

"Yeah, but…"

"But nothing! He's headed over this way, and I'm going to the ladies' room!"

"Joy, you better not leave me here. I'm not playing, Joy!"

"Have fun, see ya."

As Joy hurried off to the ladies' lounge, a well-groomed man of about six-foot-five approached Sharelle. The gentleman was meticulously dressed in an exquisitely tailored navy-blue suit, a butter-yellow, silk knit pullover shirt, and blue eel skin shoes.

In a gentle baritone whisper of a voice, he said,

"Excuse me, lovely lady, would you mind if I joined you?"

Sharelle was reluctant at first. However, she quickly reminded herself that this was nothing more than a friendly encounter with a respectful gentleman.

Sharelle thought to herself,

"Yeah, right, he's a respectful gentleman alright. A respectful gentleman who is gorgeous and charming enough to make me forget my last name, my married last name, that is!"

"I'm actually here with a girlfriend," she replied.

The gentleman looked around and turned back to her.

"Well, excuse me for saying so, but it appears your girlfriend has found some other interest."

As she leaned to one side and spied Joy on the other side of the room kickin' it with one of the Carolina football players, she mumbled under her breath,

"That lyin' heifer! Wait 'till I get my hands on her!"

"Excuse me? I'm sorry, I couldn't hear you."

"Oh, I was just saying that it's okay, you're welcome to join me if you like."

The gentleman pulled up a chair and extended his arm for a handshake while introducing himself.

"My name is Leland—Leland Alston, but you can call me Lee and your name?"

"I'm Sharelle, Sharelle Hughes."

"Well, it's a pleasure to meet you, Sharelle Hughes."

Trying to appear unimpressed, she gave a brief response.

"Nice meeting you, as well."

Sharelle just happened to notice that when Lee extended his hand to her, he was not sporting a ring on his ring finger, not that it meant anything to her. It was merely an observation. Besides, she was fully aware that men often remove their wedding rings when out alone. She, at least, knew that Eric did.

Other meaningless observations she made were the diamond-encrusted Rolex watch on his wrist and the one-carat diamond stud in his left ear.

"I hope you're enjoying your Cosmopolitan," he commented.

"As a matter of fact, I am, but how did you know that I drink at all?

"Well, I noticed you were trying to get the waiter's attention, so, I guess I assumed. I apologize if I came off as being too forward."

She thought for a beat,

"Hmm, a man that can admit to being wrong? How refreshing!" She then gives him a reprieve.

"No, it's okay. I'm just bustin' your chops, that's all."

Laughing, he charmingly stated,

"Wow, you're not only beautiful, but you're kinda feisty too."

She couldn't help but notice that his smile was a perfectly aligned string of pearls polished to impeccable perfection. His mouth, a neatly wrapped package with lips like flowing ribbons, gently curled at each end. His feathery lashes were long, lush plumes that spanned across hazel-colored eyes. His skin, though masculine in appearance, was as smooth as just melted caramel, spread evenly atop a freshly baked cake.

She intently examined every iota of his face and transcended into a place of lustful imagination. But luckily, she caught herself just short of uttering the word *delectable!*

She noticed one more thing about Lee, his hands. They were big, strong, expressive, manly hands. As he stroked the immaculately groomed facial hair on his chin, she noticed, staring her right in the face, meticulously manicured fingers! So, she figured she should give him bonus cool points simply because he wasn't a nail-biter.

Her moment of bliss was broken when he inquired, "I've never seen you here before. Is this your first time here?"

"Yeah, I recently moved here from New Jersey."

Oh really, Jersey, huh? What brings you to Charlotte?

She knew he was fishing for information about her status, but she was nonetheless impressed with his smooth approach.

"My husband's company transferred us here."

"Ohhh, so you do have one of those! That was going to be my next question, but now I'm even more curious, why isn't he here with you tonight?"

"Well..."

Just as she was about to answer, Joy approached the table, and Sharelle made the introductions.

"Lee, this is Joy, Joy, Lee."

Lee rises from his seat and shakes hands with Joy while exchanging greetings. He then turns to Sharelle.

"I enjoyed talking with you, Sharelle. So here, take one of my cards and call me sometime. I'd be more than happy to show you around Charlotte."

She gives a friendly smile and then comments,

"Okay, maybe I will. Take care, and thanks again for the drink."

"Well, he seems nice." Joy says tauntingly.

"You know I want to kill you, don't you?"

"Why? You two seemed to be enjoying yourselves."

"Joy, hello-o-o, I'm a married woman. I didn't come here for a hook-up, but I have to admit, I did enjoy talking with him."

"So, what's the problem? You met someone nice, and you enjoyed good conversation. I don't see a problem, do you?"

"I'm just trying to do what's right, that's all."

"That's cool, Shar, but ask yourself this question, has Eric done right by you?"

"Don't go there, Joy."

She looks down at the business card that Lee gave her and says,

"Wow, I never even asked him what he did, career-wise. Apparently, dude is a psychiatrist."

"A psychiatrist, get out! Let me see that," insists Joy, as she snatches the card from Sharelle's grasp. She reads,

"Leland Alston, M.D., Psychiatry. Girl, bow down!"

Joy's street-inspired expression went right over Sharelle's head. But rather than misinterpret it, she asked for clarification.

"What? Bow down? Bow down to what?"

Joy explains.

Check this out, you've heard of the two good-looking doctors called "McDreamy" and "McSteamy" on that popular T.V. drama, right? Oh damn, what's the name of that show? You know which one I'm talking about, it's, it's...ugh!"

"Okay, yeah, I know what show you're talking about, *and*...?"

Joy seizes the opportunity to spit an impromptu rhyme into the conversation, primarily because she thinks she has skills, secondarily, to emphasize her point. Complete with hand gestures, she begins,

"Did you happen to notice bruh's complexion? His skin is so smooth to the point of perfection. Just how I like my ice cream to be, butter pecan, so smooth and creamy! These hoochies in here want to kick your behind.

After all their booty-shakin', he paid them no mind. You sat here un-phased, had all his attention, yet he remained a gentleman, let's not for-get to mention. Tonight, that man was all about you. The ball's in your court, now whatcha gonna do? If I was you, I'd call him and say, doctor, doctor, c'mon over, let's play!" You saw how he looked at you with eyes so gleamy. Girl I hooked you up with Dr. "McCreamy!"

Joy simulates a mic drop, and Sharelle sits there for a few seconds staring at her with her mouth hanging open. She then rolls her eyes, unmistakably annoyed at her friend's feeble attempt at rhyming, then replies,

"Dr. McCreamy, huh? Joy, you know you're a sick girl, right? Besides, you didn't hook me up with anybody! The man came over and introduced himself."

"Yeah, but if I didn't invite you here, you never would have met him. But all jokes aside, Shar, this could be the answer to your problem. I bet he can help you remember details about your accident!"

She takes the card back and pauses to look it over again. After a long sigh, she says hesitantly,

"I don't know, Joy. If I call him, he might get the wrong impression."

"Well, of course, you would pay him, and then he'll realize that it's strictly about business. I'm serious, Shar; please consider this. I really think he can help you."

"I'll give it some thought," she replies as she reaches in her handbag and tucks the card neatly into her wallet for safekeeping.

Feeling a little woozy from the alcoholic effects of the Cosmo, Sharelle excuses herself from the table to go to the ladies' room to shake it off.

A wet paper towel dabbed on her face was all she needed to feel revived. Yet, it had no effect on the guilt she felt about her attraction to Lee.

After joining Joy back at the table, she checks her watch and says to her,

"Wow, I didn't realize it was that late! Are you about ready to go?"

"Yeah, I guess so. Besides, I don't want Eric mad at me because I kept you out too late!"

"Joy, I'm a big girl. I can handle Eric."

"I know, I know. C'mon, let's get outta here."

An Explicit Nature

Chapter Six

At 1:00 a.m., she expected her house to be dark and quiet, it was not. She assumed that he would be asleep, he was not. So, she knows what's to come. It happens every time she goes out socially without him.

She enters her bedroom and finds Eric wide awake with the television on.

"Hey, baby, how was your evening?" he asks.

"Oh, it was nice. What are you doing up so late?"

"I couldn't sleep."

"Oh, really? Is something wrong?"

"No, everything's just fine."

Sharelle proceeds to change her clothes to get ready for bed. She pulled a nightgown out of the dresser drawer. It was the soft cotton one with a high neckline in a baby blue floral print. He hated that gown. He thought it was way too matronly.

He approaches and starts kissing and caressing her despite her efforts to thwart his advances. Then using his body weight, he forces her onto the bed. She had always enjoyed making love to her husband. However, this was not lovemaking; this was sexual espionage, a form of genital reconnaissance, as it were.

She defined sexual espionage as an irrational behavior displayed by one who knows they've done wrong and, as a result, they forever expect and anticipate revenge. In her opinion, it was as if Eric was claiming what he knew was his, but knowing within, that he didn't deserve it. She hated being treated like a steer just being taken to slaughter and, upon passing inspection, being given his stamp of approval.

After the inspection, she fell fast asleep, feeling like a side of beef that had just been stamped U.S.D.A. Choice! Sharelle noticed an annoying hum in the room. She was disturbed by a radiating glow that surrounded her. It was 4:35 a.m. as she stirred in her sleep. She subconsciously pulled the covers over her head to shield herself against the humming and the radiating light, but to no avail.

Beneath the sheet, she could see haunting silhouettes wildly dancing about the room rhythmically. The distorted images flashed around her like a strobe light that sporadically illuminates the dance floor of a techno music dance club.

The humming turned to muffled sounds, and the light was fading in and out. The annoyances were so bothersome that Sharelle turned over and covered her head with the pillow to block everything out.

Eric's nocturnal habits were beginning to wear on her. It seemed like they were evolving into a nightly ritual. He was becoming more active during all hours of the night, and she was becoming more sleep-deprived because of it. While tossing and turning, it became clear why some couples sleep in separate bedrooms over time. She was awakened at about 9:00 that morning by the phone. It was her mom, Arlene, calling with distressing news. Sharelle's grandmother had become gravely ill.

Rest broken from the events of the previous hours, now she's shaken by the news of her grandmother's failing health. Her resignation to the fact that sleep wasn't in the cards drags the bleary-eyed beauty out of bed.

She hopes to escape this early morning nightmare and heads to the bathroom to wash her face. But, of course, that didn't help much because now she feels a headache coming on.

On her way out of the bathroom, she notices Eric curled up in a fetal position, still sleeping like a baby. Through clenched teeth, she mumbles,

"Hmm, look at him! He's chillin' somewhere in la-la land while I'm wide-awake feeling like crap!"

She considered turning on the TV and putting the volume on blast just to spite him. Still, once again, Arlene's infinite wisdom resonated in her head, so she opted against it. If nothing else, just thinking about doing the deed made her feel slightly better.

After taking a couple of acetaminophen gelcaps, she went into her office to organize her thoughts for the book she was supposed to be rewriting. Still, in light of things, she just wasn't feeling it. She desperately wanted to write but couldn't get excited about what she was writing about. It became clear to her what she had to do. She had no choice. She would have to abandon the subject of her book and write about a new topic.

An Explicit Nature

Chapter Seven

Final call for all passengers boarding United flight 462 to Chicago at gate twelve. This is your final boarding call. She heard the announcement over the public address system in full surround sound. The words reverberated off the walls of the airport terminal like a Philharmonic symphony orchestra performing live in concert.

But, for some reason, she wouldn't move. She had been waiting to board her flight for over half an hour. She was checked in with a boarding pass but would not move. She was stricken with grief over the loss of her grandmother.

She got the call late last night. Her other grandparents had already predeceased her, and now her last living grandparent was gone. To Sharelle, her grandmother's death signified the end of an era.

Her grandparents had been a wealth of knowledge about the past, and she never tired of hearing them tell stories about it. So, it was a devastating loss to her.

Arlene was traveling to Chicago and needed her to be there to help with the funeral arrangements. Her mother was an emotional wreck, and Sharelle had to be strong for her.

With her head bowed and eyes closed, she struggles to fight back the tears.

Opening her eyes, she notices a scuffed-up pair of round-toed black patent leather shoes standing in front of her. She hesitates to look up immediately because she is trying to figure out who might be standing in those shoes and what they could want with her.

They were familiar-looking shoes, sort of police officer's standard issue, walking-the-beat shoes. She then hears a voice inquire,

"Ma'am, are you here for flight 462 to Chicago?"

She lifts her head up to see who's speaking to her. While sniffling and twirling her hair, she replies,

"Yes I am."

She recognizes the man with the scuffed-up patent leather shoes as a ticket counter agent for the airline. He says to her firmly,

"You have to board now, ma'am. They've already made the final call for all passengers to board the plane, and they're about to shut the door to the jetway to prepare for departure, so you'd better go."

She sniffles as she gets up, grabs her designer Louie overnight carry-on tote, and scurries behind the counter agent like a puppy trying to keep up with its mother.

Once aboard the plane, she shuffles down the aisle, with "Louie" in tow, looking for her seat.

"Row six, seven, eight, ah, here we are, row nine."

She attempted to cram her bag into the overhead bin just above her row of seats. Unfortunately, it was too full, so she looked around at the adjacent overhead and saw it was also full. Since she is the last one on the plane, all eyes are on her with sneering faces. She decides the best thing to do is to just sit down and put the tote on the floor underneath the seat ahead of her.

As soon as she got settled, the fasten seat belt sign came on, and the flight attendant started her monotonous litany of safety procedures. But, of course, she paid no attention, as she already knew the safety drill like the back of her hand.

It suddenly occurred to her that seat F was the aisle seat. She had seated herself in the window seat, which was seat D. Seat E, the middle seat, was empty, but there was a middle-aged white man with a pudgy, blush-red face sitting in seat F, her seat. She looks at the man, he looks at her, and they exchange a friendly *how do you do* smile at one another.

Then, finally, she thinks, hey, why trip? I prefer the window anyway.

On practically every flight, it seemed that she would inevitably be seated next to somebody with a bad case of diarrhea of the mouth.

"Maybe this trip I'll get lucky, and this old dude will cut me a break," she hopes.

Once they became airborne, she was determined not to allow the man seated in her row to engage her in some of his corny, white folk humor. He just looked like the type that, if given the opportunity, would start letting the racial jokes fly. So, she avoided the possibility by facing toward the window, assuming a universally understood posture, a universally understood, not today, I'm in no mood.

Moments later, the flight attendant announced,

We would like to invite you to enjoy our in-flight movie...

"Oh, good. This guy can't possibly annoy me if I'm into a movie with earbuds plugged in my ears," thought Sharelle.

She had hoped that the in-flight movie would be her way of keeping him at bay. It seemed like the best way for her to run interference until she heard the flight attendant announce the selection.

...today's feature presentation is "Scoop," starring Woody Allen..."

Having absolutely no desire to partake of the selected movie feature, she simply rolled her eyes toward the ceiling and mouthed silently,

"Damn! corny, white folk humor!"

The flight attendant continued her announcement.

The flight crew will begin making their way throughout the cabin for our in-flight service.

Sharelle decided it would be a good time to feign sleep to thwart any possible attempts at meaningless chatter.

Sometime later, the pudgy, red-faced man taps on her shoulder and says,

"Excuse me, ma'am, I'm sorry to wake you, but I just thought you might want something to drink. The attendant is here serving refreshments."

She gives a smile and politely replies,

"Oh yes, thank you."

Though her parents didn't raise her to be rude, her thoughts were still operating in bitch mode.

"Maybe I didn't want refreshments, perhaps I just wanted to sleep…

She quickly adjusted her attitude and conceded,

…however, that was really thoughtful of him."

After a hearty yawn, she graciously accepted the honey-roasted nuts. She requested a Bloody Mary mix over ice before plucking the SkyMall magazine from the seat pocket. She wondered, *"whatever happened to the real food they used to give you on airplanes?"* After lowering the tray table, she leafed through the magazine while sipping her drink. She didn't have much appetite then, so she retrieved her Louie satchel hand-bag that matched the carry-on tote and tossed in the honey-roasted pea-nuts for later.

The man in seat F leaned in slightly toward her and, in a soft-spoken voice, asked, "So, is Chicago home for you, or are you just visiting?"

"Okay, here we go," thought Sharelle.

Looking up from the SkyMall magazine, she turned to him and gave him a brief,

"No, just visiting."

To her surprise, the man just smiled and said,

"Same here. Good thing this is a short flight."

She nodded affirmatively, smiled, and reached for her tote bag to retrieve her laptop. Over the next hour and a half, she played with ideas for a new book topic. Unfortunately, her focus was interrupted by yet, another announcement.

"Ladies and gentlemen, the captain has turned on the fasten seat belt sign. We will be making our approach for landing at O'Hare International Airport in approximately ten minutes. As we make our descent into Chicago, please ensure that your seat belts are securely fastened and your seatbacks and tray tables are in their full upright and locked positions. Again, thank you for flying Allova Airlines, and we hope you have a safe and pleasant stay here in Chicago."

"Finally!" exclaimed Sharelle.

As soon as the aircraft touched down on the tarmac, she hurriedly unzipped her handbag to find her lip gloss and her compact mirror to touch up a bit. They hadn't even reached the jetway before she had unbuckled her seat belt, hoping to be one of the first ones off the plane. When the exit door of the aircraft opened, the aisle was already jammed with other passengers who were also anxious to deplane. Though she was impatient, she had to wait. Finally, the pudgy, red-faced man in 9F arose from his seat, removed his coat and briefcase from the overhead bin, and stepped out in line behind the others. She grabbed her matching Louie travel duo and attempted to side-step the row to get in line behind him, but the lady from across the aisle in 9C jumped out first. A courteous gentleman bringing up the rear motioned for Sharelle to proceed in front of him, which she graciously did.

Once she deplaned, she stopped in the waiting area at the gate and put down her overnight bag to retrieve a breath mint out of her handbag. After two hours of travel and a Bloody Mary mix, her breath could use a little freshening up. So, after adjusting her clothes, she picked up her bag and proceeded. Since it had been a while since her last visit to Chicago, she was a little confused about which way to get to the baggage claim. She first looked left, right, then left again, trying to find the sign that pointed her toward the baggage claim area. Then seemingly, out of nowhere, a rather handsome thirty-something-year-old guy came walking briskly toward her. Their eyes locked on one another, and he flashed a big beautiful smile as he approached. Sharelle nervously sized up the situation.

Okay, I was warned to watch out for the crack-heads and crazies in Chicago, but can I at least make it to the baggage claim before I'm forced to call upon my MMA self-defense training?

When the man met her face-to-face, he exclaimed,

"Excuse me, I was just on the same flight as you, sitting two rows back on the other side of the plane and…."

Sharelle interrupted,

"Oh, did I leave something on the plane?" Looking him up and down as though he had something that belonged to her.

"Oh, no, I was just wondering if you realized who was sitting next to you."

"No, I can't say that I do. Who was it?"

"That was Ted Kennedy! You know, the U.S. senator of Massachusetts?"

She just stood there, stuck on stupid. Racing through her mind were all sorts of thoughts.

"Ted Kennedy? I love Ted Kennedy! How could I be so stupid? How could I not know Ted Kennedy? He looks nothing like he does on TV! Why was he sitting next to me in business class? Why wasn't he in first-class? Oh, my God, I can't believe I totally dissed Ted Kennedy!"

She gathered herself, and trying to play off her embarrassment, she uttered,

"You know, he's aged quite a bit. I didn't even recognize him."

"Yeah, and he's gained a lot of weight too, probably all the drinking," the young man replied.

The man, realizing that she was unsure of where she was going, asked,

"Are you looking for the baggage claim area?"

"Well, I thought it was this way, but I see they've changed things since I was last here."

"Yeah, it's crazy, they're expanding the terminal, and they've screwed everything up. Well, listen, I'm going that way. I'll walk you there if you like."

"Thank you, I'd appreciate that."

As they walked to the baggage claim, the man introduced himself to Sharelle.

"My name is Greg."

"Nice to meet you, Greg. I'm Sharelle."

"Nice meeting you. Are you in Chicago for a special occasion, or...?"

"No, no, I wouldn't call it a special occasion. But unfortunately, my grandmother passed away."

Greg put a hand to his mouth and ashamedly said,

"Oh, I'm so sorry,I didn't mean…."

"No, it's okay; you had no way of knowing, but thanks for your concern. What about you?" "Do you live here in Chicago?"

"No, I'm here for a pharmaceutical symposium."

"Oh yeah? What do you do?"

"I'm in pharmaceutical sales."

"Oh, so you're a drug dealer?"

Looking for clarification, he asked,

"Excuse me?"

"I'm sorry, but I couldn't resist, it was a bad joke."

After a slight delay, he got a clue and responded,

"Oh, now I get it. That's pretty funny."

Once arriving at the baggage claim, Greg asked Sharelle if she would need help with her luggage. She replied,

"No thanks, I'll be fine. Thanks for all your help, it was nice meeting you, Greg."

"No problem. Nice meeting you, too, Sharelle. My sympathy to you and your family."

"Thank you, bye."

"Take care."

Once outside the baggage claim area, she took a deep breath and smelled something familiar. Chicago always seemed to have an aroma in the air. Not a stench, but a smell—a not-so-pleasant smell. It smelled like burned sour cream and onion-flavored potato chips; at least, that's what Sharelle likened it to. Apparently, the scent has been around for centuries. So much so that the Potawatomi Indians originally named the city Checagou, the meaning of which has reference to wild onions. After taking in a deep breath, she thought,

"I guess some things just never change."

The following days were exhausting. There were visits back and forth between the mortuary, the church, and the florist. On the day of

the funeral, there was an outpouring of love for Sharelle's dearly departed grandmother, which was evident by the mourners attending the
service. As she viewed her grandmother for the last time in death, and as
she said her final goodbyes, she whispered,

"Sleep well, grandma sleep, eternally well."

Chapter Eight

It had been an entire week since returning from her grandmother's funeral, and Sharelle was still mentally exhausted. Worse yet, she still hadn't decided on a new premise for her book, and the first draft deadline was growing near. Weary-minded and clueless about what to write, she decided that tending to her flower garden, which she had been neglecting, might be therapeutic. While weeding her garden, her neighbor happened to drop by. The neighbor was Rhonda Strange and the name couldn't fit her any better because strange she was. She and her husband Curtis were two of the few blacks that lived in Allyson Heights. Rhonda seemed normal enough in the beginning and was always very pleasant. However, after a few months of knowing her, she revealed some rather peculiar behavior.

Rhonda had come over to ask Sharelle for a ride to the store. She had misplaced her car keys and had run out of cigarettes. Though she was a little taken aback at the request, she said to her,

"No problem, Rhonda, I'll take you. Just let me get cleaned up and change my clothes, and I'll be ready in about ten minutes."

With gratitude, Rhonda replies,

"Oh, thank you so much, I'll go get my purse, and I'll be right back."

When she returned, Sharelle was shocked to see that she was still in her nightgown. She thought it was bad enough that she came out of the house like that in the first place. Now she's actually going to the store in her nightgown. Thoroughly disgusted at the sight of Rhonda, she says to herself,

"Talk about a wardrobe malfunction. Thank God it's not the short, frilly kind with the plunging neckline and matching thong."

It was more of a nightshirt, but sleepwear, nonetheless.

During the ten-minute drive to the store, Rhonda explained that she needed to smoke before her husband and children got home. However, they didn't know about her habit, and her husband disapproved of it. Sharelle asked her how long she had been smoking, and she told her she had smoked for thirteen years. She was amazed that she could keep up the ruse for so long. She asked her how she kept them from finding out. She told her that she would smoke outside wearing a plastic bag on her head so that the smoke wouldn't get into her hair, and she wore a rubber glove as a barrier to keep the smell off of her hand. Sharelle wondered, "Why bother at all if you have to go through all those changes?"

Throughout the conversation, she noticed a slur in Rhonda's speech and her nodding between sentences. Apparently realizing that Sharelle was suspicious of her strange behavior, she declared,

"I know it looks like I'm asleep, but I'm not. I hear everything you're saying; it's just that I have two lazy eyes, and when the sun gets in them, they start to close."

Completely at a loss for how she should respond to such ridiculous rationale, Sharelle replied with a drawn-out and exaggerated,

"O-o-kay."

Though she played along, she wasn't going for the okey-doke. Obviously, this crazy chick had a secret that even Victoria couldn't rival. At that moment, she recalled her friend Tracy telling her sometime back that she would meet a woman with some mental problems and to beware. If there were ever a time to give credence to any psychic presage from Tracy, this was it. She started to suspect there was something else up with Rhonda. She thought,

"Oh, it's the old lazy eye syndrome excuse. Yeah, right; not only

does this chick look a hot mess, but she's high as a kite!"

Then, to add insult to injury, she really gave herself away when she asked,

"Hey, how's your boyfriend doing?"

Sharelle took her eyes off the road for a second. She looked her up and down as if trying to help look for her lost mind. She then fired back,

"My boyfriend? I don't have a boyfriend. I'm married."

"Uh-uh, oh, I'm sorry, I must be getting you confused with someone else who was telling me something about her boyfriend the other day. That's right, Eric is your husband."

She couldn't get this space shot out of her car fast enough. The more Rhonda talked, the heavier her foot pressed on the accelerator. After getting the cigarettes, she drove back to her house to drop her off. Rhonda thanked her for the ride, and with her eyes half closed, she stated,

"It's got to be after twelve o'clock 'cause I'm starving. Don't you want to come in and have lunch?"

Sharelle chuckled at the ludicrous statement, then replied sarcastically,

"Uh-no, thanks, Rhonda. It's only nine-thirty, and I haven't even had breakfast yet."

She felt sorry for Rhonda once she started putting two and two together. She had been in and out of the hospital for a while now. After she was released this last time, she remembers Rhonda telling her that the medication prescribed for her was too strong and had to be changed.

When Sharelle asked what type of meds she was prescribed, she told her that it was Webufrin. Sharelle thought she had seen something on a TV commercial that advertised the drug.

Scratching her head, she tries to remember what it was prescribed for.

"Webufrin? Hmm. Isn't that for bipolar people?"

A few weeks later, Rhonda called with some startling news.

"Sharelle, I just called to tell you I'm moving."

She stood with her mouth stretched wide open.

"What? You're kidding! You've only been here a year!"

"Yeah, well, Curtis left me for another woman, and I don't want to stay around here and have to run into him out somewhere with the bitch!"

Surprisingly, Rhonda went on to speak candidly about Curtis' requests for Rhonda to dress up like a hooker and have sex with his best friend while he watched. When she repeatedly protested against the idea, he brazenly stated that if she didn't comply, he knew someone that would. Apparently, he made good on his promise. Curious, Sharelle asked why he wanted her to do something like that. She went on to admit that it was an obsession of his. Judging by her candor, she didn't think it would appear too rude of her if she inquired further. Rhonda was all too willing to share. In tears, she spilled more twisted details of Curtis' sexual exploits.

Satisfied that she had heard enough and sickened by what she was told, she offered her condolences.

"Rhonda, I'm so sorry to hear that. Where are you gonna go?"

"I'm going back to Raleigh to live with my mom. I just put the house up for sale yesterday, and already I have two offers, so I should be outta here in a couple of weeks."

"Rhonda, please let me know if there's anything I can do to help."

"Thanks, Sharelle. I'll talk to you later. Bye."

Sharelle hung up the phone, sat on her bed, and turned on the television. While channel surfing, something caught her attention. It was a commercial advertising Webufrin. She watched the ad intently as the narrator recited the drug's side effects.

Webufrin is not for everyone. As with all medications, you may experience side effects when taking Webufrin. The most common side effects associated with Webufrin are nausea, anxiety, dizziness, and frequent urination. There is a low risk of sexual side effects associated with taking Webufrin. Ask your doctor if Webufrin is right for you.

Sharelle sat straight up and blurted out,
"Sexual side effects? That poor girl just didn't stand a chance!"

An Explicit Nature

Chapter Nine

Maya must have visited every clothing store in the mall. They had already been there for over three hours, with the difficult-to-please teen having purchased only one blouse. All the while, Sharelle's patience was getting thinner by the minute. She had promised to take her daughter shopping for clothes for her eighteenth birthday. Because graduation was just around the corner, they would shop for the perfect dress together. Since she was out of town on Maya's birthday, she wanted to make good on her promise. Though she was subjected to a cruel form of parental abuse by being dragged through the mall for several hours, she persevered.

A weary Sharelle decided to give Maya some money and let her go it alone. So instead, she went into Binder's bookstore. She loved that particular bookstore because they had cozy seats where you could sit quietly and read. She browsed through the non-fiction section and found something that captured her interest. She was attracted to a book by an unknown author named Jamie Tolbert.

She took the book from the shelf, sank into one of the comfortably cushioned, button-tucked chairs, and began diving inside.

She was already fifteen pages in and intrigued by what she had read. The book was a true story about a 17-year-old girl who was rescued from a life in the child sex-slave trade. She had been sold into the trade at the age of eight by her methamphetamine-addicted mother. She had endured horrors that were just plain unconscionable to the average person. But, as she read, she realized that atrocities like that must be brought to light. Suddenly, it hit her. This was it.

Sharelle realized that she had tapped into something that she could write about and, at the same time, be proud that she was raising the consciousness of her readers. Finally, she would write about a powerful phenomenon that can alter human behavior and destroy lives...sex addiction.

This must be what Joy was talking about when she asked me to find a subject that I'm passionate about and just write, she thought.

Her mind began to race with ideas about how she would research the subject, find people dealing with the issue, and tell their stories. It would be an exposé of sorts, an exposé of their indiscretions. Her eyes lit up at the very thought.

That's a perfect title for it; An Exposé of Indiscretion! I'll call my publisher first thing tomorrow. Right in the middle of her brainstorming, her attention was diverted to an incoming text message on her phone. It was from her girlfriend, Tracy. The confusing text read as follows:

> CRIMSON VISIONS, YOU WILL HAVE
> RESULTING FROM IRAM'S WRATH.
> IT ALL COMES DOWN TO SIMPLE MATH.
> LET 2 + 2 DIRECT YOUR PATH.

Stunned and wholly absorbed in the strange message, she didn't realize that Maya was standing right in front of her with several bags in hand. In an agitated tone, she tries to get her mom's attention.

"Mom, I'm finished. Are you ready to go? Mom! Mom!"

Though Maya startled her back to awareness of her present surroundings, she was delighted to hear the words that her daughter had spoken. Those words were music to her ears, especially after spending five hours and as many dollars times a hundred at the mall.

"Yeah, let's go home," Sharelle says.

When they got home, she was pleasantly surprised to see that Eric had prepared dinner. It was no gourmet meal, just some tacos, but as tired and as hungry as she was, she was happy to have anything as long as she didn't have to cook it. She says to him,

"Hey there, oh, I see you made tacos."

Somewhat perturbed, he responds,

"Yep. I got tired of waitin' on y'all. You took too long, and I'm about to starve to death."

Completely ignoring the dramatics, she replied,

"Well, I'm glad you cooked 'cause I'm beat."

She didn't dare speak the words of sarcasm that were dangling off of her tongue, as that would only discourage him from ever cooking again.

After dinner, she went upstairs to her office to work on an outline for her new book topic. She jotted down some notes she recalled from recently watching a documentary about the human male brain and how visual cues stimulate their sex drive. Then she logged onto the internet to begin research on sex addiction related to child molestation. As she continued to take notes, she was surprised to see the seemingly, endless amount of information on the subject. She said under her breath,

"Wow, this is more prevalent than I would've thought."

Something she found interesting was how the articles used sex addiction and porn addiction interchangeably. She had been under the impression that they were two different behavioral disorders. This revelation piqued her curiosity even more. After reading this, she made a notation of the next question that she wanted to find an answer to. She wrote:

What is the statistic on porn addicts that eventually graduate to become sex offenders?

Suddenly, she stopped cold and leaned back in her chair when a critical thought occurred.

"Wait, something just doesn't sound quite right about that question. Graduation and porn addiction don't belong together in the same sentence. There's no such thing as graduating to become a pervert. It makes sex addiction sound like an accomplishment! That would be like saying

congratulations on your outstanding achievement of graduating to sex of-fenderhood."

She shuddered at the mere thought, then revised her notation:

So, what percentage of porn addicts escalate to being sex offenders?

Satisfied with the revised verbiage, she proceeded with her research and note-taking.

As she filled the last page of the notebook, she looked through the desk's drawers to find another one, but none were there. She remembered packing a box with office supplies when they were moving and putting it in the storage closet of her office. Unfortunately, it was one of a few boxes that she hadn't gotten around to unpacking.

"I guess this is one way to get me to finally unpack these boxes," she thought.

She drags the heavy box out of the closet and, with a letter opener, slices through the packing tape that sealed it. Inside, she found her favorite Swingline stapler that she thought she had lost, some computer software manuals, and a couple of Eric's job training manuals. But, of course, her notepaper was on the bottom, so she was forced to unpack everything.

While unpacking the items, one of Eric's training manuals slipped out of her grasp and fell to the floor. It was the big, bulky one that had to weigh at least four pounds. She noticed something fly out between the book's pages as it fell. It was a couple of photos. One photo was of a plus-sized woman wearing a skimpy bikini, a thong bikini. The bottom of which was buried somewhere deep within two gargantuan butt cheeks. Sharelle had no idea who this woman was. The curious thing about the photo was that it wasn't taken on any beach or around any poolside. It appeared to have been taken in a hotel room, though she couldn't swear to it. She knew that the circumstances surrounding it were anything but benign wherever it was taken. The other photo landed face down on the floor. She picked it up, turned it over, and saw that it was a picture of Maya at about two or three years old. She smiled as she looked at her daughter's chubby-cheeked image. She almost forgot how adorable she was some fifteen years ago. It almost brought tears to her eyes to think about how the years had passed. Now, her baby girl was about to graduate from high school. As she reminisced about Maya as a little girl, she noticed something in the photo's background.

There was a car parked just behind and to the left of Maya, a red sports car. She could see that there was a building in the background. It was an office building, an office building with sun-deflecting mirrored windows. There was a vanity plate on the front end of the car. It could be seen in the reflective windows of the building. However, the image was too out of focus to make out the plate's lettering. Still, it was apparent that it wasn't a state-issued license plate. She tried to make out the numbers on what appeared to be a temporary license in the car's rear window, but they were also obscure. Apparently, the car had just recently been purchased. She tried to place the location where the photo was taken, but she saw nothing in the background that looked familiar.

"Where was Maya when she took this picture? Was I there?" She pondered.

She often blamed her inability to recall things on the amnesia she had suffered since the accident. Her memory was sketchy about some things, and she remembered others just fine.

"Whatever, I can't even remember what I did yesterday, never mind where I was fifteen years ago," she thought.

But it wasn't so much about where Maya was when she took that picture as it was that car. Something about that red sports car gave her an uneasy feeling. She started trembling. It appeared to her, at first, that she had just gotten a chill, but then, she began to sweat, and her right arm began to twitch. The symptoms were all too familiar, this was the onset of another episode of tremors. As her arm writhed violently, she braced herself against the closet door. Her heart was beating so hard that it felt like it would jump right out of her chest. She tried not to panic by closing her eyes tightly so as not to see the arm as it wildly convulsed. She grabbed the appendage and squeezed it as hard as possible, trying to restrict blood flow to the spasmodically out-of-control muscles. She prayed silently as she tried to regain control of the arm, then the tremors slowly stopped. Out of breath, she sat down in her office chair to calm herself. Just as she caught her breath, Eric walked into the room while taking a break from playing a video game. He noticed a frightened look on his wife's face.

"Sweetness, is everything alright? You look like you've just seen a ghost."

"I'm okay. I just had a sharp pain in my shoulder, that's all."

"I guess so, Ellery Queen. Your shoulder probably does hurt the way you've been tapping away on that keyboard! Do you want some Typenol or something?"

"No, I'm fine, really."

Eric left the room, and she sat there thinking about her upcoming appointment with the neurologist. It would be just a couple more days until she would get some answers. Sharelle thought she should note the events leading up to the episodes so that she could inform the doctor during her visit. She wanted to get to the bottom of this awful problem. She was sure that, once and for all, there would be a permanent solution. She was confident that he would prescribe something or recommend some physical therapy. Then, she would finally be free of the curse. A few minutes later, Eric returned with a glass of water in one hand and handed her a muscle relaxant in the other. She looked at him and said,

"I'm fine. I told you I didn't need anything."

But he insisted that the medication would make her feel better and that she should take it anyway. Conceding that he might be right, she thanked him, popped the pill in her mouth, and took a gulp of water to wash it down. Then, satisfied that she had taken his suggestion, he smiled at her, kissed her on the cheek, and then left the room to return to his video game.

Apparently, her mother, Arlene, must've sensed something was wrong because she decided to call at that moment.

"Hello?" answered Sharelle.

"Hi, what'cha doin'?"

"Oh hey, Mom. I'm just doing some writing. How're you doin'?"

"Everything's okay with me, but you don't sound so good. What's going on?"

"Nothing. I'm fine."

"Something's wrong. I hear it in your voice."

"Mom, really, I'm okay. I just…"

Sharelle didn't want to tell her mom about the tremors she was having. It would only bring about too many questions that she couldn't answer, and she didn't want her mother to worry needlessly. Still, Arlene continued pressing for information.

"C'mon now, you know I can tell when something's wrong with my child, what is it?"

"Mom, I'm fine. I'm just a little tired, that's all. I was at the mall shopping for five hours with Maya."

"Good Lord, I guess you are tired. Well, better you than me, 'cause I know how hard to please she can be. Well, why don't you go and get a nice hot bath and get some rest, and I'll talk to you tomorrow, okay?"

"Okay, I'll talk to you later, Mom. Bye."

Almost immediately after hanging up with Arlene, the phone rang again. Startled by the loud ring of the office phone, she rushed to answer.

"Hello?"

She got no response, then tried again.

"Hello?"

There was still no response, yet it was evident to her that somebody was on the other end. So, she firmly told the caller how much the game-playing was getting on her nerves.

"Look, whoever you are, stop calling here if you have nothing to say."

Slamming the phone down as hard as she could, she hung up on the rude caller. She then wondered what kind of person has that little excitement in their lives that they equate prank phone calling with fun. It had been happening more frequently and was starting to become a nuisance.

After getting back to organizing the items she removed from the box, she started feeling intense drowsiness. She took one more look at the photo, then tacked it onto her bulletin board. It was such an adorable picture of Maya that she thought it would be nice to have it enlarged and framed. Exhausted from the shopping spree earlier that evening, she took Arlene's advice.

Chapter Ten

"**P**ig intestines? They're Chitterlings, better known as chitlins. If you had done your research and asked people who know, they would've told you." Sharelle sternly admonishes the so-called "food expert" featured on Good Morning America. She had tuned into the telecast when she woke up Monday morning. But, for her, it wasn't such a good morning. For some reason, she was in a terrible mood.

The supposed food expert on the show discussed unusual foods and how to prepare them. He commented that some people eat things that shouldn't be eaten, like pig intestines. Hearing those words was all she needed to send her off on a tirade. As though the food expert could hear her through the television, she fired back passionately,

"Some people? We all know what people you're talking about, what about people who eat monkey brains and Madagascar cockroaches? Of course, those things shouldn't be eaten, but you didn't say anything about them."

Of course, her moodiness had nothing to do with chitlins. She didn't even eat them, except maybe once every five or six years if Arlene made them for New Year's Day dinner, and that was because her mom was the only one she trusted to clean them properly. But, after realizing that she needed a serious attitude adjustment, she felt that maybe there was a point to what the man on Good Morning America was saying after all.

Besides, her real issue wasn't with him anyway. She didn't sleep well last night. She tossed and turned all night long. She remembers having a dream, a nightmare, actually. In the dream, she was running down the street while being chased by a car. It was a red car, a sporty red car like the one in the picture with Maya. She didn't recall seeing who was driving, nor did she know why she was being chased. She just remembered screaming at the top of her lungs and running for her life.

This incubus, in the form of a car, seemed to come out of nowhere. It chased her for miles. It seemed to her that she ran for at least an hour or more, trying to get to somewhere safe. Sharelle recalls not knowing where she was, so she kept running until she came to a meat-packing warehouse.

Just as the car was right on her heels, she made a bee-line for the safety of the warehouse. The vehicle having no success in its evil quest, sped off, fishtailing and leaving behind a thick cloud of dust. She gasped for air as the heart-stopping nightmare shocked her back to full consciousness.

For the rest of the night, she tried, hopelessly, to get back to sleep. First, she got up to get a drink of water and then went to the bathroom. She got up a third time to turn down the heat because the marathon she had run in her dream had her wringing wet with sweat. Sharelle was well aware that her foul mood didn't have anything to do with chitlins, it had everything to do with that red sports car.

She tried to extract some meaning from this strange apparition, but it only led to more questions. She wondered,

"What's the deal with red cars all of a sudden? I don't know anyone with a red car. I don't even like the color red."

Despite her sleepless night, she was not about to let the nightmare ruin her day. It was a beautiful day out, and she was determined to get out and enjoy it. Whenever she felt a little down, there was one sure way she could cheer herself up, power shopping. Since moving to Charlotte, she had taken note of some interesting-looking boutiques and outlet stores and was dying to explore them. They looked like perfect targets for power shopping.

63

Power shopping is an art form. It requires one to be shrewd, discriminating, and, most of all, stealthy, just like a lioness when she stalks her prey. First, she lay in wait, checking out all possibilities. Then, she pinpoints her target, and before it knows what hit it, she's all up on that bad boy like white on rice.

Power shopping is defined as having no idea what you're looking for. Simply go out on the prowl for high-end items at discount prices. For Sharelle, shopping with Maya was exasperating, but power shopping by herself, that's what she calls exhilarating.

She jumped in the shower and hurried to get dressed. She wanted to return home in time to watch her favorite celebrity talk show because she had seen the promo of the day's topic about Curt Franklin and his porn addiction. She thought it was probably just a publicity stunt, so she had to see the show to believe it. She tried painstakingly to wrap her mind around the notion.

"Curt Franklin? Not Curt "Stomp" Franklin.

Can this possibly be true? First, we hear about Catholic priests secretly molesting altar boys, and now Christian gospel singers are gettin' their freak on with porn? I know gospel music has come a long way, but Curt "Lookin' for You" Franklin? *Get outta here!*"

Sharelle started her quest for high-end bargains at a store that Joy raved about—Veronique's Boutique. As soon as she walked into the shop, she knew that she had discovered a well-kept secret.

She felt like Harriet Tubman traveling through the underground railroad of designer fashion. Moshimo khaki pants, Brunolo Macetti gold lamé sweaters, and Preshda wicker wedgies, all at drastically off-retail prices. It was a power shopper's paradise.

As she made her way around the Parisienne-inspired boutique, she saw two other fashion-savvy women feverishly sifting through a rack marked:

CLOSEOUTS

All items on this rack up to eighty percent off.

One of the ladies was a tall, big-boned type. The other was about five-foot three and shapely about the same as Sharelle's height and build.

She headed to the rack to see what all the frenzy was about. Immediately, she was drawn to an adorable little Jacques Pozen waistline jacket. The only problem was: They only had it in red, and Sharelle didn't like wearing red.

She then spotted a bronze metallic, knee-length Guocci trench hanging towards the end of the rack, size eight, her size! The tall lady was looking through the size twelves. She didn't have to sweat her. "Miss big-bones" posed absolutely no threat.

It was the shorter savvy shopper that she was concerned about. She was looking in the size eight section and was dangerously close to the bronze metallic Guocci number that Sharelle spotted.

She had to think fast to devise a way to out-maneuver the competition. She knew the woman hadn't yet noticed the trench, but she was uncomfortably closer to it than she was. Then, finally, opportunity came knocking when Miss "Size Eight" pulled a Dolbe & Grivanna silk tunic from an adjacent rack to admire. She inspected the tunic long and hard, allowing Sharelle time to ease closer to her prey, the Guocci trench.

As she approached, Miss "Size Eight" continued sifting through the garments, clinging to the tunic, and getting closer to the Guocci trench. Just as she was about to move in for the kill, Miss "Size Eight" reached for the trench. She knew if she was going to be victorious, she had to make her move. It all came down to survival of the fittest. In a move of desperation, she disoriented the competition by saying,

"Excuse me, where'd you find that tunic? That's really cute."

Pointing Sharelle in the direction of the rack in question, the woman replies,

"Oh, there's another one like this over there."

When the woman turned to show her where she had found the tunic, she made her move. She quickly snatched the Guocci trench from the rack and scampered down the aisle. Unfortunately, Miss "Size Eight" didn't have the slightest idea that she had just been hoodwinked. Worse yet, she had been jacked Jersey style.

Feeling a slight twinge of guilt, she turns to the woman and says, "Oh, thank you so much."

Looking at the tag on the trench, she saw that it was originally priced at four hundred thirty-five dollars. She immediately did some mental math and was ecstatic about her conquest.

Eighty-seven dollars, for Guocci? Yes!

She no longer felt guilty about her deceitful maneuver. That's the beauty of power shopping, you have to be quick and calculating, otherwise, to quote a popular phrase, if ya slow, ya blow.

An Explicit Nature

Chapter Eleven

"Well, Sharelle, I've got good news. After reviewing your EEG and CT scan results, I see no evidence of any nerve damage. In addition, the MRI of your spine looks fine except for a slight bulging of the disk between the third and fourth cervical vertebrae. Therefore, the tremors you've complained about are not a result of any neurological concern," explains Sharelle's neurologist.

"What about the memory loss? Did the tests show anything relative to that?"

Well, that's what's interesting. I know that you suffered some trauma to the head in an accident that you had some years ago, but I find no physical damage. However, I believe your symptoms might be psychosomatic; therefore, I'd like to refer you to a psychiatrist.

Her eyes welled up after hearing the neurologist's findings. One might think that she would have been thrilled to know that there was no physical damage to her brain and she did feel some relief in knowing that she didn't have a disabling injury.

However, the report was bittersweet, now she was back at square one, she was still unsure of the cause of the tremors that plagued her.

"So, doctor, are you saying that I'm imagining these tremors?"

"No, not at all. I'm saying that I believe the tremors are real and the memory loss, but that the cause is psychological, not physiological. At worst, the bulging disk may cause numbness in your right arm, but it wouldn't cause the tremors you describe.

Sharelle, you had a very traumatic experience, and sometimes, emotional trauma can result in debilitating physiological responses."

She left the doctor's office in a daze while clenching a referral to a psychiatrist and a prescription form in her hand. She sat in her car, trying to make sense of everything the doctor told her.

"Psychosomatic. What does this guy think, I'm crazy?"

She looks down at the referral form and then at the prescription form and tries deciphering it.

"What is this prescription for? He didn't tell me anything about a prescription. Lord have mercy, what does this say? W-w-wuh, web, Oh, hell no! I know this man did not prescribe Webufrin for me!"

Sharelle was highly insulted. Actually, she was pissed. She couldn't believe that this quack, who was obviously only masquerading as a doctor, dared to imply that she was psychologically challenged. She was willing to accept that maybe she was hormonally imbalanced or even emotionally fragile, but psycho? Although he didn't say it quite like that, she had sense enough to know that psychosomatic and psychotic share a common prefix.

She ripped the prescription form into little pieces and threw them out her car window. She then folded the referral form several times into a perfect two-by-two square. Finally, she searched for a prominent place in her wallet for safekeeping. Searching for a vacant spot within the credit card slots of her wallet, she noticed a glossy black business card with embossed gilded lettering. It was neatly tucked behind her American Impress card.

She didn't recognize the card as having any real significance at first glance. However, after reading it, she realized she had a good reason for squirreling it away. It was the business card of Dr. Leland Alston, the psychiatrist she met at the Jazz Café.

She smiled at the irony of the moment. She was being advised by a neurologist to seek psychiatric help when she had Lee's business card in her wallet all along. Maybe Joy was right; perhaps it was fate meeting Lee. Maybe it was divine intervention. But, more than likely, Joy was right. She almost always was.

Still sitting in the parking lot of the medical arts building, Sharelle unzipped her handbag to retrieve her phone. She stared at Lee's card for a minute, trying to talk herself out of making the call to his office. Finally, she dialed the number, let it ring once, then hung up.

"Uhhh! Why am I trippin' about this? I have to do this and I have to do it now."

She makes another attempt at making the call. This time, she waits for someone to answer. She hears a woman answer in a sing-songy tone of voice.

"Dr. Alston's office, please hold."

Before she could open her mouth to speak, the receptionist had cut her off and disappeared, leaving her to be entertained by the toe-tapping tunes of Lawrence Welk.

After holding throughout what sounded like an entire big band rendition of The Itsy-Bitsy Spider, the receptionist finally came back on the phone.

"Dr. Alston's office, may I help you?"

"Uh, yes is Dr. Alston available, please?"

"I believe he's just finishing up with a patient. May I tell him whose calling?"

"Yes, this is Sharelle Hughes."

"I'll see if he can take your call. One moment, please."

She withdrew the phone from her ear in anticipation of another auditory assault by Lawrence Welk. When she placed it on speakerphone, she was somewhat surprised to hear a more pleasant selection playing this time. It sounded like one of those Broadway show tunes. Maybe a Rodgers & Hammerstein show tune, though she couldn't be sure.

Still, she was a little suspect of Lee's choice of music.

She respected that he was a doctor and that gangsta rap might not be the most appropriate choice for a professional setting. Yet, her contention was that he's not just a doctor, he's a doctor that happens to be a brotha.

70

Basically, he had a responsibility to represent, in her opinion. It wasn't that she didn't enjoy the more refined music genres. In fact, she had a genuine appreciation for classical music from the impressionist era. It was Lawrence Welk and his polka music that, for her, was a bit of a stretch. Her thoughts drifted over to the many alternatives that Lee could've chosen.

"Why not rock a little Miles Davis or Wynton Marsalis, maybe even some Barry White, if it's orchestras that he's into?"

She thought perhaps she'd make the suggestion to him if the opportunity presented itself.

Just as she felt like hanging up after being placed on perpetual hold, the receptionist came back on the line.

"Ms. Hughes?"

"Yes."

"Thank you for holding. I'll transfer you to Dr. Alston now."

She immediately tensed up and tried to quickly gather herself before Lee answered. Sharelle closed her eyes, took a deep breath, and then heard that deep, smooth, sultry voice. He sounded just as she remembered when they first met.

"Dr. Alston speaking."

"Hi, Dr. Alston. This is Sharelle Hughes. I don't know if you remember me, but...."

Lee laid on a thick layer of charm as if she wasn't nervous enough.

"Sharelle, of course, I remember you, how could I forget such a beautiful face? How are you and to what do I owe the honor of hearing your lovely voice?"

"Oh, I'm doing good. I'm doin' pretty good, and I'm calling because I was hoping to meet with you."

"Hey, that sounds good, how 'bout lunch, say, one-thirty?"

"Oh, no, I guess I wasn't too clear. I meant that I want to meet with you professionally. You know, an appointment?

"Ohhh, I see, I see. Okay, well, my three o'clock just happened to call and cancel an appointment for today. Can you come then?"

71

"Three o'clock today? Umm, yeah, okay, that'll work."

"Okay, Sharelle, I look forward to seeing you. Let me transfer you back to my receptionist."

"Oh, wait, wait! What is your fee?"

"Well, the initial consultation is free, and we'll discuss further when you come, okay?"

"Alright, thank you, Dr. Alston—I'll see you later."

"Hey, let's cut the Dr. Alston crap. Call me Lee, okay?"

"O-o-kay, Lee."

"Now hang on while I transfer you back to the receptionist so she can book your appointment, and hey, thanks for calling. I'll see you later."

"Okay, bye."

She was relieved that Lee remembered her, and was even more relieved to hear him sounding so cordial with her on the phone. She knew she was about to reveal much of herself in her sessions with him, which was a scary thought. Still, at least he wasn't a total stranger, and she felt she could trust him not to take advantage of her vulnerability. Besides, that's what he's been trained to do, to help people.

She pulled out of the parking space and glanced at the clock on the dash. It was 12:45. She debated whether to go home to get lunch or grab a bite while she was out. Lee's office was about forty-five minutes from her home in Allyson Heights. The area where she was at the moment was a mere fifteen minutes away from his office.

She decided that it might be best to go home and change first. She wanted to look fresh and fabulous when she saw Lee for the first time in weeks. It had nothing to do with wanting to look attractive for him, it was more about how she felt about herself. It was a power thing. Sitting in the office of a successful doctor who seemed to have it all together while confessing to him how screwed up in the head she was, could potentially being ego-crushing. She knew it was shallow, but she had to do something to level the playing field, and the best that she could come up with was to, at least, look as good as he does.

Once back home, she went into her bedroom to check her answering machine for messages. She was annoyed that two out of three messages recorded were hang-up calls.

"Fools! If you don't have something to say, don't call!"

She had intended to change the greeting for a while because the number of hang-ups had increased since she recorded a greeting posing as a British housekeeper, complete with cockney dialect. She thought that maybe this was karma for all the times she had called someone's voicemail box just to hear their clever greeting and then hung up without leaving a message.

After checking her messages, she went into her bathroom to freshen up.

Dashing into her closet, she hoped to find something that could be quickly and easily thrown on. She immediately thought about her sage green Indian-inspired silk shirt. She prayed for it to be among the articles she had recently picked up from the cleaners. Unfortunately, it was already a quarter 'til two, and wearing something that needed ironing was not an option. After a five-minute expedition through her closet, she located the shirt, slipped it on, and headed back into the bathroom to give herself a final check. After a quick once-over, she approved what she saw and headed out the door.

Chapter Twelve

"1805 Lafayette Pike, Building C. Yep, this is the place," Sharelle said as she confirmed Lee's office address. She pulled into the parking lot of his office at precisely 2:55pm. She lucked out because, at that time of day, traffic happened to be running smoothly. She was relieved that she was able to find the place with no problem as well.

The office was in a part of Charlotte that she had never ventured into, and she wasn't sure where she was going or what to expect. However, it was apparent that this was a predominantly Jewish section of Charlotte. The huge synagogue she had passed down the street was a distinct indication. There was no doubt when, three blocks later, she realized that all the men in town were sporting all black, long beards and side locks.

As she walked toward the building, she heard a buzzing noise. Although it was a faint buzzing noise, it was still loud enough where it could be detected and it wasn't a steady buzz, it was a buzz with a pulse.

She looked all around her but couldn't find the source of the sound. She thought the sound would intensify as she approached the building if it were coming from there, but it didn't. It should've been getting fainter as she walked farther away from the parking lot if it were coming from there, but it didn't. Still, with every step she took, the buzzing was right there with her, seemingly coming from her own body.

She became so tuned in to the noise that it started to annoy her, like a mosquito hovering around her ear. Then, suddenly, the buzzing stopped for just a few seconds. Then the buzzing started again, this time with a short buzz, then two short beeps.

Finally, it registered with her what was happening.

"Oh my God, it's just my stupid cell phone!"

She had forgotten that she had set her phone to vibrate while at the neurologist's office.

She pulled her phone out of her handbag to see who had called, it was Eric. He had left her a message, but she didn't listen to it; instead, she called him back.

"Hello," Eric answers.

"Hi, you just called me?"

"Oh hey, yeah, I just left you a message."

"Yeah, I see. I didn't listen to it. I figured I'd just call you back. So, what's up?"

"Oh, nothing really. I just wanted to see how you made out at the neurologist's, that's all. Everything's alright, I take it?"

"Yeah, everything's fine. He said I just have a bulging disc in my neck, which is causing the pain in my shoulder, but other than that, I'm fine."

"That's great. I knew you'd be okay. Did he give you a prescription or anything?"

"No, he just told me to take Ibuprofen when the shoulder starts bothering me."

"See, I told you. You have to stop running to the doctor every time you get an ache or pain. There's nothing at all wrong with you. You're probably just on that damn computer too much. Maybe what you need to do is find another hobby. Besides, I know what'll take that pain away…."

With an exaggerated rolling of her eyes and a look of total disgust, she cut him off and said,

"Hmm, let me guess, sex?"

"Hey, how'd you guess?"

"I'm just a good guesser, I guess! But, look, I gotta go. I should be home in a little while. I'll see you when I get in."

"Okay, I'll see you later."

"Okay, bye."

Sharelle had no intention of telling Eric what the neurologist had told her. The last thing she wanted him to know was that she had been advised to seek psychiatric help. She hadn't even come to grips with it herself, let alone give him more ammunition to shoot her down with.

Not that he would believe that she was a head case, but he would think she was stupid for letting someone mislead her into seeing a shrink in the first place. His problem was that he had little trust in doctors, lawyers, and ministers. He believed people in those professions get rich by preying on others' sensibilities.

She thought his position was unfair. Her opinion was that all three professions provide the public with valuable, even necessary, services. She'd be the first to admit that there's always that proverbial bad apple in every profession, but she also knew there are good ones.

She would really become unnerved when he made derogatory remarks about lawyers. Especially since her father, Paul, is an attorney of good moral character.

Two minutes 'til three was the time that she saw displayed on her phone. If she hurried, she was sure she would make it on time. Inside the lobby of the building, she made her way to the bank of elevators on the left. There were three elevators, and all were sitting there with the doors open, so she chose the one on the end closest to the lobby entrance.

Lee's office was suite number 409, so she pressed the button for the fourth floor and waited, nothing happened. The doors wouldn't close. She pressed the button to close the doors and waited, nothing happened. The elevator would not move. She exited the elevator and entered the one next to it, and the same thing happened, nothing.

When she exited the second elevator, a maintenance worker noticed the flustered look on her face. He informed her that the elevators were being serviced; therefore, she'd have to take the stairs.

Annoyed, she mumbled to herself,

"Oh, that's just lovely. Not only will I be all sweaty and out of breath, but now I'm going to be late too!"

As she climbed the final flight of stairs and reached the landing, she took a tissue out of her purse to dab away the shine that started to form on her forehead.

She opened the stairwell door leading into the hallway of office suites and saw a sign pointing to the right for suites 400 to 414.

Finally, she entered suite 409 and approached the reception desk to tell the receptionist that she had an appointment for three o'clock.

She noticed that the clock on the wall behind the receptionist read 3:05. When asked to have a seat in the waiting area, she didn't feel so bad about arriving a little late. It was apparent he wasn't ready for her either. She looked around the waiting area and saw it was exquisitely decorated. There were custom satin drapes, burgundy leather furnishings, mahogany wood tables, and a beautiful Persian rug. She noticed a large arrangement of exotic flowers on the sofa table, and suddenly a strong feeling came over her, it was her gaydar!

"Any man who pays this much attention to detail has to be gay," she thought.

Just then, the receptionist opened the door to the waiting room.

"Ms. Hughes?"

"Yes."

"Dr. Alston will see you now."

She got up from the burgundy leather sofa and walked through the door. He was standing in front of his desk looking magnificent, even better than when she first met him. A big smile on his face and outstretched arms greeted her. As he gave her a gentle hug, he said to her in as gentle a voice,

"Well, hello, Sharelle. It's wonderful to see you, how have you been?"

"I'm fine, Lee. How are you?"

"Much better now that I see you."

She looked at him through scrutinizing eyes that searched for the slightest indication of gayness and concluded,

"This brotha sure doesn't seem gay."

Then, after realizing that her scrutiny was approaching the point of being just plain rude, she commented,

"Beautiful digs you have here, Lee, I'm impressed."

Obviously tickled by her compliment, he replied,

"Well, thanks, but I have to give all the credit to my interior designer. If it were left up to me, I would've been okay with a few folding chairs and a magazine rack."

After engaging in a brief laugh together, she was totally convinced and silently rejoiced,

"That confirms it. This brotha is definitely NOT gay!"

Lee regrouped and steered the focus in a more professional direction.

"C'mon, have a seat, Sharelle. Tell me, what brings you here to see me today."

Never having been in a psychiatrist's office before, she was surprised not to see the classic psychoanalyst's couch as she'd seen in the movies.

In fact, the office was set up much like a cozy living room, a living room with two buttery-soft leather club chairs, both of which faced each other and were flanked by a side table on one side. On the side table was a heavy bronze replica of Auguste Rodin's "The Thinker," along with a pen and notepad. Lee's desk sat on the other side of the room, paired with a high-back leather office chair. On either side of the room were built-in bookcases filled with beautiful leather-bound reference books and trade publications. He didn't sit behind his desk during sessions. He sat in one club chair while his patient sat in the other. He made sure that both he and the patient sat barrier-free, face-to-face.

"Well, Lee, my neurologist advised me to see a psychiatrist, so, I called you."

"Okay, good. Well, I must tell you I'm glad you chose to come to see me, Sharelle. Now, let me tell you how this works. First of all, have you ever sought the help of a psychiatrist before?"

"No! And I really don't think I need one now," She replies adamantly.

"Okay, okay, that's fine. I want you to understand something. Just because you've been advised to see a psychiatrist doesn't make you crazy, okay? Let's just make that clear from the very beginning. That's a common misconception that people have about my profession.

People like me are here to help you work through things that might be causing you difficulty in your life, things that you probably aren't even aware of.

Everybody has experienced some event that may have been difficult to deal with. Many have experienced something traumatizing enough to affect them to some degree or another. Some of us work through these events without requiring help, and others need a little guidance to cope.

Now, my role is simply to provide you an unbiased, impartial ear. I am here to help you recognize the things that may be causing you hardship and dysfunction in your daily life."

Once we identify the root cause of what's impacting your life in a disruptive way, we can work on ways to overcome these things together. How does that sound to you, Sharelle? Sharelle?"

She sat staring out of the office window at the picturesque skyline while paying little attention to Lee's psycho mumbo-jumbo at first. Then suddenly, she responded as if she'd been listening attentively all along.

"Oh, uh, that sounds just fine."

"Now, Sharelle, you have to want to do this for yourself; otherwise, I can't help you, no one can, do you understand?"

"Yes, I understand. I apologize"

"Okay, great! I'd like to learn a little about you, okay?"

"Okay, fire away! What would you like to know?"

"Well, I know you're married, but how long have you and your husband been together?"

"We just had our 25th wedding anniversary."

"Wow, that's a long time these days! So, you have kids, I presume?"

"Yes, two, a son and a daughter."

"What are their ages?"

"My son is twenty-three, and my daughter is eighteen."

"Are they still at home?"

"Well, my son is away in graduate school, and my daughter just graduated from high school and went back to New Jersey.

"Wow, so you have an empty nest, huh? How do you feel about that?"

"It was strange at first, but I'm getting used to it."

"What about your parents, are they still living?"

"Yes, they're still with me."

"That's good, you're really blessed. So, tell me, Sharelle. What was your childhood like?"

"It was a normal childhood, I guess."

She held back, thinking how corny this was of him to use the Freudian analysis method on her. She was a Psychology major in college and knew where this was going.

"Normal is a very subjective term. What does normal mean to you?" Lee asked.

"I just mean that I had a loving mother and father and was nurtured and cared for the way a kid should be. There was no abnormal behavior or abusive treatment in our family."

"So, your parents got along well?"

"Well, no, not necessarily. I mean, they ended up getting a divorce, and wait, you asked me about my childhood. I didn't think we were talking about my parent's marriage."

She felt that this was a cheap shot. She was there to discuss what was happening in the here and now with her own life. She was not there to talk about what went on forty-some-odd years ago with her parents. Fortunately for him, Lee knew when to back off. It became apparent to him that he had struck a nerve. He immediately altered his approach and replied,

"Okay, no problem. We'll come back to that later. But, first, tell me, what are some of your fondest memories about your childhood?"

"Hmm, I guess I'd have to say vacations with my family, holidays, you know, the basic stuff."

"Can you think of a specific time with your family that is most memorable?"

"I guess if I had to name something, it would be Christmas when I was 10 years old."

"Why is that such a special memory?"

"I guess because it was one of the best Christmases I'd ever had. I had been asking my parents for this candy apple red bike I had seen in the toy store for two consecutive Christmases. I was disappointed each Christmas morning when I didn't get it. It was the prettiest bike I had ever seen, and I really wanted it. I had forgotten about it by the third Christmas and didn't even put it on my Christmas list."

"Then why would it be such a fond memory of yours if you were disappointed?"

"Well, as it turned out, I was shocked when I got up that Christmas morning to find that bike next to the Christmas tree. I guess it was a magical thing as a child to realize that if you wished hard enough for something, you would eventually have it."

"Why do you think they waited so long to get it for you?"

"My guess is because it was a 10-speed bike meant for an older girl. They probably didn't feel I was big enough to handle it until at least age ten, in hindsight, they were most likely right."

"What makes you say that?"

"Well, let's see. If I remember correctly, our next-door neighbor's daughter, LaDonna, asked to ride my new bike one day. She was about two years younger than me and was only accustomed to the kind of bike with foot brakes. You know the kind that you pedal backward to brake?"

"Yeah, sure."

"Well, she was riding downhill and saw a car backing out of the driveway and panicked because she was gaining speed too fast. She grabbed the caliper handbrakes suddenly, and the bike flipped her."

"Wow, was she alright?"

"The car backing out of the driveway never saw her and rolled right over her. I saw the paramedics cover her face with a sheet, and after that, I never saw LaDonna again."

"Hmm, that had to be really difficult for you to deal with at such a young age. What happened to the bike?"

"My parents got rid of it. It was just too painful a reminder for all of us."

"I can imagine. That's really too bad."

Unbeknownst to her, she had already given Lee incredible insight into some possible reasons the neurologist referred her to him.

However, he decided not to push it any further on this visit. He had a good feeling that it wouldn't be long before the levee would break and reveal what was happening in Sharelle's head.

"Tell me what you hope to accomplish throughout our sessions, Sharelle?"

"Well, I had a bad accident about fifteen years ago. I don't remember much about it, only what I was told. It took me about a year and a half to recover fully from my injuries. Still, my memory never fully returned, and recently I've developed tremors. My doctor says there's no medical explanation for the tremors, so he advised therapy. Basically, I'm hoping that you can help me determine the cause."

"Hmm, okay. I'd like you to talk a little more about these tremors. How often do they occur, and what part of your body is affected?"

"It's only my right arm, and I guess over the last two months or so, they've become more frequent, maybe once or twice a week.

"Okay. Have you noticed what usually happens just before the tremors start?"

"I haven't noticed, except maybe this last time."

"What happened the last time?"

She was embarrassed to tell Lee about the events leading up to her last episode of tremors. It was just too ridiculous. If he didn't think she was crazy before, this would definitely cause him to think twice.

Just then, she noticed that the notepad and pen on the side table next to him were no longer there. She wondered when he picked them up off the table, how long he had taken notes, and what he had written. She realized that she must not have been looking directly at him for a while; otherwise, she would have noticed him picking up the pad and pen. She recounts the details of her most recent seizure.

"I was looking for something in my office at home, and a picture of my daughter fell from one of my husband's old job training manuals. It was an old picture; she couldn't have been more than three years old.

Then, I noticed a car in the background. For some reason, I got this awful chill, and before I knew it, the tremors began. I know it sounds stupid, but that's what happened."

"No, Sharelle, it doesn't sound stupid at all. Actually, I'd like to discuss that car some more. Unfortunately, we're out of time, but I have a little assignment for you for your next visit."

"An assignment?"

"Yes. I'd like you to keep a notepad with you everywhere you go over the next week. Make a point to notice what you were doing just before any episode of tremors occurred. Then, write down your thoughts and what you feel after the tremors subside."

"Lee, you can't be serious. So, what is that gonna do?"

"Yes, Sharelle, I'm very serious. You just have to trust me on this, okay?"

"Okay, but I really don't see the point."

"You want to get to the bottom of these tremors, right?"

"Oh, most definitely."

"Alright then, that's the point. Now, I'll see you next week, okay?"

"Okay, when should I come?"

"See my receptionist on the way out, she'll book an appointment for you."

"Okay, thanks a lot. I'll see you next week.

"Take care, Sharelle."

Chapter Thirteen

A rriving home around a quarter to five, Sharelle pulled into the driveway and noticed that Eric's car wasn't there. Although it struck her strange enough to notice, she didn't think too much of it. He was usually home from work by three, and it was his day to pick up Maya from school. So, she assumed maybe he had called her from home when he called earlier. After thinking about it, it was indeed possible that he wasn't at home when he called because he had called from his cell phone. Assuming he had just stopped at the store, she parked her car in the driveway without further thought.

She entered the house through the garage entrance and headed for her bedroom. Her bed was still made just as she had left it, a clear sign that Eric hadn't been home from work.

Again, she thought it was odd that he didn't tell her when they spoke earlier that he wouldn't be home when she got home. Not even as much as a message on the answering machine. Although it was a little out of character for him, she simply dismissed it.

She went into the kitchen to pour herself a glass of iced tea. Then, she returned to the bedroom to change into something more comfortable to relax and watch a movie on DVD. As she turned on the DVD player, she noticed that the TV screen displayed the word reading, indicating that there was already a DVD inserted. Before hitting the eject button, she waited to see which movie was already loaded. She thought maybe it might have been one of the many DVDs that Eric brought home that she hadn't gotten around to watching.

When the movie finally cued up, she was horrified at what she saw displayed before her. It was the most shocking thing she had ever seen on a television screen. It was the last thing that she would ever expect to see, a pornographic production featuring teenage girls! These girls were very obviously adolescents. They had the most innocent, youthful baby faces and newly developing breasts that every fourteen or fifteen-year-old girl has. They looked as if they were in agony as the forty-something-year-old men molesting and exploiting them performed anal sex and other deplorable acts on them. All the while robbing and raping them of their youth, innocence, and mental stability.

She watched as young lives were being destroyed, all for the profit derived from the sick and perverted pleasure of their demented audiences. The video was filmed in Brazil where, as Sharelle learned from her research, young girls are forced into prostitution and sexual slavery, often due to limited economic means.

In the Amazon River basin, young girls are made false promises of employment as waitresses or cooks in gold mine camps. What she found most shocking was that recruiters take these girls to brothels to have sex with men, and those who try to escape are beaten or killed. The wealthy owners of these gold mine camps often hold "virginity auctions," whereas girls, sometimes as young as nine years old, are sold to the highest bidder.

In that country, many police officers are paid bribes to look the other way. As a result, the laws that protect innocent victims from opportunists and pedophiles looking for a way to skirt American laws meant to protect minors from such abuse aren't enforced. These young girls aren't paid much, if at all, yet the profits are enormous for the gutter rats that distribute the illicit material.

She sat there in shock and disbelief. Tears streamed down her face, staining her white gauze tank top as she cried for the young molested girls on her TV screen, as she cried for her eighteen-year-old daughter,

Maya.

She was terrified that she had been married to a man for 25 years without truly knowing him. They have an eighteen-year-old daughter. She silently questioned Eric's judgment. What if she appeared in one of these pedo-pandering productions, he would be ready to kill both her and the freak that put her in it. Yet, it's okay for him to lust after someone else's precious baby girl? He should be repulsed at the idea of lusting after girls Maya's age and younger, whether on DVD or otherwise. He should advocate for swift and severe punishment for the monsters that exploit these young girls and the pieces of shit that distribute the filth they produce.

Eric considered none of those things. Instead, he had allowed himself to become desensitized to it. He no longer saw human beings, God's creations. He no longer saw someone's daughter or sister. There was nothing wrong with his eyesight. His twisted mind only saw young, tight vaginas and anuses, too small to accommodate the adult penises that ripped them apart repeatedly.

He had become that dirty old man that mothers warn their daughters about. She wondered how he would explain this, especially since he had an excuse for everything. She began to think out loud how she would incorporate this into her book, though it was much too disgusting to talk about, she could at least write about it.

Suddenly, she felt a sharp pain in her neck, which began to shoot down her right shoulder and arm. She stood still for a second, bracing herself for another seizure. Her arm started to quiver, and her lips suddenly felt parched. She gripped her toes deep into the carpet in anticipation of the tremors taking control of her body. She stood there waiting, but the quivering in her arm never developed into a full-blown seizure, not this time. Had she had a seizure or not? She wasn't sure, although she was relieved that it wasn't any worse than it was.

She was supposed to follow Lee's instructions and write down the events that led up to any seizures she had, but she couldn't decide whether to count this one or not.

"I guess it won't hurt to jot it down anyway," she thought.

After settling down from her near-miss, she began thinking about the changes in Eric's behavior in recent months. The late-night creeping around the house, the elusiveness, and the preference for solitude. But then, there was that picture of the stripper that he was allegedly promoting. Suffice it to say, something was wrong, something was very wrong.

She was reminded of one night recently in which she thought she had been dreaming. She remembers being disturbed by a radiating light and low-level moaning sounds. She recalls squinting and seeing that the television was on. She saw Eric seated on the chair across the room, watching it with the volume turned down low.

To her disgust and dismay, she saw pornographic images of sodomy being performed on the 52-inch television screen. She had awakened to look between a woman's legs spread so wide open that if you looked hard enough, you could probably see her tonsils. The woman was obviously drugged out of her mind. She was being devoured by several men at once and she devoured them, each of them, likewise. No orifice went ignored or unexplored.

All the research she had done for her book had come in handy. Now she was able to recognize the signs. There was absolutely no doubt Eric was addicted to porn.

When she and Eric were first married, there were no DVDs. There was only primitive cable television with the Playboy channel and pornographic magazines. Now, she was subjected to widescreen formatted, high definition enhanced, lewd sex acts at 4:30 in the morning, courtesy of the technological wonders of digital video discs. Eric had volumes and volumes of them. They contained no passion, no love, just raw, animalistic, perverted sex between two or more people with no identity.

She remembers when DVDs first became popular. One of the first ones she discovered was entitled Pissy Champagne. The title alone piqued her curiosity enough to watch it.

However, her curiosity had nothing to do with any interest in the material itself. Instead, her curiosity was more about finding out what

Eric had an appetite for.

One afternoon, she decided to play the DVD when he wasn't home. She couldn't believe her eyes. Featured were men and women having a party or, more appropriately, an orgy. The depicted acts reminded her of a grainy amateur video featuring a famous R&B singer who could clearly be seen hosing down a 15-year-old girl.

Sharelle could go along with certain things, purportedly, in the name of love. However, relieving oneself on the body of another can only be done in the name of derangement. Anyway, featured in the DVD was a virtual pissing party where the men were urinating all over other men and women in between having sex. Toward the end, the men would pee into champagne glasses, and everyone would make a toast and drink.

After watching the video, she felt nauseous. She remembered being frightened to the point of trembling. She wondered what kind of monster she had married. She eventually confronted Eric about it. His defense was that he had no idea what it was about until he started to watch it, but it disgusted him also. *"No idea?"* she thought. For her, the absurdity of it was mindboggling. She wondered,

"At some point, wouldn't your thought process say to you, hmm, that's an unlikely combination? Or, even if you don't know what it's about, you would have to know that the two don't belong together, so why wouldn't you just leave that one alone?"

She pondered further,

"How many sex acts can a person watch other people engage in any way? And why would anyone want to watch other people having sex?" Doesn't he realize how demeaning and disrespectful this is to women? But, more importantly, does he even care? He has a mother, a wife, and a daughter, is this how we're perceived by him, as objects to be sexually exploited?"

This damaged her sex life with Eric, yet he blamed her as the problem. Instead of protesting against it, she should have watched it with him, from his point of view. The pornography served as a constant reminder of an affair that he had some years prior, for which she forgave him and from which they ultimately reconciled. She was reminded of his ability to be unfaithful and what she felt was her inadequacy as a wife. After twenty-five years of denying that this was destroying her self-esteem as someone desirable and sexually adequate, she was emerging out of her fog of denial. She was starting to realize that he was the one that had the problem, not her.

Despite her disappointment in Eric, she was willing to work through this problem with him, as she had in other situations that impacted the marriage. Regardless, she knew that it would require a little tough love. He was an addict, and just like a drug addict or alcoholic, the addict, first, has to admit that there is a problem and then want help before anyone can intervene.

Instead of confronting him, as usual, she went quietly back to sleep without uttering a word.

He had exhibited all the classic signs for a while now; however, Sharelle didn't previously know enough to identify them. So instead, she simply thought she wasn't the right one for him. She felt she didn't have what it took to keep him happy. But that's what he wanted her to think to coerce her into joining him in his world of sordid sexual fantasy.

Until now, she wasn't aware of the consequences of porn addiction. She realized that no matter who Eric was involved with, he could never have a normal, loving, passionate relationship with anyone. He absolutely had to get help for his addiction. Eric was out of touch with what a real relationship was. He had forgotten what it's like to enjoy a meaningful and loving intimate relationship because that's not what's reinforced in images of pornography. It's all about instant gratification, more importantly, self-gratification.

Chapter Fourteen

When she heard Eric entering the front door, she closed her eyes. She took a deep breath, trying to regain her composure so that when she confronted him, she'd be rational. Therefore, Sharelle first greeted Maya and briefly discussed details about her upcoming graduation ceremony before watching her scamper off to her room. She gave Eric a few moments to get settled in before approaching him, then she heard him call out her name.

"Shar! Where are you?"

She went downstairs, and as she entered the bedroom, she answered, "I'm right here."

"Oh, hey, I didn't see you come in. Where were you, upstairs?"

"Yeah. I was in the office doing some work."

"Oh, writing again, huh?" he says disapprovingly. Sharelle simply ignored the inflammatory comment, as she was focused on a much bigger fish to fry.

As he kicked off his shoes and reclined on the bed while turning on the TV, she couldn't hold back any longer.

"Eric, we need to talk."

"O-o-okay, what's on your mind?"

"Well, a couple of things, actually."

"Okay, talk to me."

She let out a deep sigh and began twirling a lock of hair that gently graced her cheekbone, then began,

"I went through a box that we never unpacked that was in the closet in the office, and a picture fell out of one of your old training manuals."

"Yeah, okay, a picture of what?" he asks.

"It was a picture of some skanky-looking woman in a thong bikini, Eric."

He attempts to play down the significance of the photo.

"Oh, I think I know what picture you're talking about. Was it a picture of some big ass, ugly chick?"

"I definitely didn't see anything attractive about her. However, the question is, who is she, and why do you have a picture of her?"

"Now, before you go jumping to conclusions, let me tell you. What had happened was the girl was trying to promote herself as a stripper, and she knew that I knew countless people with money. So, she asked me to spread the word about her so that she could get bookings for private parties, like bachelor parties and stuff. She gave me the picture to show people what she looked like, and that's all there was to it."

She stood for a moment, just shaking her head in awe of her husband's lack of judgment and his careless attempt to lie. She couldn't believe that he still hadn't figured out that whenever he began with *what had happened was*...she knew a lie wasn't far behind. The ridiculous explanation prompted nothing less than a facetious response.

"Oh, so what are you supposed to be, the goodwill ambassador for the National Strippers Association?" Besides that, where did you meet this chick, anyway?"

"I met her at a strip club, okay? C'mon, Shar, give me a break. I was just trying to do the girl a favor, that's all."

Eric's asinine rationalization for his stupidity was frustrating. Sharelle addresses a more troubling issue.

"You know, I'm really starting to wonder where your head is, Eric. Just today, I was about to watch a movie and happened to see the porn flick that you left in the DVD player and...."

He immediately threw his hands in the air adopting a defensive posture, then replied,

"Shar, I've had that for a long time. It's nothing new."

"Well, that only makes it worse! Those are teenage girls. You're lusting after teenage girls now?"

He yells emphatically, "NO, THEY'RE NOT. They are grown women!"

"Okay, now you're really scaring me. Do you mean to tell me that you can't see that those girls are Maya's age or younger? Their breasts are just starting to develop, Eric. Even Ray Charles can see that, and Stevie doesn't have to wonder! If you can't differentiate between a mature woman and a teenage girl, then you really do have a problem." He wiped the beads of sweat that moistened his brow, then proceeded to give a most moronic response.

"I don't know their ages, but if you had read the disclaimer in the beginning, you would see that it says that all actresses are at least eighteen." Completely dumbfounded at her husband's selective naiveté, she fires back with venom-fueled sarcasm.

"Oh well, that makes it all good then, right? If a porn movie producer says they're eighteen, then it must be true because someone of such high moral standards would never lie about something like that, now, would they?" His defense sent her reeling with anger, and instead of diffusing the situation, he only stoked the fire out of control.

"You can even see that one of them has had a baby, he insists, you can see the stretch marks! Didn't you see her?" Sharelle was now seething over Eric's relentless attempts at defending his reprehensible behavior.

"WHAT ARE YOU, SOME KIND OF IDIOT? Do you think thirteen and fourteen-year-old girls don't get pregnant? Especially in Brazil? Where they're known to have the world's second-largest child sex slave trade? YOU'RE SICK! YOU REALLY NEED SOME HELP!"

She was so angry with Eric that she couldn't stand to look at him anymore. She had such fire inside her that it felt like if she looked at him any longer, she'd burn a hole right through him. For the first time in years, she was beginning to understand why her life felt so empty.

Chapter Fifteen

A *room is not a house, and a house is not a home when the two of us are far apart, and one of us has a broken heart. Now and then…*Sharelle sang the lyrics to almost every Luther Vandross selection on his greatest hits CD from Charlotte to Macon, Georgia. It was a five-and-a-half-hour trip by car, so she had to have her tunes.

She had never attempted to drive that distance herself, usually, Eric drove. She occasionally took the wheel during road trips, but he was still there to guide her. Now, she had to make the long drive by herself.

She was going to spend some time with her mom, Arlene. She needed to get away to clear her head and to think about what she would do with her life from here.

Luther's hits seemed to speak to her in her time of confusion, to the point of tears. She loved Luther. God rest his soul. However, some of his cuts never had such an effect on her until now. Maybe it was because he was gone or perhaps it was because she knew her marriage of 25 years was gone.

It was a Friday afternoon, and she was tired of the two of them walking around the house for the past couple of weeks, not speaking to each other. So, as she paced the floor, she decided that the weekend would not catch her there, she would be gone when Eric got home from work.

Besides, Arlene had plenty of activities planned for the weekend, and she knew that if she hung out with her, there would be no time to be depressed, Arlene wouldn't allow it. Nothing was keeping her there in Charlotte anyway. Now that the school year had ended, Maya had graduated from high school, and she wasted no time returning to New Jersey.

She had been accepted to college there and was to start classes in the fall, so she decided to spend the summer there with her grandmother, Eric's mother, Evelyn. But, of course, that would prove to be a disaster. Maya and her grandmother in the same house for an entire summer?

Maya gave her grandmother very little respect. Sharelle knew it was just a matter of time before Evelyn would pull her hair out over her antics. Right now, she has enough on her plate. She couldn't worry about Maya. She would let Eric deal with that. Besides, that's his mother, the three of them would just have to work it out. She had been putting out fires where the kids were concerned all of their lives. It was time to let Eric sit in the hot seat for a change. After all, that was what this road trip was all about, leaving her cares behind.

She drove the entire five and a half hours without stopping. Luther had taken her all the way to Georgia. In fact, she had heard enough Luther to last her a lifetime, maybe not a lifetime, but for at least another couple of months. She was eagerly awaiting to attend the huge cookout Arlene had been invited to on Saturday. There's bound to be some laughs anytime you have a large group of black people eating and drinking together.

As much as she loved her black brothas and sistahs, she was the first to admit, they were a trip. It was a sure bet that there would be somebody at that cookout that would provide unsolicited entertainment by showing out. Regardless, she knew she would have some fun this weekend.

During the trip, Eric had been blowing up her phone, trying to reach her. However, she wouldn't answer any of his calls, Sharelle was still too angry to talk to him, so she thought it best to avoid all contact with him for a while. He started leaving her nasty messages and threatening to report her car stolen. Which, in itself, would have been a stupid thing to do, seeing as the vehicle was registered in her name. Despite his threats, she paid no attention to his messages. He had no right to be angry with her, she hadn't done him wrong. His idle threats only added insult to injury.

Apparently, she had really struck a nerve. She had called Eric out on his porn addiction. She had offended his true love, his passion for porn. Now, she was the enemy. It was clear that he had made his choice. She was trying to interfere with his obsession in life, and therefore, she had to go.

Upon arrival at her mom's house, a delicious dinner awaited her, typical Arlene style! She hadn't had an appetite all day. However, she suddenly became hungry when she smelled the tantalizing aromas wafting through the kitchen. After dinner, they sat out on the lounge chairs of Arlene's patio. They enjoyed talking and relaxing in the balmy breeze of the late spring evening. As she and her mom sat there engaged in laughter, she immediately realized that the tension in her body was melting away. The healing process was already taking place, even if, just for a weekend, her broken spirit would begin to heal.

On Saturday, the big cookout was on and poppin'. There had to be over 300 people in attendance at the lakefront resort where it was held. People of all ages were there, from the very young to the very old. As predicted, somebody amongst the crowd had to show out. This time, it happened to be a woman of at least 67 years of age.

As soon as the DJ got warmed up, the woman started doing the "booty" dance. It was such a sight that she drew an entire crowd of on-lookers. Once she realized that she had an audience, she became more and more outrageous. As if doing the "booty" dance wasn't enough, now this sixty-something-year-old grandmother was droppin' it like it was hot! It wasn't long before she dropped it so hard that she hit the floor and couldn't get back up. People laughed as she scrambled up off the ground with her legs in the air and her granny panties exposed. To Sharelle, it was just plain embarrassing!

To spare this woman and her family any further humiliation, she contemplated sharing a piece of advice with her. If only she could've gotten nerve enough, she imagined what she would say:

"Ma'am, no disrespect, but you're somebody's grandmother, and you're out here droppin' it like it's hot, my suggestion is to please stop, 'cause, I assure you that, it's NOT!"

After rethinking it, she realized that it could've been much worse. It could have been Arlene out there acting a fool. Just thinking about it gave her the willies.

All in all, it was a fun day at the cookout. Everyone was on good behavior and came there to have a good time. Sharelle came there expecting good food, fellowship, and fun and she got just that. She was so glad that she came that she even vowed to return the following year again.

On Sunday, she and her mom got up early to prepare for church. She was looking forward to going because Arlene's church has a close-knit congregation and a rockin' choir. It's something that she had been missing ever since she moved to Charlotte. She knew Arlene's church would be a much-needed feast for her spirit.

Soon after they arrived at the church and were seated, the choir started to sing, and the musicians began to play. Before long, everyone in the congregation arose to their feet and started singing a joyful noise unto the Lord. Sharelle clapped her hands and swayed side to side, feeling the spirit filling her soul with divine energy. She firmly believed there was nothing like getting your praise on to lift your spirits.

After the service, Arlene must have stopped ten times to introduce her daughter to people she knew in the church, despite Sharelle's efforts to make a quick exit. Instead, she simply obliged her mother by smiling graciously. While, at the same time, welcoming hugs from the church ladies with their little white nurse shoes and ridiculously ornate hats.

Chapter Sixteen

"Joy, it's four o'clock in the morning. What on earth are you doing up calling me at this hour?" protested Sharelle. Like a mother hen, taking account of her chicks, Joy cries out frantically,

"Girl, I've been going crazy trying to reach you. I didn't know if something terrible happened to you or what, I just couldn't sleep. Where are you?"

"I'm on my way back to Charlotte from Georgia. I went to visit my mom in Macon."

"Why haven't you answered my calls? I called your house over the weekend, and Eric didn't know where you were; then I tried your cell phone, and all I got was your voicemail. So what's going on, Shar?"

"Yeah, I know. Eric and I had a big falling out, and I was really upset and wasn't taking any calls."

"Well, why didn't you call me?"

She exhaled a huge sigh and leaned her head over so her free hand could latch onto a curl or two. She anxiously replied,

"Joy, I didn't call you because I knew you were away on business, and that wasn't the time to bother you with something like this."

"Shar, I thought I was your friend. Even if I was in the middle of a meeting, which I wasn't, at least if you had called me, I would have called back to talk to you."

"I know, Joy. I apologize, I just needed to get away."

"Well, are you okay? I mean, did he hurt you?"

"No, not physically. Look, I'll call you when I get back to Charlotte, okay?"

"Alright, you better call me!"

"I promise I will. Bye."

"Okay, Shar, I'll talk to you later."

Joy was furious with Sharelle for not calling on her in her time of need. She believed that's what friends are for, to be there for one another through the inevitable trials and tribulations that life brings. Sharelle believed that too. However, what she was going through wasn't something that she could easily discuss with anyone. Though, it would definitely lift a heavy load from her heart if only she could talk about it.

Just then, she looked in her rearview mirror only to notice a sporty little compact approaching behind her. It looked to her like a tricked-out European sports car. Unfortunately, she wasn't very good at identifying the various auto makes and models. But nevertheless, she knew whatever it was, it was coming up on her a little too fast.

She started to break out in a cold sweat and could feel herself hyperventilate. She pleaded.

"Dear God, no, I can't possibly be having a seizure now. Please, please, not while I'm driving!"

She checked her passenger side view mirror to see if it was clear for her to change lanes. She regulated her breathing and began to regain her composure. She had to. She wasn't trying to be the one to set the odds for surviving a seizure on the highway, traveling at 70 mph.

"The odds probably wouldn't be in my favor," she reasoned.

The nearest car to her right-hand lane was almost two car lengths back. She quickly seized the opportunity to move into that lane to allow the driver in the sports car to proceed.

She watched as the reckless, speeding compact approached closer to her side. When the vehicle got evenly parallel with hers, the driver of the compact slowed down. She could barely keep her car in the lane. She kept trying to watch both the road and the vehicle's driver next to her.

She could now see who was driving and saw it was a middle-aged Hispanic man with a long ponytail, wearing a leather vest with no shirt. Just as she made eye contact, the man winked and licked his lips at her in a suggestive manner. She sucked her teeth, rolled her eyes, and in disgust remarked,

"Ugh! Perverts and flies, I do despise!"

After the excitement wore off and she realized she wasn't in danger, she received another phone call. She expected it to be Eric calling with more threats. However, when she looked at the caller ID, she noticed that it was a number that wasn't immediately familiar to her. She was reluctant to answer, not knowing who would be on the other end of the call, but curiosity got the best of her.

"Hello?"

"Hello, Sharelle. This is Candace, you know, Rhonda's friend?"

It was Candace Porter, an acquaintance introduced to her by her former neighbor, Rhonda Strange.

"Oh, hey Candace, how have you been?"

She was a little taken aback by the impromptu phone call from Candace. She didn't recall exchanging phone numbers because they had never had casual phone conversations before.

"I've been doing alright. How 'bout yourself?"

"I'm doin' pretty good. I'm really glad you called, 'cause I've been wondering how Rhonda's doing. Have you talked with her lately?"

"Well, that's why I'm calling Sharelle, Rhonda's dead."

"What! Rhonda's dead?" Oh no, Candace, what on earth happened to her?"

"Well, from what I'm told, she committed suicide."

"She committed suicide? Oh my God, how did she do it?"

"Apparently, at least from what I'm told, she overdosed. "Uh–uh–uh, that is such a shame. Well, thanks so much, Candace, for notifying me. I would have hated to have to hear it from one of the other neighbors."

"Yeah, I know. That's why I wanted to call to give you the news. Well, listen, Sharelle, I've got to run, but I'll be seeing you."

"Yeah, okay, Candace. You take care and thanks again for calling, alright?"

"No problem, take care, Sharelle."

"Okay, bye."

She was stunned at the news about Rhonda, although she knew that she had problems, but certainly not to the point of suicide! *"Nothing could be that serious,"* she thought. Then she remembered. Tracy had warned her. She remembered Tracy telling her about her vision of death in association with a woman that Sharelle was connected with that had mental problems. What Tracy didn't say was that Rhonda would be the woman who ended up dead. During the remainder of her drive back home, she tried to make sense of the whole thing. She wondered if Rhonda's husband leaving her caused her to become so distraught as to make her want to end her life or if the medication made her suicidal. After all, one of her last conversations with Rhonda was about her medication being too strong. She told Sharelle her prescription needed to be changed. Just thinking about that conversation with her sent chills down her back. Finally, she cringed and said under her breath,

"And to think, the neurologist tried to prescribe Webufrin for me. Thanks, but no thanks!" Strangely, Sharelle derived strength from the tragic news. Although she was saddened by the death of her former neighbor, she somehow felt better about her own situation. As much turmoil and confusion that she thought was a part of her life, she never once considered ending it all, at least not ending it all by taking her own life.

After finally arriving home, she felt drained from the more than six-hour road trip. It had been so much easier on the drive going than it was on the return trip. Probably due to the construction that was taking place on the eastbound side of the interstate crossing through South Carolina. Traffic had come to a virtual stand-still for a good stretch, and Sharelle never did do traffic jams very well. As much as she dreaded coming back home to fight with Eric, she was, on some level, relieved to be back in her own home again.

Chapter Seventeen

As Sharelle turned the corner onto her street, she pressed the automatic garage door opener button. When she pulled into her driveway, the garage door had opened about halfway by then, and she could see that Eric's car wasn't in there. It was around 10:00 a.m. Monday morning. It was the first day of a two-week vacation from work for him.

"He's probably out running some errands," she thought.

She was relieved that she didn't have to face him immediately after returning home. Besides, the peace and quiet would allow her to get some writing done. The long drive home allowed her to come up with new ideas for her book, and she was anxious to put pen to paper as soon as possible.

After unpacking and changing clothes, she headed straight to her office to take advantage of her precious moments of solitude. As usual, checking her email before immersing herself in her work was a must. As expected, upon connecting to the web, she noticed at the top of her email page there were fifty-six new email messages.

She blew away about three dozen junk email messages. She then ran across an unopened email confirming airline travel plans. She was puzzled because she hadn't recently booked any air travel. This was her computer, used solely by her, and her email address, also used solely by her. She started to wonder if she had been the victim of identity theft.

Had someone hacked into her computer and then stolen her credit card information? Had one of her greatest fears come true? Was it a fact that she had been hacked and jacked? she wondered.

Curiosity would not let her rest. While her fingers nervously twirled her hair, she opened the email. It read:

Your flight is confirmed. The ticket type for this reservation is an e-ticket. No ticket will be mailed to you. Please print this flight itinerary for your records.

Flight reservation

Traveler(s)

Eric Hughes

Leave

Friday, May 15, 2020

Sigma Air Lines 1882

Depart: 11:45am   Charlotte, NC
                             Charlotte/Douglas Airport (CLT)

Arrive: 2:05 p.m.   Newark, NJ
                             Newark Liberty Int'l (EWR)

Return

Saturday, May 23, 2020

Sigma Air Lines 821

Depart: 4:45 p.m.   Newark, NJ

Arrive: 7:12pm   Charlotte, NC

Charlotte/Douglas (CLT)

She couldn't believe Eric's audacious act of revenge. With bitterness in her tone, she murmurs,

"Ohhh, he's mad because I left, so he decided to do the same and take off for Jersey, how very mature of him."

Though she was annoyed at Eric's childish behavior, she breathed a sigh of relief that she wasn't a victim of identity theft as previously thought. Additionally, she felt that Eric was only digging a deeper grave for himself by displaying such immaturity. She was determined not to lower herself to his level by continuing this little game of tit-for-tat.

Instead, she called him to let him know she was back at home. Besides, she was curious to see how far he would take his little charade. She wondered,

"Would he be stupid enough to refuse to tell me where he was while being utterly ignorant of the likelihood that I would see the email from the airline? Or would he refuse to take my calls as a form of payback?"

She absolutely had to find out just how much more capable he was of lowering her opinion of him.

"Hello, Eric?"

"Well, well, well, look who finally decided to surface. How're you?" he replies sarcastically.

"I'm fine."

"Good, that's good to hear. Now that I know everything's okay, where the hell have you been? I'm sure you know I've been blowin' up your phone, and you've obviously been ignoring my calls."

"I needed to get away to clear my head, so I went to Georgia to visit my mom."

"Well, I figured that's where you were after a while, but you could have at least let me know that you were alright. If I hadn't heard from you by today, I was going to report the car stolen. I didn't know if you had been carjacked and left for dead somewhere or what."

His frail expression of concern highlighted his propensity to be cold-hearted when things don't go his way. Determined not to allow him to think that he could rattle her, she said,

"Well, isn't that thoughtful of you. By the way, where are you?"

"Why? You didn't tell me where you were going."

"Eric, I believe I had good reason for leaving the way I did. It would not have been good for me to stick around as angry as I was, but if you'd rather not …."

"I'm in Jersey, Shar, if you must know."

"Here we go again, always planning to go to Jersey without me."

"Well, nobody knew where you were, remember? I didn't know if you were coming home before I left or not, so I booked a flight for myself."

Not allowing him to rattle her only lasted so long before she eventually lost her cool and went off on him.

"Let's keep it real, Eric. You booked a flight to Jersey just to spite me. You had no intention of taking me. Besides, whatever happened to all this concern about me possibly being carjacked and left for dead. You must have been really concerned, so concerned that you thought it would be a good time to leave town. Never mind trying to find my lifeless body!"

She ended the conversation by telling him to enjoy his hiatus, doing whatever he does when he's not in her presence. She then dismissed him by saying she would see him whenever he decided to come home.

In the meantime, an idea came to her mind, she decided to check his call activity on his cell phone using his online account. She figured this would give her some insight into what goes on when he takes his solo jaunts to Jersey. Once into his account, she attentively scanned each call until she ran across a number that begged her attention for some unknown reason.

He dialed this number three times, back-to-back, at around midnight the previous Saturday. Almost instantly, two words shot through her mind...*booty call!* Something about that number just didn't smell right, and she was about to go on a mission to clear the air. She decided to call the number to see who would answer.

As suspected, it was a woman. However, it wasn't an actual woman. It was a woman's voice that greeted her by voicemail. In her greeting, the woman gave her first initial and last name, C. Williams. This allowed Sharelle to address the woman by name in the message that she left without raising too much suspicion.

In her message, she didn't leave any details about the nature of the call. Instead, she simply asked the woman to return her call and identified herself only as Mrs. Hughes. She didn't expect a return call from Ms. Williams, but she figured it was at least worth a try.

Once her fact-finding mission was over, she began jotting down some notes that she wanted to include in An Exposé of Indiscretion.

Then, an alert popped up on her computer. She checked her computer's calendar and saw that she had an appointment to have a facial and massage at one o'clock.

As she scanned the page, she read:

Nerdstorm's 3-day shoe sale starts today…do Bible study assignment…she continues reading,

…complete next three chapters of manuscript…Due tomorrow.

"Oh my God, that's right, she exclaimed. How did I ever forget the deadline?"

She absolutely had to have the last three chapters finished today and ready to email to the publisher by eleven o'clock tomorrow morning. It was crunch time for her to meet her deadline, which meant she'd have to reschedule her "me time" for another day.

After calling the day spa to reschedule her appointment and working on a couple of pages of revisions and additions to her manuscript, she became drowsy and just couldn't stop yawning. She didn't realize just how much the drive from Georgia had taken out of her.

After fighting fatigue, she thought a short nap might be just the thing she needed to rejuvenate her mind. Afterward, she would begin putting the finishing touches on her manuscript.

She headed toward her bedroom to lie down, but the phone rang before she could even make it to her bed. She answered, obviously agitated,

"Hello!"

"Uh yes, hello. May I speak with Mrs. Hughes?"

Neglecting to check her caller ID before answering, she responds,

"This is Mrs. Hughes. Who's calling?

It was C. Williams; the woman who Sharelle called and left a voicemail message.

"This is Ms. Williams. I'm returning your call."

She immediately adjusted her disposition once she realized who she was.

"Oh, yes, hello, Ms. Williams. I called because I was looking over my husband's call detail and noticed your number appearing several times. Honestly, I was curious about who he was calling at twelve o'clock on a Saturday night."

"Last Saturday night?"

"Yes, by chance, do you know an Eric Hughes?"

The woman pondered for a beat,

"Hmm, Eric Hughes, Eric Hughes. You must be talking about the guy who tried to get with me at the bar Saturday night."

"You met him at a bar?"

"Yeah, if we're talking about the same guy. He never told me he was married, and to be honest with you, your husband doesn't conduct himself like a married man, Mrs. Hughes."

"What did he do?"

Sharelle asked the question hesitantly. She wasn't sure she really wanted to hear what Ms. Williams was about to say. But she had gone this far, so she couldn't wimp out now.

"Well, at first, he seemed okay. He bought me a drink and behaved like a gentleman, and after we talked for a while, he asked me for my number, so I gave it to him. Then, after a few drinks, he started acting like a real asshole. He kept trying to feel all over me and asked me if he could go home with me. He made it very clear that he wanted to get with me."

Sharelle's voice cracked as she attempted to ask for more information. She cleared her throat and then asked,

"What did you do then?"

"I told him he was an asshole, and I left."

"So, nothing happened?"

"Well, this is probably where the phone calls on the phone bill come in. First, he followed me out to the parking lot, then he got in his car and followed me to my house. Then, he called my phone and begged me to let him go home with me. I told him no and hung up. Then he called again."

"But I see where you called him once."

"Yes, I did. By then, his number was registered in my phone, so I called him back to tell him to stop following me."

"And did he?"

"No, your husband has a problem. He was really scaring me. He followed me all the way home. Then he called me again begging, and because he wouldn't leave me alone, I let him come up on the front porch to try to convince him to leave because I didn't want him to start any trouble."

Sharelle still wasn't sure if she believed Ms. Williams' story. She wondered,

"Was she making this up just to get the wife off her back? Was she covering for Eric because he threatened her not to tell?"

In a devious attempt to get at the absolute truth, Sharelle resorted to a rather cruel scare tactic.

"Well, Ms. Williams, you're absolutely right. Unfortunately, Eric does have a problem, he has herpes. So, if anything did happen, I would suggest you see a doctor as soon as possible. You might potentially be infected now too."

"Oh wow! Mrs. Hughes, I assure you nothing happened, not even as much as a kiss! He was drunk and acting a fool, so please don't get it twisted, I definitely don't want your man. But wait, you still wanna be with him, and he has herpes?"

"Oh, I've already filed for divorce because he infected me. I'm just trying to make sure you understand what you're dealing with because I know he wouldn't come right out and tell you 'cause he didn't tell me until it was too late."

Though none of it was true, Sharelle thought it was well worth the deceit to get to the truth.

"Anyway, thanks for being so willing to talk with me. I'm sorry that you had to go through that with Eric, but I would appreciate it if you didn't mention that we spoke. I'd like to use your testimony as evidence in court. If I need it, would you be willing to give a statement as to his behavior with you?"

"Oh, I can't take time off from work to go to court."

"No, you wouldn't have to go to court. If you could write down what you just told me about what happened Saturday night and have it notarized, you won't ever have to hear from me again. Would that be okay?"

"Okay, I can do that."

"Thank you, Ms. Williams, have a nice day."

"Okay, bye."

For some reason, the conversation with Ms. Williams was exhausting. Now, even more than before the phone call, Sharelle needed a good nap. So, she turned the ringer off on the phone and was sound asleep before her head could hit the pillow.

Around 1:30 that afternoon, Sharelle was awakened by the doorbell. She dragged groggily to the door to see who it was. She wasn't expecting anybody and the last thing she wanted was company. Still, she was curious about who it could be. She peeped through the peephole of the door. There was nobody there. They only rang the bell once, so it couldn't be that she took too long to answer.

Now she was even more curious, so she opened the door. Just as the door opened, she saw the FatEx truck pull out of her driveway, and she noticed a package was left on her doorstep. Then she remembered.

"Oh, this must be the stuff I ordered from Nerdstorm. It's about time!"

She brought the package inside and closed the door. Just as she was about to open it, she remembered she had promised Joy she would call when she got home. She didn't want her to worry any more than she had already. So, she gave her a call while she was thinking about it.

"Hello?"

"Hey, Joy. It's Shar, how're you doin'?"

"Oh, hey Shar, I'm good. How're you doin'?"

"Aw, girl, I'm fine."

"Are you sure, Shar?"

"Yeah, I'm just a little tired from all that driving, but other than that, I'm good."

"Well, can you talk?"

"Yeah, Eric's not here."

"Well then, tell me, what's up? What the hell happened between you and Eric?"

"Well, I really don't know how to tell you this…."

"What do you mean? Just tell me."

"Joy, how do you feel about pornography?"

"Pornography? I mean, I'm not into it, but it doesn't really bother me either; why?"

"What if your man watched it all the time and it started affecting how you feel about yourself, or you noticed that his sexual behavior was changing?"

"Whoa, wait a minute! What are we talking about here? Are you accusing Eric of some kind of sexual abuse?"

"No, not at all, I'm saying that I believe that years of overindulgence in pornography has influenced his behavior to the point that I feel he's addicted to sex. He doesn't even care how it affects me. I believe he deliberately puts himself in situations where he can be tempted into sexual encounters."

Joy interjects some sarcasm into the conversation.

"Wait a minute, which Eric are we talking about here, Hughes or Bonet?"

"Are you kidding? Eric Hughes makes him look like a boy scout."

"Well, according to Haillie…."

"Yeah, well, only she knows for sure. Besides, I'm not totally convinced that Eric is having an affair, although he has in the past. I'm saying that his judgment and respect for women have been compromised. I believe he's losing sight of the fact that the females he's being entertained by, in the form of pornography, are no longer seen by him as human beings. To him, they're merely objects of pleasure, whether age fifteen or thirty-five."

"Wow, Shar, that's deep! Actually, I do believe that when a guy gets married, he should leave that crap alone. Still, I didn't think it would cause any harm if he were to occasionally sneak a peek at some. I've even heard of some couples that use pornography as a marital aid, not sure how that works, but I've heard of it."

"Believe me when I tell you, it doesn't work when one or both parties become obsessed with it." The obsession is in the imagery, not the partner. The partner is only the vehicle with which the obsessed person acts out their fantasies. So, you see, it's not important who the partner is, just as long as that partner is a cooperative participant."

"Sounds like Dr. McCreamy's been giving you a real education in Psychology, huh?"

"Oh, I've been learning a lot from Lee, but nothing about this topic. I've been doing my own independent research concerning the porn issue, and I found the subject so interesting that I decided to use that as the premise for my book."

"So, because Eric was watching porn, you got angry enough to leave home?"

"Well, it wasn't just that. I mean, it's not simply because he was watching porn, even though I don't condone any of it. It was the nature of the porn he was watching, coupled with my suspicion that there's been a little bit of life imitating art thrown in."

"Wait a minute, I'm confused."

Sharelle explains,

"Put it this way, my real concern is the maturity level of the young ladies he seems preoccupied with. The more porn he's exposed to, the more he seems to be leaning into exploitation of minors' territory. It indicates to me that he's incapable of distinguishing the little saplings from the full-grown trees."

"Oh, hell no, I don't play that, that's just sick!"

"Okay, so you feel me now?"

"I feel you, Shar, the man needs some help. But I don't blame you one bit. I would've left too, after I killed his ass."

"Well, believe me, I've wanted to kill him many times, especially whenever he seems to get into these precarious situations with woman after woman."

"Girl, I don't blame you!"

"Well, Joy, I just wanted to let you know that I made it home, and everything is fine, okay?"

"That's good. So, how are you and Eric getting along now?"

"Well, that's another story. He's in New Jersey, probably getting himself into more precarious situations. I guess this is supposed to be payback, but I don't have time to play those games. Besides, I have a book to finish and, as a matter of fact, I have got to go. I've got a deadline to meet by tomorrow."

"Okay, girl, hang in there, and I'll talk to you later."

"Alright, Joy, talk to you later, bye."

"Bye, bye."

An Explicit Nature

Chapter Eighteen

The blinding rays of the morning sun streamed through the sheer curtains of Sharelle's bedroom windows, waking her rather abruptly. She turned to look at the clock on the nightstand to see what ungodly hour the sun had chosen to wake her.

The unfinished glass of Merlot on the nightstand from the previous night obstructed her view of the clock's digital display. She could only make out the distorted numbers on the LED panel by shifting her position to view it from a different vantage point. Even that was more effort than she cared to put forth that early in the morning.

It was 6:19 a.m., and she was nowhere near ready to get up. Her rest had been broken from waking up repeatedly during the night. She woke up practically every hour on the hour. Finally, after about the third hour, she decided to get up and pour a glass of wine, hoping it might help her sleep through the rest of the night. Apparently, her idea worked after a couple of glasses because it was the third glass that remained unfinished on the nightstand.

She contemplated what might have kept her from sleeping. She wasn't sure if it was the mild case of heartburn, the guilt over not finishing that last chapter or the fact that she hadn't heard from Eric all night.

It seemed that it was actually a combination of all of the above. Sharelle concludes,

"I guess Doritos and nacho cheese dip at 1:00 a.m. don't exactly

qualify as comfort food. But so help me God, if I don't finish this chapter in time for submission to my publisher I'll never forgive myself. And, huh, I like "Mr. Man's" nerve! He's out in Jersey and calls himself mad at me and didn't bother to call not once last night. Well, he can go straight to…"

She caught herself just as she was about to, once again, wish him to that awful place of eternal damnation. That was yet another thing she vowed to work on. But, regardless of how she felt this morning, it was a must that she get an early start. The final paragraphs of the last chapter still had to be completed, and all work had to be submitted by 11:00 a.m. With that in mind, she sluggishly lumbered out of bed and saw that she had an unread text message. It read:

> "TWENTY-SIX LETTERS FROM A TO Z;
> IN TWO OF THEM, THERE WILL IRAM BE.
> TRUST THE MIND'S EYE TO HELP YOU SEE,
> HOW DANGEROUSLY CLOSE DEATH
> CAME TO THEE."

Rubbing her eyes to get clearer vision, she couldn't believe what she was reading. It was much too early to dwell on the nonsensical message. However, there was no question about where it came from, and she would confront the source at another time.

She decided, for now, to ignore the message and scrolled through her menu to the calendar option. It was a good thing she decided to check because, to her surprise, she found an entry she had previously forgotten.

"Oh wow, that's right, I have a two o'clock appointment with Lee today."

She smiled, anticipating entering Lee's office and boasting about not having had a single seizure since she last saw him. There was, of course, that near miss on I-77 while being stalked by that creep in the sportscar. Yet, in her mind, that didn't count.

She hadn't seen or spoken to Lee since their last visit. After giving him a good report, she wondered if he would still expect her to go through those silly little exercises that she never wanted to do in the first place. She could only wish that Lee would find that she didn't really need his psychotherapy. She wanted nothing more than for him to say that she was cured of this awful thing that plagued her for so long.

Conversely, she felt this fleeting moment of sadness at the thought of no longer having reason to see Lee again. However, simply staring into "McCreamy's" gorgeous hazel eyes while fantasizing about the possibilities was some serious therapy in itself.

She hurried into the bathroom with a sense of urgency, praying that she'd make it before the floodgates opened. Once seated securely upon her porcelain throne, she exhaled a sigh of relief, thankful that she had made it entirely without incident. Apparently, doing all those Kegel exercises throughout the years really did have some benefit after all. While at the sink washing her hands, she gazed into the vanity mirror. She was mortified when she noticed two newly forming zits sitting side-by-side smack dead in the middle of her chin. Gasping in disbelief, she remarked,

"I cannot believe this. As soon as I cancel my facial, my skin starts erupting like Krakatoa."

After treating herself to a do-it-yourself-at-home facial, she patted her face dry with a fluffy towel. She then realized that her little crisis was far too trivial to waste time trippin' over. So, she quickly got over herself and went upstairs to her office to finish working on the book's finale, which she should have done by now. However, she now had under five hours to finish before emailing the three completed chapters to Kirsten.

The third and last chapter she was working on dealt primarily with how sex addicts transfer guilt or blame onto their partners to create a smokescreen for their addiction. She includes another one of the interviews that she conducted with her former roommate from college.

Three years after graduating, her roommate became the loving, caring wife of a man who constantly devalued her by calling her frigid, stuffy, prudish, and physically unattractive. He got her to believe that if she were more adventurous in trying different things, (things usually derived from situations he'd seen in porn movies) he wouldn't need the porn or the other women. He went so far as to humiliate his wife by telling her how "fine" another woman that he was sleeping with was. She writes:

Carly F., a dutiful, loving wife, had been expected by her husband to go out and buy a blonde wig and a French maid's costume to reinvent herself. He told her to act out some kind of sick fetish he'd obsessed over in porn movies. When she refused, he said he was no longer attracted to her and that she should do this to make herself more appealing to him. He blamed his wife for his state of moral bankruptcy, and rather than insist that her husband seek help, she chose to turn the other cheek to his dirty little secret. Finally, his emotional and professional demise came when he solicited an undercover police officer posing as a prostitute.

Unfortunately, Carly's story is not unique. There are countless stories like hers. The circumstances may vary, but the outcome is the same. Porn addiction destroys lives. How many more lives caught in the grips of porn addiction must be destroyed before we finally face the facts?

She finished in plenty of time. It was just 10:00 a.m., and she had time to review the chapters for last-minute revisions. When she was satisfied that everything was in order, she went downstairs to open the FatEx package she had just received. Once opened, she discovered it wasn't from Nerdstorm as previously thought. The box contained a bubble wrap insulated mailer. She got the surprise of her life when she opened it. With eyes wide-stretched and jaw dropped downward, she squeals,

"What the...? Oh my God, it's Tootsie!"

Inside the mailer were the collar and two photos of her adored miniature Yorkshire Terrier, Tootsie. Tootsie had gone missing six years prior. She had been let out in the backyard for about three hours. When Sharelle went to let her in, she was gone. She had simply vanished without a trace.

The entire family was devastated at her loss, especially Sharelle and Maya. They had searched for the following six months trying to find her, but Tootsie was never found. Now, six years later, it appeared that someone thought it would be amusing to torture her by sending pictures of her beloved Tootsie.

Since no note was included, she looked at the box containing the mailer to find its origin. The only information she could glean was that it was mailed from Detroit, Michigan. As she broke down and cried, she couldn't believe the cruelty that this anonymous person was capable of, and was even more puzzled as to the reason behind it. Since she didn't know anyone in Michigan, the most she could do was wonder.

An Explicit Nature

Chapter Nineteen

Murphy's Law was what crept into Sharelle's mind as she attempted to e-mail the final pages of her manuscript. The term suggests that some dominant force, predestined set of circumstances, or even deviltry can rear its ugly head at the most inopportune times. There is nothing you can do about it, and it is entirely outside one's control. Simply put, whatever can go wrong, will go wrong.

Sharelle resisted that brand of thinking. She wasn't trying to claim it in any way, shape, or form. Instead, her attitude was unless it was Eddie Murphy knocking at the door, Murphy was definitely not welcome. She tried time after time to connect to the web, and all she got was Internet connection failed. Finally, after about the sixth attempt, she called her internet service provider and was given the worst possible news. There was a service outage in her area, and the estimated resolution time could not be determined.

She had to think fast. Suddenly, her extra time turned into crunch time. She had to figure out a way to e-mail her publisher the requested chapters on schedule, absolutely no excuses. There was no way that she could afford to screw this up.

Her publisher, Poole & Rofford, didn't have much patience or sympathy for her right now. So, she had to prove herself again worthy, productive, and, more importantly, marketable in their sight.

She began to think as her index finger instinctively searched for that readily available lock of hair. She thought aloud,

"Okay, no biggie. I'm not gonna sweat this. Worse things could've happened, not much worse, but worse things could have happened. Alright, think Shar, think, what else can I do?"

She considered going over to a neighbor's house; however, she didn't like asking for favors from her neighbors, especially at 10:00 in the morning. Really, the only neighbor she would've been comfortable asking was Rhonda and she's dead. So, she came up with a better idea.

"I know. I'll take my flash drive down to Eric's office and ask his assistant if she would email it for me. Voila! You are brilliant, Shar, simply brilliant!" she exclaimed.

She had spoken to Eric's assistant, Charminesha, a few times over the phone when she called the office to speak with him. She seemed to detect a slight chill coming through the phone, but dismissed it as part immaturity and part poor phone etiquette on the assistant's part. Still, she didn't think asking her to help the boss' wife out in a pinch would be a problem. Besides, she thought, how much time would it take from her work schedule? Practically none, but I'll be sure to express my appreciation by sending her a lovely bouquet of flowers for secretary's day.

It only took her 20 minutes to get showered and completely dressed, undoubtedly a personal best. She was on her way to Eric's office within half an hour. Once at the office building, she was greeted by the receptionist at the front desk.

"Good morning, ma'am. Can I help you?"

She paused to contemplate the question for a beat and read more into it than it was worth.

"Ma'am? At what point did I stop being a "Miss" and become a "ma'am"?

She responds,

"Yes, I'm here to see Eric Hughes' assistant, Charminesha."

"And who shall I say is here to see her?"

"Sharelle Hughes, Mr. Hughes' wife."

"Oh, okay, Mrs. Hughes, I'll let her know you're here."

"Thank you."

As the receptionist dials Charminesha's extension, Sharelle peruses the visitor's log. She was curious to see if she recognized any of the names of the people who had recently visited, as though they would be familiar to her.

Almost immediately after the receptionist hung up the phone, a young woman, who looked to be about 22 years of age, appeared at the front desk.

"Hello, what can I do for you?" the assistant says.

Sharelle was immediately struck by Charminesha's youthful appearance, she figured she couldn't have been much older than her daughter, Maya. Yet, her voice didn't quite match up with her appearance. She had this raspy, kind of throaty-sounding voice. When speaking over the phone, she thought she was much more mature in years than was the case.

The young woman's trendy hairstyle was becoming to her. It was intricately styled in the front with basket-weave patterned flat twists. The twists then segued into what must have been a thousand cinnamon-hued microbraids that cascaded midway down her back.

However, what struck Sharelle the most about her was her bone structure. Her facial features looked as if they had been precisely and expertly chiseled by a master sculptor. Her dramatic jet-black eyes twinkled under the lights like the most exquisite "FL" grade diamonds. Charminesha was absolutely gorgeous.

With a warm smile, Sharelle extended her hand for a handshake to consummate the face-to-face meeting with her husband's assistant for the first time.

"Charminesha? Hi, I'm Eric's wife, Sharelle, it's nice to meet you."

She noticed immediately that the young assistant had no intention of reciprocating the shaking of hands, so instead of wasting time, she got right to the purpose of her visit. Surprisingly, her tone of voice was somewhat dry for a first-time meeting with the boss's wife. Usually, after speaking with someone by phone a few times without ever seeing them, it's nice, at last, to be able to put a face with a name and voice. Yet somehow, she wasn't getting that warm and fuzzy feeling. Charminesha cut right to the chase and asked,

"What, pacifically, is the e-mail address?"

Stunned by the poor grammar, she stood there staring at her and thought momentarily,

"Pacifically? Really? Home girl is a college grad and can't pronounce the word *specifically?*"

Despite the situation's awkwardness, she overlooked the assistant's apparent ignorance. She handed her a sticky note with the e-mail address on it. Charminesha agreed to bless her with her cooperation and proceeded from behind the receptionist's desk. A camel toe was plainly visible when she appeared in full view from behind the desk.

Once again, appalled at the level of unprofessionalism, she thought,

"Those pants are entirely too tight. Where does this girl think she is, the club?"

As she escorted Sharelle back to her cubicle, she couldn't help but notice her BBL jeans. They begged for attention to her rotund rear end. Then, of course, there was the tiny waistline, which accentuated her outrageous butt even more.

As she swayed and sashayed down the hallway, she stumbled, almost losing her balance in the five-inch high pole-dancing pumps she wore. In addition, the corporate hood-rat sported a curve-hugging white shirt with three-quarter length cuffed sleeves, which would've been cute had it actually fit her. The shirt was buttoned down so low that nothing was left to the imagination, absolutely no-thing.

To be fair, there was one thing that Charminesha was modest about. That would be wearing a bra. The girl was packing two beach balls with fully extended blow tubes under that Baby Gap shirt.

Though terribly put off by the girl's unprofessional appearance, she thanked Charminesha for her willingness to assist her but was completely thrown for a loop when she replied,

"Well, I'll do it for you this time, but me and Eric never conversated about this, and I work for Eric and Eric only," as her neck rocked from side to side.

Sharelle bit down hard against her bottom lip and was at a loss as to how she should respond. She did have a few choice words that she wanted to fire back at her, but she knew she had to keep her cool because of the jam she was in. She desperately needed Charminesha's cooperation and could not afford to get into a sparring contest with her. Regardless, she was terribly tempted to inform her that *conversate* was improper English. Simply because some idiot decided to put it in the dictionary doesn't make it right.

She humbly handed her the flash drive and couldn't help but notice her two-inch, neon orange acrylic nails. They were accentuated with detailed artwork reminiscent of fireworks displays, only replicated in glitter.

Sharelle wanted to get through this uncomfortable situation as quickly as possible, so she was relieved to see that things were moving along without incident. Which was good because it was getting close to the time she should be preparing for her visit with Lee, something she looked forward to with eager anticipation.

Once the e-mail went through successfully, Charminesha handed the flash drive back to Sharelle. Then, behind gritted teeth, she thanked her for her help.

"Thank you, Charminesha, I really appreciate you taking the time to help me out, and it was a pleasure meeting you."

The rude assistant responds with a smug look and a shoulder shrug, "No problem."

In earnest, Sharelle got absolutely no pleasure out of meeting Charminesha.

In fact, she wanted to give her a good smack up beside her head. However, she was the mature one. Therefore, it was up to her to keep things polite and civil, even though she really did hate the whole make nice-nice routine.

As she left the office building, she couldn't help but wonder why Eric would hire someone so unprofessional looking and with such a nasty disposition.

Does he not realize that she's the first point of contact when people need to do business with him? Isn't he aware of her impression to the rest of the business world? She wondered.

She was glad she didn't have to deal with the silly girl any further. Yet, she would definitely be *conversing* with Eric about his decision to hire her...that is, whenever he planned to come home.

Chapter Twenty

"C ome on back, Sharelle. Good to see you. How's everything going?"
The aroma of Lee's cologne wafted through the air and into Sharelle's voracious nostrils. She inhaled deeply as she walked past him and into his office and savored the sensual scent. She thought she recognized the fragrance, but it really didn't matter what it was. The brotha just smelled so good. Reminded about the nickname that Joy had given Lee, she luckily caught herself before making what would've been a most embarrassing Freudian slip.

"I'm great, Dr. McCrr... I mean, Lee."

"Ahh, man, it's only been a week since our last visit, and already you've forgotten my name? Wow, that's messed up, I feel slighted."

"No, no, I was thinking about another one of my doctors and...."

"I'm just teasing you, Sharelle. You know, ha-ha-ha, it's okay, really."

"...I'm sorry," she says, giggling nervously like a young girl who's just been approached by the cutest boy in school.

He simply smiled and changed the subject.

"So, Sharelle, tell me, what's the good news?"

She looked at Lee in astonishment and wondered how, on earth, he could've known that she had good news to tell in the first place.

"Well, as a matter of fact, I do have some good news to report..." she says proudly.

"Fantastic! Let's hear it."

"...I haven't had one seizure since my last visit. So, whatever the issue was, I think I have things under control now, isn't that great?"

By the look on Lee's face, there would be no champagne bottle-popping in celebration of this news. On the contrary, it was apparent that he was not encouraged. In fact, his countenance changed to that of extreme concern.

"Well, Sharelle, I wouldn't get too excited if I were you. Let's first talk about what's been happening in your life since we last spoke. Did you keep the list we talked about?"

"Yeah, I made a few notes here and there, but it's not much because, fortunately, there hasn't been much to write about."

Lee cautiously downplayed the sudden cessation of seizures. He would have liked nothing more than for her to be free of her torment, but this was something he had seen before, the proverbial calm before the storm.

Nine years ago, Dr. Alston had a patient with a similar issue. This patient was a woman in her late forties. Involuntary movements caused her head to jerk violently from side to side. She, too, had been to several physicians who all concluded that, in her case, psychiatric help was warranted.

The woman came to Dr. Alston and told him she had witnessed her 17-year-old son being killed by two police officers a few years prior. The young man had never been in trouble before but apparently fit a robbery suspect's description.

The day a squad car pulled up alongside her son, the woman's life was forever changed as he approached his house while walking home from the store. As the officers approached him for questioning, the young man's cell phone vibrated in his pocket, and he reached for it. Unfortunately, although he was unarmed, the officers mistook his actions as an imminent threat.

The young man's mother came out on her front porch to water her potted plants as both officers tragically discharged three rounds from their weapons into her son's chest. The woman explained that she had sustained no injuries during this altercation. However, it left her severely traumatized. Soon after her son was killed, she noticed that sudden loud noises would trigger violent involuntary convulsive movements in her neck.

After several sessions with Dr. Alston, the woman came to the office one day absolutely exuberant. She excitedly told him she would no longer need to be under his care because she had miraculously overcome the involuntary movements. Though Dr. Alston was tremendously happy to hear the good news, he was skeptical. Nevertheless, his professional opinion is that years of therapy are usually required when someone has such a traumatic experience, as did this woman.

Subsequently, the woman went without treatment for about six months, which led to tragic consequences. She was under the influence of mind-altering drugs when taken into police custody after a routine traffic stop. When the police officer approached her car, the woman viciously stabbed his arm with a nail file. She apparently had hallucinations of him drawing his weapon. The officer merely reached into his shirt pocket to retrieve an ink pen so he could issue her a speeding ticket. Regrettably, the altercation landed the woman a lifetime membership in the Broughton Psychiatric Facility.

Lee was determined that nothing like this would happen to Sharelle, at least, not on his watch. So, he had to ensure she didn't get a false sense of security and abandon her therapy.

"Well, let's look at what you wrote down, Sharelle."

She reached into the outer pocket of her handbag, then pulled out a crinkled half-folded sheet of notepaper. Hidden within the fold of the notepaper was an empty tampon wrapper. As she unfolded the paper, the wrapper freed itself, littering Lee's spotless office as it fell haphazardly onto the floor. She hurriedly handed Lee the page, hoping he didn't notice the wrapper. A chivalrous act on his part, such as insisting on picking it up for her, would definitely, not be appreciated in this situation.

"How embarrassing would that be," she thought.

Trying not to call attention to herself, she eased her arm to the floor to retrieve the tampon wrapper while Lee skimmed over her cryptic notes.

With the wrapper securely balled up in hand, she says smugly,

"See, I told you it wasn't much."

"Well, that you did, Sharelle, that you did, but I just have one question for you."

"Okay."

"Why do you think your tremors have stopped?"

"Oh, well, maybe because I've started writing again, and I'm writing about something substantive. As a result, I have more confidence in myself now."

She really didn't have a clue about why she hadn't had a seizure in such a long time, but, to her, the rationale, at least, sounded good. Except, there was one problem with her analysis, Lee knew it was a bunch of bull.

"Pretty clever, Sharelle, but it doesn't fly."

"What do you mean by that?"

He knew that she wouldn't like what he was about to say, but Lee had to make sure that she took her treatment seriously, and he wanted to help her work through whatever was troubling her. Lee was not about to lose another patient to complete and total insanity.

"Well, let me explain. I don't want to frighten you, but I'm just going to break it down so you'll understand the severity of your condition. You have what's known as post-traumatic stress disorder or PTSD, and, in your case, the PTSD presents with essential tremors."

"Gee, thanks for breaking that down for me, Lee, I have complete and total clarity now!"

He belts out a hearty laugh and explains.

"Forgive me, Sharelle, it really isn't that complicated. What I'm saying is you have a stress-related and somewhat extreme condition. The tremors are the end result of the stress disorder. In other words, if we successfully treat the stress disorder, the tremors will take care of themselves. However, if the PTSD is left untreated, the tremors will undoubt-edly worsen."

"Wow, okay, I think you broke it down this time, except there's one thing I'm still unclear about."

"What's that?"

"You referred to the tremors as essential? Let me assure you, I'd be much better off without them."

He again enjoys a hearty laugh.

"I realize the name is somewhat misleading, but the term is just a fancy way to describe the severity of the symptom. The word essential simply refers to something basic. See, there are various types of tremors, each with its unique root cause. You're fortunate that the type of tremor you experience has no known cause and does not damage the central nervous system. Just please understand that PTSD is nothing to play around with, it's paramount that you continue with your therapy be-cause you are a long way from complete recovery."

"Okay, Lee, whatever you think is best. I'll continue the therapy."

"Very good. Now, Sharelle, let's talk a little about your marriage."

Lee begins to ask some very poignant questions about Sharelle's life with Eric, starting from the very beginning of the relationship. Of course, she didn't see the relevance in some of the questions, but she just vowed to cooperate and continue her therapy. So, she played along and answered the questions, regardless of their perceived absurdity.

Eventually, he got around to asking if either Eric or she had ever had an affair. She explained how Eric had an affair some years ago when she was pregnant with their daughter Maya and how it continued well after Maya's birth.

"Yes, Eric had an affair. Her name was Mari. She would call the house and hang up on me if I answered the phone. When the hang-up calls started, I dismissed them as a pathetic form of entertainment for some weirdo with nothing better to do, but then I found out it was her."

"How did you find out who she was?"

"Well, I was cleaning up after opening Christmas gifts and found a receipt from Vintoria's Discreetness for some lingerie I never got. She got the lingerie, and I got luggage! And as for the phone calls, Eric always denied knowing anything about them until one day, "Miss Thing" called the house demanding to speak to him. It just happened that he wasn't at home. In fact, as I found out later, he was on his way to see her, but apparently, he wasn't there soon enough."

"When she finally spoke to you on the phone, what was the conversation like?"

"Well, I asked the rude, demanding hussy who she was, and her answer to me was, "you know who I am, now let me speak to Eric.""

"I'm sure that had to make you very angry."

With raised eyebrows and head shaking in disagreement, she downplayed her emotion.

"Actually, I was quite proud of myself because I kept my cool and simply insisted that the belligerent bitch announce who she was, excuse my French."

"Oh, not at all. Please say whatever comes to mind."

"Finally, she told me that she was Eric's girlfriend and that he had told me all about her. I told her that he told me no such thing and that he must've just told her that lie to shut her up. He probably was trying to steer her away from the subject. He wanted her to think that he was planning what he was going to do about me."

"What do you mean when you say what he was going to do about you?"

"Well, apparently, she felt like she was now the queen "B." She said something about them planning to be together and that Eric was just waiting to be free of his wife, whatever that meant."

"Did you believe her?"

"In hindsight, I probably should've. After all, Eric did give me luggage. But, of course, I guess that was his plan all along—to send me packing! Actually, my initial thought was, duh, men will say anything when they're afraid you're gonna stop giving up the booty."

"Uh, not necessarily, Sharelle. Not all men are created equal, you know."

"I'm sorry, Lee, I didn't intend to offend you."

"No, no offense taken. So tell me, how did the conversation end?"

By then, tears streamed down Sharelle's face. She paused momentarily to blow her nose and then continued.

"The conversation got heated when the side-chick dared to ask me when I was leaving?" Finally, the conversation came to an abrupt end with me hanging up on her when she said,

"You only had that damn baby because you think that'll make him stay with you, but he doesn't want your ass nor that baby, and you're just trying to keep us from being together!"

"How did that make you feel to hear her say that?"

With lips trembling and voice straining, she answers,

"I was so crushed that I actually did leave Eric. I didn't know what to believe anymore, so I took Darius and Maya and moved to California for six months. I wanted to sue the skank for alienation of affection, but New Jersey didn't make provision for that under the state's law."

"You obviously came back, how'd that happen?"

"Eric begged for forgiveness, and I believed him when he said he simply made a big mistake. So, I forgave him, and we reconciled."

"Hmm, Sharelle let me ask you on a scale from one to ten, how safe and secure would you say you and your kids were with Eric before the affair? Ten being the safest and most secure."

With a contemplative look, she answers.

"I guess I would say at least a nine?"

"Okay, good. Now, on the same scale, how safe and secure would you say that you and the kids felt you were with Eric after you learned of the affair?"

"Hmm, probably a three or four."

"Really? What changed to cause you to feel so unsafe?"

Once again, tears started raining down her face. The trembling of her lips intensified as she spoke, but she was determined to answer Lee's question.

"Before she made herself known to me by phone, she would sit in her car outside my house and watch us; therefore, she knew what I looked like."

"Sounds like stalking to me," Lee interjects.

"Yeah, but back then, stalking laws weren't in place, and besides, I've never actually seen her because I didn't know she existed. So even if I had seen her, I wouldn't have known her from a can of paint."

"If you've never seen her, how'd you know she was stalking you?"

"My son kept talking about seeing this red car outside our house. So, I never really gave it a thought until after Eric finally confessed about the affair and after her phone calls became more threatening."

"I'm sure that must've been disturbing."

"Who're you telling? It's scary to know that someone out there wants you to fall off the face of the earth, and you don't know who they are, where they are, or what to look out for. Eric could've been putting me and the kids in harm's way. He had no way, of knowing what that psycho was capable of until, possibly, it was too late.

I mean, the only thing on his mind was keeping her a secret so that he could keep making the booty calls. Do you know what I'm saying? I mean, I could've bumped into her at the grocery store, and she could've, at any moment, walked right up to me and boom! Shot me dead in the face! I'll never feel the same about him again because of that."

Lee handed her the tissue box after realizing that the tissue she had was already saturated with her tears. He then asked,

"Are you okay, Sharelle? We can stop here if you like."

By this time, she was sobbing uncontrollably.

"Okay, Sharelle, that's all for today. I think we've accomplished quite a bit, and believe me, I'm really proud of you. I think you did a great job."

Chapter Twenty-One

Dead silence. That's what Sharelle got when she asked Eric who he was talking to at 3:00 in the morning. It had been a week since he returned from New Jersey, and they both walked around the house, still not speaking to one another.

She had moved out of their bedroom and was sleeping in one of the upstairs guestrooms when she could faintly hear him having a conversation on this particular night. She picked up the house phone extension upstairs to see if he was on the phone, all she heard was a dial tone. She wondered if he could be inconsiderate enough to have another woman in her house, in her bed!

"If there's anyone in that bedroom with him, somebody's going to jail tonight," she vowed.

Determined to catch him wrong, she eased downstairs to eavesdrop at the closed bedroom door. She could see the familiar flickering of light from the TV coming from underneath the doorway and could hear him talking in a little louder than a whisper of a voice. Still, she was bewildered as to whom he could possibly be having a conversation with when the only audible voice was his.

By this point, curiosity had gotten the better of her, so she suddenly swung open the door in hopes of catching him off guard. There was no one in the room but him. He was sitting on the ottoman watching a porn movie, his typical late-night pastime. However, there was one atypical thing about this scenario. Just as she flung open the door, she heard

Eric, who was obviously startled, saying,

"I'll call you back."

She was totally perplexed by his suspicious behavior and the putrid smell of infidelity that filled the room. She asks him,

"Were you talking to someone just now?"

"No, you probably heard the TV. I couldn't sleep, so I decided to watch a movie. You don't mind if I handle my business, do you?"

"Look, Eric, I know your voice when I hear it. So, it's three o'clock in the morning, and you're on the phone and watching a movie? Be for real, you were having phone sex with somebody, why don't you just man up and admit it!"

He abruptly got up and went into the bathroom without uttering a word, slamming the door behind him. Ever since he left for New Jersey, it was as if his entire personality had changed. He, all of a sudden, had this kiss my ass kind of attitude.

She tip-toed over to the nightstand where his cell phone was. She hurriedly scrolled through the call log to see who the last call was registered to or from. The log showed that the previous call was sent or received many hours before she went to bed. She wondered how it could be. Nothing was adding up. She began to doubt if she actually did hear him having a conversation. It might have been just the television, or maybe he was simply playing games, trying to make her think that there was someone else and then expecting her to break down and beg his forgiveness.

"Dear God, I hope he's not that childish?" she thought.

He came out of the bathroom and saw her with his phone. He bum-rushed her and tried to wrestle the phone away while yelling,

"Give me my phone Sharelle, give me my phone!"

At that very moment, she noticed something in him that she had never seen before. His eyes had a particular look, a stern, demon-possessed look. He had this insolent look on his face that suggested to her that he was getting some type of sick pleasure out of seeing her tormented. She also realized that her opinion of her husband had diminished significantly.

All of a sudden, she saw in him no redeeming qualities. She could no longer see any value added to her life by being in a marriage with Eric. She could only wonder how it got to this point. They were optimistic about their future with the move to Charlotte. There were new possibilities with the kids finally out of the house and on their own. It was supposed to be a beautiful new beginning, a renewal of their lives together. But, instead, it appeared that their life together had taken a different turn.

She went back upstairs to the guestroom to get back into bed. She tried to make sense of the madness that just took place in her home but couldn't. She knew that she heard Eric talking to someone, but couldn't process why there were no recent calls registered in his call log, neither in nor outbound. All she could do was lie there, tears rolling down her face while staring at the ceiling. Finally, she cried and twirled her hair until she fell fast asleep.

A few weeks went by, and Sharelle and Eric were finally, at the very least, acting civil toward each other. It wasn't long before he was assigned to go to Detroit on business. He often traveled to Michigan on business, but this time he would have an extended stay, approximately six months, give or take a month or two.

His assistant, Charminesha, had arranged for his apartment and car, and he was to leave in two weeks. For some strange reason, Sharelle felt really uneasy about this business trip. Still, she ignored the chills that undulated down her spine whenever it came to mind. This trip would test a relationship already on life support to its very limits.

An Explicit Nature

Chapter Twenty-Two

Three days and counting before Eric's departure, and the frenzy was on. He and Sharelle scurried around the house, trying to make sure that clothes got packed, the lawn was mowed, and hedges were trimmed before he left for Michigan.

"Hey Shar, do you know where my gloves are?" asked Eric.

She often wondered how she won the distinction of being the official finder of all lost things in the relationship. Living up to the title, she replied,

"Yeah, they're in the hall closet with the hats and coats."

Since moving to Charlotte, there hadn't been much need to wear heavy winter gear. So, Eric found himself unearthing things he hadn't seen since leaving Jersey, i.e., his winter gloves. It was now February, and getting caught without your heaviest gear in Michigan was no picnic in the dead of winter.

In contrast, Charlotte had been unseasonably warm so far this winter. It had been so warm that there was some confusion within the plant realm about what they should be doing. As a result, residents found themselves doing yard work well into winter.

"Oh, okay, here they are. I found them", he chimed.

After finding his gloves, Eric went outside to mow the lawn. At the same time, Sharelle continued gathering sweaters and warm socks for him to pack. While in his closet, she happened to rise up from a crouched position and felt something weighty bump against her forehead. It was something in one of Eric's jacket pockets.

She wondered what it could be that had that much bulk to it that he would put it in a jacket pocket. Fully aware that it might be a gun, she carefully reached into the pocket to retrieve the item.

"A cell phone? Whose cell phone is this?" she asked herself.

In the pocket was an older model cell phone. It was one of those sleek models with a generic black LED display. The only icons on the screen were indicators for the battery life and the signal strength. Sharelle was the one who bought Eric his first cell phone.

Around that time, this was the same model that everybody and their grandma bought. For this reason, she knew she didn't buy him this one. Following the crowd had never been her style. She stood there for a moment, trying to rationalize the whole thing. Then it dawned on her this must be the phone that he was talking on that night.

That night, about a month ago, when she was sleeping upstairs and vaguely heard him talking at three o'clock in the morning. It all made sense now. She wasn't losing her mind after all. No wonder she only heard a dial tone when she picked up the house extension. No wonder there was no indication that a call had been made or received in his call log. So, this was how he did it. He had a secret phone all along.

She mustered up the nerve to power the phone on. As she navigated through the call log, she noticed that the last call made was a couple of months prior, just after Christmas. However, the phone registered a call received within the past couple of weeks at around 2:45 a.m.

She started to tremble upon going through the phone book, and her shoulders became extremely tense. Homeboy's phone book read like Hugh Hefner's guest list at the Playboy mansion, it consisted of nothing but females. She scrolled endlessly through girls' names. There was Charminesha, Patricia, Reneé, Pam, Brenda, Sheiba, Janice, Karen, Chantal, Stacy, and the list went on and on, including someone he logged in as "Sweetness."

Sweetness, the pet name he had given her going back to college. She couldn't believe that he didn't even have the decency to devise an original endearment term for his other women. She investigated further and noticed his assigned phone number had a Charlotte area code. Apparently, he acquired his "secret" phone on a three-day business trip before they moved to Charlotte the previous year.

When she checked his voicemail, it was apparent that he didn't know much about his "secret" phone, particularly how to perform certain functions. The voicemail message he intended to forward to "Sweetness" was erroneously recorded as his personal voicemail greeting. The message shockingly said,

"Yeah, hello, Sweetness. Uh, sorry I missed your call, but I do value that. Uh, I will certainly get back to you.

Um, please keep the faith, heh-heh, and keep the love strong. I'll talk to you soon, Sweetness, bye, bye."

She felt as though someone had kicked her in the stomach. Her hands became clammy as she started to feel light-headed and her right arm quivered. She braced herself for what would surely evolve into a full-blown seizure.

Running into the bathroom, she hid the phone in her bathrobe pocket and burst into tears. She sat on the toilet lid, her head in her hands, sobbing uncontrollably. Then, inexplicably, the crying stopped. What happened next was enough to scare her to death. As soon as she raised her head from her hands, her arm jolted away from her face. It happened so suddenly and with such force that her thumbnail grazed her and scratched her right cheek, actually drawing blood. Her arm extended straight down at her side, as though rigor mortise was setting in. Whichever way she tried to move the arm, it would forcefully snap back into the same position.

Seconds later, the quivering started up again. The quivering escalated in intensity until it gradually developed into a full-blown seizure. She wrestled with the unruly arm for a good five minutes until it finally stopped.

After standing motionless for a few seconds, a frightened and distraught Sharelle fell to her knees on the bathroom floor, completely out of breath, exhausted, and crying. It appeared that Dr. Alston was right. The tremors stopped temporarily, only to start again and worsen with each stressful event thereafter.

When Eric came back into the house after mowing the lawn, he found her sitting on the bathroom floor, sniffling with a tear-stained face.

"Baby, what's wrong? Why are you crying?" he asked.

She stared blankly into space, not responding to his question or presence. She was in a trance-like state, numb to the world around her.

Finally, stunned at her lack of response, Eric yells at her out of sheer terror.

"Shar, Shar, answer me! What is wrong with you?"

He got down on his knees and placed his hands on her shoulders to look her in the eye. Repulsed by his touch, she pushed his hands away.

"Get your hands off me!"

"Shar, what the hell is wrong now!"

"I found your little secret phone."

His reaction was entirely indicative of a person with an addictive personality. First, he went into a rage about his privacy being violated. Then, he ranted about how he was sick and tired of her snooping around in his things. His reaction was exactly how someone deep into addiction was expected to respond.

As an addict, he could only see his source of pleasure being compromised, in this case, the pleasure sources were various women that Sharelle was to know nothing about. He never once thought about how his actions have impacted others. The federal crime here was that his private world of deception had, yet again, been breached.

He went into a frenzy by tearing up the bedroom, emptying all of Sharelle's dresser drawers, and dumping her clothes onto the floor. His primary concern was to get his treasured secret phone back. She looked into his eyes as he ranted and raved and cursed. This was not the person she had loved, married, and produced children with all those years ago. This maniac belonged to someone else.

By now, she was convinced that Eric had been giving himself to other women, several of them. But, strangely enough, that wasn't the most troubling part anymore. What really scared her throughout everything was that he had given himself to a much more formidable entity.

Unknowingly, through his attempts to play her, he, too, was being played. He thought he was the supreme "Mack daddy," having the kind of game that could conquer even the most resistant panties. However, little did he know that he was being pimped by an even craftier deceiver than he could ever be.

Sharelle could see it just as plain as the nose on her face. It was an evil force that had Eric cloaked in complete darkness. This same evil force had succeeded in shielding him from the light that would have otherwise enabled him to see. Oddly, during his conniption, a biblical scripture came to her mind, Luke 23:34. Defiantly, she thought,

Oh, he knows exactly what he's doing. He just doesn't care.

The scripture was a divine slap in the face. It reminded Sharelle of what she was supposed to do in this situation. It reminded her that she didn't have to stay with Eric, but she did have to forgive him.

An Explicit Nature

Chapter Twenty-Three

"C'mon Joy, just one more, you can do it." Sharelle couldn't believe she was speaking these words of encouragement regarding Joy engaging in physical exercise. Finally, though, somehow, she was able to talk her into running laps with her at the gym.

There was a new man in Joy's life, and the relationship was starting to get serious. So now, she actually had something to motivate her to get moving.

"One more? Look, Shar, now you're starting to piss me off. Enough already!" Joy shouted.

"Alright, alright! Boy, are you grouchy today. Is there something bothering you?"

"Sorry. Look, can we just go sit down for a few minutes?"

"Yeah, sure are you feeling okay? I hope I didn't push you too hard."

Strangely enough, Joy had been excessively fatigued lately. She had been falling asleep earlier in the evening and could barely make it through a day's work without needing a nap.

She assures, "I'm okay. I'm just tired, that's all."

Sharelle became concerned when she looked into her eyes and saw a far-away look. Even though they had both broken a sweat while jogging, she noticed that Joy started to perspire profusely only after they sat down. Then within seconds, she slumped over and passed out cold right into her arms.

"Oh my God! Joy, Joy! Joy, wake up. C'mon now, wake up! Joy puh-leez, wake up!

A welcome sight was seeing Joy's eyes start to flutter, and her body begin to stir. Sharelle slowly propped her up and pulled the towel from around her neck to make a pillow for her head. Then, she leaned her back so she could lie on the bench with her head resting on the make-shift pillow. Meanwhile, she ran to get a wet towel and water to cool Joy down.

"Hey, how're you feelin', any better?"

"Whew, yeah, I feel much better, thanks Shar."

Relieved that the crisis was finally over, Sharelle rested her back against the bench and tilted her head back to take a few sips from her water bottle. Still concerned about what she just witnessed; she probes.

"Joy, when was the last time you saw a doctor?'

"Uhh, it's been a minute, maybe two and a half, three years, but...."

"Joy, you need to get a physical, why do you keep neglecting your-self? If I have to make your appointment myself, I'm...."

"Shar, calm down, I was just about to say I have an appointment scheduled for next week."

"...Well, that's good, but something tells me that this must not be the first time that something like this has happened for you to have made an appointment just out of the blue. Is there something you're not telling me?"

She couldn't have been any less prepared for what her friend Joy was about to tell her.

"Shar, I think I'm pregnant."

"Whaaat!?" she shrieked.

She almost choked from the strain on her vocal cords when she shouted out in response to the shocking news. She didn't know if she should be happy, angry, or sad about it, so instead of taking a position one way or the other, she decided to follow Joy's lead.

"I've been feeling so tired here lately, and my cycle has been on again, off again, so I bought one of those home pregnancy test kits, and it read positive. So, that's why I called the doctor to make an appointment."

"Wow, this is such a shock, um, how accurate do you think that test is?'

"The home pregnancy test? They say it's about 98% accurate, if you do it right."

"If you do it right? I think it would be pretty hard to do it wrong unless you just have really bad aim. I mean, how hard is it to pee on a stick?"

"Yeah, pretty much."

She posed her next question delicately to avoid sounding like she was passing some kind of moral judgment.

"Well, if you are pregnant, what will you do?"

"I don't know. I just can't believe I'm in this position at my age. I mean, this is something that happens to teenaged girls, not mature, responsible women like me."

"Have you told the father?

"Yeah, I told him."

Until now, Joy hadn't talked much about the man in her life. Sharelle assumed he was merely someone to kick it with in between relationships. She never thought that Joy would consider him a qualified sperm donor. Now, she had to rethink her original assumption. Obviously, this mystery man had made a deposit that yielded quite a significant return, and Sharelle had to know who that man was. She delved further.

"Well, in light of this new development, no pun intended, I have to ask, who is the father?"

"His name is…Robert."

"Robert? Oh, okay. Well, do I get to meet this Robert?"

"Yeah, if I don't kick him to the curb before then."

"Well, Joy, you know I would never judge you, but why on earth wouldn't you use protection? I mean, you know the risks that are out there."

148

"That's just it, I insisted on him using a condom. I ain't that crazy. But I stopped using birth control pills right after my divorce and never went back on them."

"So, the condom failed?"

"Either that or the son of a bitch set me up."

"Well, that would be a switch, usually it's the female that pokes holes in the condoms 'cause she wants to get pregnant, not the other way around.

Chapter Twenty-Four

When in doubt, go find out was the new battle cry that Sharelle recently adopted, and that's precisely what she was going to do. She decided on one of Eric's visits home that she'd sneak and make copies of his Michigan bachelor apartment keys. The plan was to have keys handy and at her disposal whenever she decided to pay him a visit. And she was definitely going to pay him a visit—a complete and total already-sittin'-in-his-apartment-when-he-comes-home surprise visit.

He called home every night, and they would talk briefly before bed. However, she had a gut feeling—some call it women's intuition. He occasionally seemed preoccupied when she would call. Whatever it's called, it raised a red flag with her. There were times that he even seemed disinterested in speaking with her. However, she was well aware that those instances may have been her perception rooted in her rapidly mounting insecurity.

Although she was preparing for a surprise visit to Eric's bachelor pad in Michigan, it was probably one of the last things she wanted to do. Despite her clever undercover surveillance tactics and her super sleuth maneuvers, this was not a source of satisfaction for her. She was not having fun. Her clandestine acquisition of privileged and withheld information was merely the result of being deceived for so long.

Without a doubt, and to her chagrin, the relationship had evolved into this game of who can outwit who. With respect to this little exercise in wit battling, Sharelle had latched onto a Latino colloquialism—¿"quién es más macho"? The phrase basically translates in English to who has more balls? Aside from the phrase having a nice ring, she thought it was a clever alternative to the corny phrase, *"bring it!"*

To be clear, she, in no way, had a desire to be saddled with a couple of itchy gonads between her legs. She simply refused to be outwitted by any man. So, as Eric stepped up his game of deceit after each episode of getting caught, she sharpened her keen detective abilities with each new lie that he told.

He had been working in Michigan for about two months, and she was getting used to him not being there. In fact, she was starting to be able to see herself living as a single person—no more headaches. Yet, on Eric's visits home, he always seemed so happy to see her, and in some twisted way, she was glad to see him too.

At the same time, she felt uncomfortable with him. It was as though she had built a fortress around her emotions to protect them from any further hurt or harm. He sensed it too. He became frustrated with her because she seemed distant and emotionally encumbered. She just wanted to be at peace with her husband—the way things used to be.

Even though he still could make her laugh, the synchronization between them was off. Their hearts no longer shared the same cadence. That intuitive ability to finish one another's sentences had waned, and the comfort of being two people in love—no longer provided comfort.

For the first time in twenty-five years, she realized her love for him was fading. She hoped that maybe he was simply going through mano-pause and that things would return to normal again. However, she didn't count on that by the time he got his priorities in order, she would have lost all respect for him and would be completely fed up with the mar-riage. Still, she hung in there, staying in prayer and believing God for a miracle.

It was Friday, and Eric's flight was due at 7:45 that evening, his second trip home for the month. As usual, she looked forward to his arrival. She prepared dinner that afternoon so she would have time to get her mani/pedi and shower before picking him up from the airport.

She often wondered why she even bothered anymore—to go to all the trouble, that is. Then again, she had always been meticulous about keeping herself well-groomed. It was not for Eric or for any man per se. It was and still remains about taking pride in herself, for herself.

After arriving home from picking him up from the airport, she changed into her nightgown and poured herself a glass of merlot. He made a fire in the fireplace in the great room and grabbed a beer out of the refrigerator. The timing was perfect because his favorite basketball team was playing on SportsNova, and he turned on the television just in time for tip-off right after changing his clothes. After they settled in, Sharelle decided that this would be an excellent time to ask about Charminesha.

"Eric, I went to your office back when you were out of town on vacation, and I met Charminesha."

He responds in short blurbs, hoping not to be engaged in a drawn-out conversation, thus taking attention away from the game.

"Oh yeah?—that's nice."

Intent on getting answers, she refuses to be ignored and continues.

"The internet went down, and I needed to e-mail something a.s.a.p so I took it down to your office."

"Oh, okay. So, did you get it done?"

"Yeah, Charminesha e-mailed it for me."

"That was nice of her," was his delayed response, only after the Nets regained possession from turning over the ball.

"Eric, what made you hire her?"

She was startled when he suddenly jumped to his feet and yelled at the television, "And one!" His excitement over the Nets getting a rebound and scoring trumped the need to answer her question. After calming down a bit, while still intently focused on the TV, he asks her to repeat the question. Then, in an exasperated tone, she asks again.

"I was asking, what made you hire Charminesha?"

"Oh, why did I hire her? She has good administrative skills. I mean—what's this about?"

She believed that about as much as she believed men buy Playboy magazine for the informative articles. However, she did think he hired Charminesha for her skills, but they had nothing to do with administration. She presses for more answers.

"She's kinda trashy looking, don't you think?"

"No, what makes you say that?" he responds begrudgingly, tearing his attention away from the game.

"Well, when I saw her, I felt she was inappropriately dressed for the office, and I'll bet other people have the same impression."

He tried to play it off as though he hadn't noticed the beach balls bouncing around the office. "Really?—I mean, maybe she doesn't dress as conservatively as you do, but let's face it, she's young—you know how they dress these days."

"Eric, do you think going braless at the office is acceptable?"

He paused momentarily, realizing that the braless question might somehow be a "booby" trap. So, he decided that it might be best to give her his undivided attention throughout the rest of the discussion. As much as he hated it, the game would simply have to be put on the back burner.

"Uh, no—of course not," he answers.

"Well, do you think walking around the office wearing five-inch high pole-dancing pumps is cool?"

Sharelle's colorful yet brazen description of Charminesha's shoes caught him entirely off guard. He tried hard to stifle his amusement but couldn't contain himself. Attempting to keep from choking, a chuckle and a mouthful of beer escaped through his nose and came out a forceful spray of snot-laced Heineken.

With hands on her hips, she says,

"Okay, so you get my point?"

After wiping his mustache with a napkin and blowing his nose free of beer residue, he responds,

"Shar, I've never even noticed her not wearing a bra, nor these so-called pole-dancing pumps. I don't even know what you're talking about, but then I don't play her that close, either. So what's the point you're making here—you don't think something is going on between Charmine-sha and me, do you?"

She had her doubts but didn't intend for the discussion to end in an argument. Besides, Eric's ghetto fabulous assistant was, basically, a non-entity as far as she was concerned. She most certainly wasn't worth placing that much importance on as to be a hot topic of conversation in her household.

"No, Eric, I wasn't implying that at all, she replies. I just didn't think she was very professional or friendly toward me, especially considering I'm her boss' wife."

"Oh, so you just don't like her—that's what this is all about?"

"Well, as a matter of fact—I don't. And let me just go out on a limb here and say that her own mother must not have liked her very much either to have named her after something you wipe your butt with!"

"Shar, what the hell are you talkin' about?"

"You know, Charmin—toilet paper? Charminesha? Who would name their child some stupid name like that unless they didn't like them?"

"Okay, Shar, now you're just trippin', and on that note—I'm going to bed. Good night."

"Tell the truth, you know just as well as I do—it's a stupid name!"

"Good night, Shar."

"Oh, whatever!"

That night they both went to bed angry and with their backs turned toward each other. Of course, each knew it wasn't supposed to end up that way, but neither wanted to give in to the other, so they just went to sleep.

The next morning, Sharelle dreaded him heading back to Michigan. It wasn't that she would miss him, as much as it was her lack of trust in him. Actually, it was her inability to keep an eye on what he was doing which was what she dreaded most of all.

Common sense told her that it was only a matter of time before he would lose control and do something that would cause more damage to their marriage. Any reasonable person on the outside would ask, why would a woman stay with a man she has to babysit to keep him out of trouble?

She often asks herself that question, though she hasn't decided that she will stay. The fact is that Eric is not just a man who needs a babysitter; he is a sick man who needs to overcome an addiction, and she feels it's her obligation to help him.

Chapter Twenty-Five

Apparently, Poole & Rofford Publishing was pretty psyched about Sharelle's submission of the final chapters of An Exposé of Indiscretion. She had just concluded a 45-minute conference call with her publishing agent, Kirsten, and the editors. So naturally, they were anxious to finalize things and get the book immediately into circulation.

Kirsten was already planning a book signing in New York and was discussing plans for a huge launch party. She even mentioned contacting the producers at several daytime talk shows and putting several magazine publications on notice. Sharelle couldn't help but think about the absurdity of it all. Just a couple of months ago, how disposable she was. Today, they're practically ready to erect a statue in honor of her. She concluded,

"When they love you, they really, really love you; when they hate you—you're dog crap on the bottom of someone's shoe."

All things considered, it felt pretty good to be back in the good graces of her publisher again. Although she wanted to, once again, have her publisher's approval, she didn't need them to validate Exposé and the fact that it had all the makings of a best seller. Somehow, she just knew that this project was something special.

If, for no other reason, she knew that she was educating people about the effects of excessive use of pornography. More importantly, this book may even help porn addicts realize what a slippery slope they're on. It just might prevent someone on the verge of losing all self-control from potentially becoming predatory, thus harming others.

Even if not one copy of her book was sold, she was still extremely proud of her work. Conversely, if not one copy of her book was sold, she would unleash all kinds of hell when it came down to her friends and family.

She thought the good news called for a mini celebration, but first, she had to make a few calls to let everybody in on it. Her girl, Joy, was the first call on her list, right after her mom and dad.

"Joy, hey, how you doin'?"

"Nauseous as usual. What's up with you?"

"Aahhh Joy, I feel so bad for you—sounds like you could use some cheering up."

"Nah, I'll be alright in about an hour or two; it's really not that bad."

"Well, Joy, are you sitting down?" asks Sharelle.

"Why what's going on, Shar?"

Joy wasn't really feelin' the whole surprise thing. She needed to conserve every ounce of energy just to get through the day.

"Well, you'll never guess who I just heard from."

"Hmm, let's see, your publisher, and they absolutely love your submission, right?"

Somewhat disappointed that Joy didn't allow her the opportunity to make her big announcement, she states,

"Well, dang, thanks for stealing a sistah's thunder. How'd you know?"

"Because A, all you talk about lately is your book, and B, I have more confidence in you than you have in yourself, that's how."

She was stunned by Joy's painfully blatant and unbelievably terse remarks. Ever since she got a positive pregnancy diagnosis from her gyno, now obstetrician, she's been almost impossible to get along with. She was trying her best to be understanding and non-confrontational toward her friend, realizing that right about now, she was extremely hormonal. However, some of the comments she's been making lately constitute friend abuse, and to put a stop to it, she thought she needed to get her good and told.

In a firm tone of voice, she gives Joy a tongue-lashing.

"Okay, Joy, you know what?—my work is important to me, and I believe in what I'm doing. If I bore you by talking about something that happens to be of great importance to me, then I'm so sorry. I listen to whatever cares or concerns you have as any caring friend should. However, if you're saying that I shouldn't expect the same of you, in that case, then I promise you'll never hear me utter another word about my book or any other concern I have. From now on, we'll deal with each other equally on those terms, capisce?"

Sharelle paused for a moment. She couldn't believe her ears. She heard sobbing coming from the other end of the phone. Could this possibly be her tough-as-nails, hard rock of a friend, Joy—showing an emotional side? Feeling sorry, she tried to console her.

"Ah, c'mon Joy, don't cry. I didn't mean to hurt your feelings, but you've been a little selfish lately, and I thought I should tell you."

"I'm sorry, Shar. I know I've been selfish and mean. It's not that I intend to, but it just comes out that way. I look at you and get so angry sometimes. You have a husband, two beautiful children, a gorgeous home, and a great career—not to mention you're beautiful. You have the life that every woman dreams of, yet you don't appreciate your blessings.

Then, look at me. I'm 47 years old, divorced, with no children, at least, none 'til now that I'm almost ready to retire. Of course, my baby's father is married, so I'll be a single parent raising a child at least 'til I'm age 65. Oh yeah, I almost forgot. I do have a great career well, whoopdee-doo!"

Something that Joy said gave Sharelle great pause. Out of all the things she said throughout her entire rant, one little tidbit grabbed her attention. So she rewound the tape back to that part of her speech and requested a more detailed explanation.

"Whoa, whoa, hold up a minute, he's married?!!" You sort of left that part out."

"Yeah, well, now do you see what I'm sayin'? Who would've thought I would be one of those women talkin' about *my baby daddy*. Shar, my life is so screwed up!"

"Okay, Joy, stop beating up on yourself. First of all, let's not forget. I'm not exactly sleeping on a bed of roses either. And, like you say, let's look at you. You're also beautiful. Do you realize how many women out there have been trying to get pregnant and, at age 47, have to resign themselves to the fact that it just ain't in the cards for them?"

At least you were able to get your career up and running, whereas you're in a position to support a child entirely on your own if you should have to. Besides, girl, don't you know that "Auntie" Shar just can't wait to babysit?"

Joy laughs half-heartedly between sniffles.

"You're right, Shar. I've always wanted to be a mom, but I just thought it would happen the traditional way. You know, the old husband, wife, and then kids—model of the American family?"

"Well, Joy, I've always believed that a child is a blessing from God. Okay, so maybe the way in which the child was conceived might not be in line with God's perfect will, but the child is no less one of God's divine gifts. So hey, be happy about your pregnancy. This is a time when, as a woman, you're the most beautiful that you'll ever be in life, and if you're healthy and happy, your baby will be born healthy and happy. So no more feeling sorry for yourself. I ain't tryin' to hear it, ya got that?"

"Yeah, I guess so, 'cause the way you just read me the riot act, I'm scared that I might be looking at a good old-fashioned beat down."

Sharelle belts out a hearty laugh and says,

"Nah, you don't have to worry about that, at least not until after the baby's born."

Chapter Twenty-Six

The mind is undoubtedly the most fascinating element of all the physiological processes. The mind enables us to retrieve information from our memory banks. However, some people are said to have selective memory. It suggests that they have consciously decided not to remember something for their own selfish convenience or benefit. Basically, selective memory is thought of almost as a form of deceit.

In actuality, selective memory can result involuntarily in the mind's effort to block out the recall of certain traumatic occurrences, thus allowing one to cope with everyday life. Dr. Alston was a champion at peeling back the layers. Sharelle had packed away the recollection of certain painful events in her life. Lee was relentless in his mission to exhume her memory out of the deepest recesses of her mind. She had been working with him for a few months with little to no real progress.

However, during this therapy session, she would experience a sudden unexpected breakthrough. Dr. Alston would get some insight that would help to send her on the path to recovery. Once again, his questions were probing and provocative, intended to strategically summon Sharelle's subconscious mind to higher and higher levels of awareness. He delves right in during this session.

"Last time we met, Sharelle, you'll remember we talked about Eric's affair and the two of you eventually reconciling."

"Yes," she replies.

"After you left, do you recall having any other feelings surface resulting from that discussion you may want to talk about?"

"No, not really, but I would like to talk about the seizure I recently had."

"Oh, you had another one? When was that?

"It was a couple of weeks ago."

"Sharelle, why haven't you told me?"

"I just couldn't talk about it then. It was so disappointing."

"I understand. Well, today, we're going to try something a little different. I'm going to ask you to stretch your imagination. I want to see how creative you can be."

Lee pressed the wrong button with that one. She couldn't believe he had the nerve to challenge her creative ability. Her work stood for itself, and she had the reviews to prove it. Yet, she sat there, expected to jump through hoops to validate herself. She wasn't about to let him belittle her in that way. Apparently, he didn't know the deal, but she was going to ensure he recognized.

"Are you serious? If I'm nothing else, I'm creative—creative enough to make a living off of it," she insisted.

Little did she realize that Lee knew exactly what he was doing. She had been holding something back, and he had to go hard to evoke some deep-rooted emotions from her. He was a master at diplomacy, and he knew how to appeal to her sense of pride. He pulls back a bit to disarm her.

"Oh, without a doubt!—which is why this exercise should be a breeze for you! Now, here's what I want you to do. I'll give you a list of five objects, and from that list, I want you to rate which of them you would rather be if you had to choose. You'll rate the objects from one to five, one being the most favorable and five being the least. Also, give some thought as to why you make those choices." She leans to one side, crossing her legs, and with an arrogant stare, she says,

"Sounds easy enough."

"Good. Here's a pad of paper and a pen. Now, I'd like for you to write these things down."

She sits up nice and tall in her seat like an elementary school child trying to impress her teacher. She then places the notepad squarely on her lap, preparing to write.

"Alright, ready?" asks Lee.

"I'm ready."

He rattles off a series of flower varieties for Sharelle to jot down.

"A pink carnation—a yellow daffodil—a purple violet—a red rose—and a white lily."

"Okay, I've got it. Should I start now?"

"You may start now. I'm going to step out of the office for a few minutes while you tackle this, and I'll be right back."

"Okay, but I'll be done with this in no time."

After Lee leaves the office, Sharelle focuses on the assignment and completes it in as little as 30 seconds. About another 30 seconds later, Lee returns and asks,

"So, how'd we do?"

"I'm finished."

"Okay, let's see what you wrote down."

She hands Lee the notepad, and he scours over her responses.

"Well, I see you chose the white lily as your number one choice."

"Yes, I did."

"Can you explain why?"

"Uhh—because I like—lilies?"

"What do you like about them? Is it the fragrance, the color, or just the flower itself?"

"Well, I like the flower—I guess."

"Alright, and I see that your least favorite choice is the red rose. Why is that?"

"I don't know—I just rated it last, that's all."

"Well, what do you like least about the rose? Is it the thorns, the color, or roses in general?"

"Oh, I love roses—I don't know, maybe it's the color."

"Hmm, that's interesting".

She started to become annoyed with what seemed to her to be a monumental waste of her time. Even more annoying was the feeling that Lee was trying to find some significance in this juvenile exercise when there absolutely wasn't any. She abruptly challenges him.

"What's so interesting about it? I hate the color red, so what's the big deal?"

"Okay, this is good. Let's examine that for a moment. Why do you hate the color red?"

"For no real reason other than it's just not a color that appeals to me. You know, for example, if I gave you four color choices and one of them was pink, you'd probably choose pink as your least favorite color out of the four, right?"

"You're probably correct in that assumption, Sharelle. However, I probably wouldn't say that I *hated* the color pink. It would simply, as you say, be my least favorite of the choices. Which brings me back to my question—why do you *hate* the color red?"

"I don't know, I just do."

Now, the shoe was on the other foot. Lee challenges Sharelle.

"No, you don't."

"Huh?"

"I said, no, you don't."

"Lee, how can you tell me what I hate and don't hate? I absolutely hate the color red, I always have!"

"Sharelle, if you've always hated the color red, then why did you dream of getting, what you called, the most beautiful bike you had ever seen for Christmas when you were a young girl? That beautiful bike that you wanted for so long was red, was it not?"

Sharelle sat back in her chair, stunned, with her eyes fixed on Lee for about five seconds. Then, for the first time, she realized that maybe she did need his help. She knew that he had tapped into something. She just wasn't exactly sure what that something was.

"Sharelle, are you alright?" he asks with a look of concern.

She leaned her head to one side and grasped a lock of hair. While feverishly twirling an already tightly wound coil, she answered,

"Uh—yeah. Yeah, I'm fine."

"Okay, our time is up for today, and hey, perk up! You should be pleased with our session today. I really think we made some headway."

"Oh, I am pleased. Thanks a lot, Lee, and I'll see you next week."

"Okay, Sharelle, enjoy the rest of your week."

An Explicit Nature

Chapter Twenty-Seven

"What's wrong? Cat got your tongue? Nah, that's just too corny," Sharelle says as she tries to decide on a clever line, she would use when Eric comes home to find her sitting in his Michigan apartment.

She had a gut feeling that something wasn't right, so she decided that this was the time to go and pay him a surprise visit. It had been three weeks since his last trip home, and he told her he couldn't come home this weekend because he would be working. It's not that she found anything unusual about him working over the weekend. He worked weekends occasionally. Still, something told her to go, and that something told her to go—now!

She had booked her reservations the day before. It was now three o'clock the next morning when the alarm sounded and coaxed her out of bed to get dressed. After showering and feeling more alert, she got dressed, threw a few last-minute items in her luggage, and was off and running. She punched it, doing 80 mph on a 65 mph stretch of highway. Luckily, there's no traffic at 4:30 in the morning, and it's still dark. So, according to Sharelle Hughes' logic, this was the perfect setting to speed without getting pulled over by "the man." Somehow she felt that speeding under the cloak of darkness afforded her a sort of invincibility or maybe it was more like invisibility.

She made a mental checklist of things she hoped she hadn't forgotten.

Itinerary... phone charger... toothbrush...

She prayed she'd get to the airport in time to make her flight. She absolutely had to make this flight for things to work as planned. The plane was due to depart at 6:00 a.m., earlier than she had ever voluntarily traveled before in her life. Although she certainly could've opted for a later flight, that would've given her a two-hour layover. That would've put her in Detroit too close to when Eric was expected home from work.

Once at the airport, she parked her car in the short-term parking lot section B, row 6. She resorted to word association to help her remember where she parked. She always found it helpful to remember her various passwords and usernames. Therefore, she figured the technique might just as well help her remember where she parked her car.

Eric tried to reach her on her phone around 5:00 a.m., but she wouldn't answer. She had to be careful not to tip him off, and background noise at the airport would be a dead giveaway. Most likely, he'd only call back again and again until he reached her. Still, she hoped that he would assume she was out on her morning jog or at the twenty-four-hour fitness center and couldn't hear the phone.

It was imperative that she execute her plan flawlessly. She couldn't afford to make any careless mistakes. The point of the matter was, she wasn't interested in a tidied-up, staged environment which is precisely what would happen if Eric had prior notice of her arrival. No, Sharelle wanted to step into his world of quasi-bachelorhood completely unawares and unannounced.

He has the opportunity to do anything he so chooses without worry or fear of getting caught. So this visit was a way to get a fly-on-the-wall perspective of just what he's been up to.

While walking briskly through the terminal, she took out her phone and checked her voicemail messages.

"Hmm, eight missed calls. I wonder who they could be from?"

She knew exactly who the calls were from. Eric had been trying to call her on the house phone since late last night. She had turned the ringer off because she had to get to bed early to ensure she would catch her flight on time. She had also turned off her cell phone, and now, apparent from the number of missed calls, she sees that he was blowing that up too.

One good thing about ridiculously early morning flights is the security check lines aren't very long.

"Oh, bet—this should be a breeze", she thought.

She removed her four-inch cork wedge-heeled shoes and placed them on the conveyor tray along with her handbag and carry-on. Just as she shuffled through the x-ray checkpoint, the TSA agent stopped her, removed her carry-on tote, and summoned her to another table. The agent told her that he had to open her carry-on for closer inspection.

Confident that she wasn't carrying a bomb or kilos of heroine, she obliged.

"Ma'am, you're not allowed to take more than three ounces of liquid on the plane. So I'm going to have to remove this."

She looked at the man as if he had a booger hanging out of his nose. She couldn't believe that he would confiscate her bottle of Farkkai curl-enhancing lotion for which she had paid an arm and a leg. That was the only thing that would keep her curly locks nice and smooth. Without it, she'd be rockin' a serious Eryka Badu. She certainly wasn't taking anything from Eryka, but Sharelle preferred the smooth and bouncy curly look instead.

She wasn't going to give in so easily. After all, they allow lighters on the plane again, knowing that some fool already tried to blow up his shoes. Certainly, she should be able to keep her hair lotion. Besides, she wondered, what harm can I do with a bottle of curl-enhancing lotion? Do they think I'll force the pilot into submission by forcing his bone-straight hair to curl as part of some diabolical plot to take over the plane?

She was so angry that she was ready to give that TSA agent a good piece of her mind. It was apparent to her that he wasn't moved by her pleading or by the fact that sistahs don't play when it comes to their hair. She proceeded with her protest. "

168

But that's a full bottle! Do you know how much that stuff costs?"

The agent calmly pointed to the sign that outlined what could and couldn't be taken on the plane and said,

"I'm sorry, ma'am, but either you have to put it in your checked baggage or limit it to three ounces if you're going to have it in your carry-on."

Heartbroken, she conceded and reluctantly walked away with her carry-on tote weighing about 16 oz. lighter.

Once at the gate, with just twenty minutes to spare, she noticed only a few people who were half asleep seated in the waiting area. She thought it was a little strange that these people weren't boarding the plane by now, so she decided to ask at the desk.

"Hi, this is the gate for the six o'clock flight to Detroit, isn't it?"

"Yes, ma'am…

She becomes slightly annoyed with the airline agent and says, between clenched teeth and under her breath,

"Here we go with that ma'am crap again."

The agent continues,

…the aircraft hasn't arrived at the gate yet. As soon as it arrives, we'll begin boarding."

Still somewhat annoyed, she again mumbled under her breath,

"The aircraft hasn't arrived yet? It's not like calling a taxi. The plane should be waiting for me, not the other way around!"

After a couple of minutes, she finally calmed down and relaxed after all the rushing around that she had done since three o'clock that morning. Once she placed her carry-on under her seat, she sat down near the jetway and made herself comfortable, at least as comfortable as she could be, in those hard vinyl seats.

About thirty minutes later, she heard the call to board the plane. As soon as she heard her group number called, she boarded, and she was up and away before long.

Chapter Twenty-Eight

Eric's apartment was on the outskirts of Detroit. It was a newly developed community of condominiums and townhouses surrounding a beautiful lake with dense forests in the background. The wildlife still frequented the lake, as the area hadn't yet become developed and populated enough to force their migration. The area was so newly developed that the cab driver that brought Sharelle from the airport was even unsure how to get there.

Once inside, she immediately noticed the view overlooking the lake from the terrace of Eric's executive condo. It was picture postcard perfect. In awe, she watched a fox in the distance prance gracefully off into the backdrop of trees away from the lake. With a smile, she thought,

"So that's why they named that dance The Foxtrot."

She began checking out the layout of Eric's condo. It was very tastefully appointed with mission style furniture. Not really her taste in home furnishings, but nice, nonetheless. Every convenience was provided him. There were two flat widescreen televisions, each one paired with a DVD player one in the bedroom and one in the living room.

Having an uneasy feeling about it, she thought,

"Uh-oh, that could be trouble."

Also, in the condo was a laundry area complete with washer and dryer and there was every type of cooking utensil imaginable in the kitchen, right down to an electric mixer—which was a total waste, seeing as he never baked anything in his life.

Nevertheless, Eric's place was nice and cozy, a sex addicts hideaway. It was like PeeWee's playhouse, the consummate bachelor crib.

Given that it would be hours before he would be home from work, she kicked off her shoes, turned on the TV, sat back and relaxed. She was in no rush to start her investigation, she had plenty of time for that. She heard her cell ringing in her handbag. After turning the volume down on the TV she ran to get it and checked the caller I.D. It was Eric.

"Hello?" she answered.

She thought it was comical that he greeted her with such anger in his voice. Apparently, she was supposed to be able to be accounted for at any given time, yet he wasn't supposed to be subjected to the same rules. He expressed his displeasure with her inaccessibility.

"Oh, so you finally decided to answer your phone, huh?"

"I see that you've been trying to reach me. My battery was dead and my phone shut off."

"Shar, I've been trying to reach you since last night. I called on the house phone twice and all I got was the answering machine and then when I started blowin' up your cell all I got there was voicemail. What the fuck is goin' on?"

"I told you, my battery was dead and I didn't realize it."

"Well, where the hell were you last night when I called around 11:30 your time?"

"I was home in bed. I went to sleep early, I was tired."

"Bullshit! You weren't at home all night. You slept somewhere with somebody else, because I called twice last night and once about five o'clock this morning and you didn't answer. 'Fess up. I know you were laid up with somebody, who was it?"

He was going nuts not knowing what to make of Sharelle's whereabouts. She remained calm and simply tried to diffuse the situation.

"Eric, I told you I was at home last night. I listened to the message you left on the answering machine when I got up this morning, but I couldn't call you back because you were at work. You said yourself that they were correcting some issues with your phone extension there in

171

Michigan and your cell phone doesn't get a signal in the building, re-member?"

"Well, I called the house a couple of hours ago and you still didn't answer the phone, but now you'll answer your cell phone? What's up with that?"

"That's because now I'm not at home."

"Where the hell are you?"

"I'm at the mall."

"Shar, why don't you just tell the truth. That's the quietest mall I've ever heard. If you were in the mall, I would at least hear some noise in the background and I don't hear shit, so just stop lyin'!"

She simply stuck to her guns even after Eric shamefully asked her to put one of the sales clerks on the phone to prove to him that she was really in the mall. Even if she really was in the mall she wouldn't humiliate herself by giving her phone to a perfect stranger to have them tell her husband that she was there. Needless to say, she adamantly rejected his ridiculous request—and needless to say, he hung up on her.

After having her R and R so rudely interrupted she began her search. She looked in his closet and saw nothing incriminating there. She checked the bathroom cabinets.

"One toothbrush, shaving cream, and a hair brush—this is good!"

She went to his dresser and checked the top drawer.

"Underwear, socks, tee shirts. Well, well, well, here's his secret phone again," she said to herself.

She tried powering the phone on, but it didn't work. It was obvious that he wasn't using it because it was as dead as a doornail and upon further inspection she found that there wasn't even a battery in it. It's been said that if you look hard enough, eventually you'll find, and sure enough there under the stack of tee shirts was a box of condoms, uno-pened. Sharelle thought, "NOT GOOD!"

She continued her search, because she had sense enough to know that wherever there are condoms there is a woman linked to them some-where. She continued her search and walked across the room over to the nightstand on the left. It was empty. She walked over to the right side of the bed to the other nightstand. When she opened the top drawer she came across an envelope.

She opened the envelope and inside were pictures of a woman—a rather matronly-looking, chunky woman that appeared to be in her late forties to early fifties. One of the pictures showed her in a full frontal view wearing a cheap polyester pant suit. The other picture was an upper body pose with her wearing a black and white prison-striped sweater under a leather, or more likely, pleather vest. Sharelle took one look at the photo and thought,

"Apparently, no one ever told her that chunky girls should stay away from horizontal stripes."

She continued her search of the drawer and saw something that she definitely didn't expect to see—another secret phone! This one was a state-of-the-art modern day model with a camera feature, a web browser and the whole nine. The brotha was equipped to do some high-tech, world-wide creepin' now.

She powered the phone on and started navigating through it, at first just trying to familiarize herself with its features. Then she checked the phone's contact list only two numbers there and they both appeared to be job related. She then checked the voicemail inbox. He had a message. There was a message from a woman which said,

"Hey sweetie, I'm sorry about last night. I just couldn't stay awake and I don't even remember what I said, I was so tired. Call me when you get this message. Bye."

She stood there scratching her head for a second and thought,

"Sweetie? I know I didn't hear her call him sweetie."

She checked the call log. There were just a few numbers there, however there were several calls to and from a recurring phone number and it happened to be the same number that the voicemail message came from. This piqued her curiosity enough to call it.

At first she called from her cell phone using * 67 to block her number. She got a pre-recorded message that said something to the effect that, the wireless customer you are trying to reach does not accept calls from unidentified callers.

When that didn't work she called the number from Eric's new-fangled secret phone and a voice answered—a female voice.

"Hello?"

"Yes, hello, this is Eric Hughes' wife and I see your number appearing several times in the call log of his cell phone. I'm not calling to accuse you of anything, but I would like to know what the nature of your relationship with my husband is?" The skank's response was,

"Oh, were just friends. I've known Eric for many years, we worked together about thirty years ago and since I became a minister he calls me sometimes for spiritual advice." The street-slick, unanticipated response completely disarmed her, almost to the point of shame. She attempted to redeem herself, by saying,

"Really? Well, that's very nice, and—I'm sorry, I didn't get your name."

"Oh, my name is Minister Leeds."

Refusing to allow the shady lady to throw her off course, Sharelle regrouped and tossed her a curve ball.

"Well, Ms. uh, Minister Leeds, do you call all of your friends sweetie?"

"Excuse me?"

"Well, I listened to a voicemail message that you left Eric and you called him sweetie."

She responded,

"Oh, uh, uh—yeah, I call all of my friends sweetie, even my guy friends, it's just a term of endearment, that's all."

"Well, I apologize for disturbing you and I won't call again. God bless you and have a nice day."

"Same to you, bye."

Sharelle wasn't really buying the whole holy-roller thing. She just wanted to get off the phone as quickly as possible. There was no doubt in her mind that the sinister minister had a bolt of lightning with her name on it, and it was about to strike at any minute. Actually, at that point, she couldn't accuse the woman of any wrongdoing anyway, so she decided to just let it go. As for Eric, he was definitely going to have some explaining to do regarding the irreverent reverend.

She continued her search for incriminating evidence against him, when she stumbled upon some recently downloaded pictures that, clearly, weren't of his grandma's church choir solo. To her dismay, she ran across approximately ten x-rated pictures of a woman who had the nerve to include captions with each and every one. There were captions like "the girls" referring to two huge breasts heading pathetically south-ward. There was a picture with a caption that said "all yours" referring to what was between her spread-eagled legs. Then there was the caption that said "the backyard" which featured a flabby rear-end speckled with red and black blotches. There were dildo shots, masturbation shots, bath-tub shots and just about every other self-deprecating pose and scenario that one can think of sent to Eric's phone. Although some photos were laughable, this was a real live woman—not clips from a porn flick, and Sharelle needed to find out the identity of the woman in these photos.

She checked the downloads' folder in his phone to determine their origin. When she discovered that Ms. Leeds' number and the number associated with the photos were one and the same, she exclaimed,

"This is Minister Leeds' phone number. Spiritual advisor, huh? Lyin' heifer!'

Now she was steaming mad. She was mostly mad at Eric for his part in it, but she was also mad at Ms. Leeds. She was mad at her because she realized that this was not the first, and only, time that she had spo-ken with her. It was all coming back to her now. The hypocritical hussy had called the house back in New Jersey asking to speak to Eric several years before. She and Eric had worked together during high school. When Sharelle inquired who she was, she introduced herself as Minister Leeds. Her full name wasn't learned until later, Sheiba Jackson-Leeds.

That's what disturbed her most. She now realized that this was yet, the second time she had given the hussy the opportunity to woman-up and be honest with her about her connection with Eric. She had called her in a non-confrontational, non-threatening tone and even wished blessings from God upon her.

However, the way things were unfolding, there would be no handing down of blessings any time soon if Sharelle had anything to do with it. As a matter of fact, she was certain that the only thing that Minister Leeds would be leading would be herself straight to hell, in her opinion. With hands shaking, she called Sheiba Leeds back, and again she answered,

"Hello?"

"I know I said I wouldn't call you again, but I just found the disgusting pictures that you sent to Eric and I see that you're just as big of a liar as he is, you two belong together!"

Surprisingly, Ms. Leeds' calm, ministerial demeanor changed quickly and upon adopting a more satanic quality to her voice, she said,

"Don't call my number again, you're harassing me!"

Apparently, the misguided minister didn't know that sending naked crotch shots via electronic means can be very risky. It's risky, partly because there is absolutely no way that anyone can guarantee where they'll end up along their journey through cyberspace. It appears that she wasn't the least bit concerned about her crotch shots ending up in the wrong hands. It's possible that risking the possibility that someone might use them as ammunition against her was of no concern. However, ammunition was precisely what Sharelle had in mind. What better proof that Eric is an adulterer than to show up in divorce court with poster-sized copies of Eric's personal porn star. Since the flabby photos reflected the exact phone numbers they were sent to and from, complete with time and date stamps, the evidence would be right there in the judge's face. Sharelle thought to herself,

"Ugh, how cringeworthy!"

Trembling and faint of heart, she reached out to her friend Tracy.

"Hello?"

"Tr—Tracy, I need your help!"

"Shar, is that you?"

Sharelle responds crying and hyperventilating,

"Whew yeah, yeah it's me."

"Shar what's wrong? You sound out of breath, are you okay?"

"No, Tracy, I'm not. I'm in Michigan. I secretly had keys made to Eric's apartment and I'm here at his apartment now. He's at work and he doesn't know that I'm here. Tracy, I really need your help."

"Yeah sure, but you're talking too fast. What happened, Shar?"

"Something told me to pay Eric a surprise visit and check things out and sure enough, I found a cell phone that I'm not supposed to know that he has. It's a new phone and some skeezer sent him some disgusting pictures.

Tracy, I need to send you these pictures and I want you to guard them with your life. Store them on your computer in a protected file. Can you do that for me?"

"Of course, sure—I'll give you my private e-mail address. Neither Darryl nor the kids know about this e-mail address. The pictures will be safe there."

"Thank you so much. I knew I could count on you. I'm gonna need to rely on these pictures when I take Eric to court. Tracy, I can deal with a lot of things, but I can't deal with crazy."

After she ended her conversation with Tracy she collapsed from exhaustion onto the couch and continued to lie there trying to catch her breath and regain her composure.

Chapter Twenty-Nine

O kay, mission accomplished! I found out what I came here to find
out, now what? Sharelle contemplated. Either crap or get off the
pot was what came to mind. She was so emotionally constipated from
taking his crap for all these years that the only movement she felt coming
down the pike was the urge to move him right out of her life.

It had been a couple of hours since the discovery, and she was still
trembling. What made it worse was that she could feel herself tensing up
even more after realizing what time it was. It was 4:00. Eric was about to
leave work and would very shortly be walking through the door.

She didn't know whether she should be sitting there as he made his
entrance, or if she should leave and then unexpectedly ring the bell making it look as though she had just arrived. She opted for the latter.

She didn't want him to know that she had keys to his apartment,
just in case she had to make another surprise visit. She had already seen
everything that could be considered damning. If not damning, problematic, at the very least. There again, problematic would be finding a female's phone number in his coat pocket. Finding a secret phone with
sexually explicit pictures and a voicemail message sent from some
hoochie is, no doubt, as damning as the day is long.

She already had the 411 on the undercover brotha. Therefore, she
would allow him to go through his ritual of tip-toeing around hiding
evidence when she wasn't looking and let him think he was one step
ahead. Despite his efforts, whether he knew it or not, Mr. *"I got hoes in*

different area codes" was definitely slippin' on his pimpin'.

She turned off the TV, remembering to put it back on the SportsNova channel beforehand. The man absolutely must have 1000 channels of cable programming at all times. Which was something that never actually made sense to her, seeing as the SportsNova channel is the only program he ever watched.

Knowing how things were when she arrived, she was careful not to leave any tell-tale signs of her presence. So, she methodically went through the apartment, making sure to cover her tracks. She waited until about 4:15 and then grabbed her handbag and her luggage and left the condo.

She went downstairs to wait at the entrance to the building. Although the door to the building was open, there were sidelight windows on either side of the front door that she could peek through to see when he was coming. During one of their long distance conversations he mentioned that the company had reserved for him a silver colored Lincoln, therefore she knew what kind of car to look for.

As she waited, her phone rang. She looked at the caller I.D. it was her son, Darius.

"Ah, Darius, your timing sucks," she thought.

She answered the phone. The line of questioning was somewhat suspicious. She wouldn't put it past Eric to put Darius up to calling so that he could fish information out of her pertaining to her whereabouts. There was no way that she was going to fall for it. As much as she hated to lie to her son, she couldn't let him interfere with her plan, so she rushed him off the phone using some fugazy excuse.

When she saw the Lincoln pull into the parking lot of the complex, she stepped back away from the door as far as she possibly could so that he wouldn't see her. Then she heard him approach. He was talking to someone on his other phone, the commonly known one. As he got closer and more within earshot, she heard him ask,

"So, did you hear from your mother?"

He was talking to Darius—she was sure of it. Her son had teamed up with his dad against her. She thought, nah, never would her firstborn

179

do that. Besides, he didn't even know the deal and God only knows what his dad told him.

He may have told him that his mom was missing, and out of worry and concern, he may have desperately been trying to help find her. She cringed to think that he would stoop so low as to play on their son's emotions in an effort to obtain information.

She could feel her knees knocking as his voice became more audible, indicating that he was approaching closer and closer. Finally, after what seemed like forever, he entered the doorway. He instantly looked to his left and saw her standing there. It was if time stood still. He looked at her and stopped dead in his tracks with his mouth held wide open. After about five seconds he regained his ability to speak and with absolutely the most dazed expression he said,

"Darius, let me call you back later."

Once he recovered from the initial shock of seeing her standing there in the flesh, he uttered,

"Hey baby, how're you doin'?"

Now, there was absolutely no sparkle in his eye, no delight in his voice, no lighting up of his face. His reaction was a very dry, hey baby, how're you doin'? Translation?

Oh shit, what the hell are you doing here?

The reception wasn't warm in the least. He was as cold and as distant as she'd ever felt him be toward her and she had felt him be cold and extremely distant many times before. However, this time, he wasn't just cold, he was stone-cold. Actually, he wasn't just stone-cold—he was stone-cold busted, and he knew it! His wife was the last person that he expected to see just show up at his Michigan bachelor crib. Besides, he thought he had that whole situation on lock.

Ωmega Sentry Security Systems made provisions once a month for spouses to visit their husbands or wives while they were away on business. He would have welcomed her with open arms had she gone through him to arrange for her to be there. He would have expensed the trip through the company and been completely aware of her itinerary and thus, would've been prepared to plan accordingly. He never expected her to forego such perks and discreetly plan the trip on her own dime. Not that she wasn't able to go wherever she chose, whenever she chose. It was a company benefit that was afforded her—so he totally expected her to take advantage of it. Sharelle loved perks as much as the next person, but this time she decided to pass. The element of surprise was way more valuable to her than any corporate perk.

Once they went upstairs and into the apartment, she put her bags down and pretended to be in awe of the condo. She deplored putting on the phony act, but since he had chosen to introduce mind games into the marriage, she figured she'd oblige him this time by playing along. After all, it wasn't any longer about honesty and truth, and she wondered if it ever really was. It was about who can outwit who. She asked him,

"Aren't you glad to see me?"

"Of course, he said, insincerely. You know I'm always glad to see you."

He was as fidgety as a crack addict in need of a fix. He paced the floor trying his best to find the perfect opportunity to stash his secret phone and other incriminating items without her noticing. Again, she played dumb and turned the other cheek. She let him think that he was slick enough to once again, get one over on her.

Relieved that he had succeeded in stashing the evidence without getting caught, he asked her if she was hungry. Although she had no appetite, she was willing to do just about anything to put an end to the excruciatingly tense 30 minutes or so of playing the game.

"I'd offer you something to eat but all I really have in the fridge is some cold cuts. If I had known you were coming, I would have taken something out of the freezer," he said facetiously.

"That's okay, I'll find something."

"Well no, if you're hungry we can go out to dinner. Do you feel like going out?"

"Sure, we can go out."

He obviously wanted to get her out of the apartment to distract her from snooping around and noticing something that he hadn't yet had a chance to hide.

They ended up going out to a lovely little Italian bistro and had drinks while awaiting the arrival of their meal. She ordered an antipasto salad trying to avoid anything that would be too filling.

Between sips of a Mojito, he asked her,

"So, how are you feeling?"

She responded,

"I'm a little tired from traveling, but I feel alright other than that."

Then he asked her a question that totally opened up the floodgates and caused her impenetrable emotional armor to melt away like butter. He looked her square in the eyes and asked,

"No, I meant your heart, how's your heart?"

Within seconds her face was awash with tears. She had tried desperately to maintain a strong outward appearance, a stiff upper lip. If only he hadn't spoken those three little words. Those words had incredible power. They had the power to bring her to her knees, the same as a boxer who's taken an upper cut square on the chin.

As if things could get any worse, Eric was about to confess something that would be the blow that would stretch her flat out cold—it would be the knock-out punch that would put her down for the count, except this time, she wouldn't answer the bell.

"Baby, I didn't want to hurt you. I wish you had never seen those pictures. It's all my fault. I asked her to send me those pictures."

"Who is she? And I want the truth, I'm sick and tired of your lies," she demanded.

"I'm going to come clean, and I'm going to tell you everything 'cause I'm tired of sneaking around and lying to cover my tracks."

"How long has this been going on?" she asked.

"Well, I might as well tell you. At first, we were just friends from high school, and we worked together at Scheindlin's. She started telling me that her husband was abusive, so as a friend, I would just be there to comfort her. Then it developed into something more. I've been going with her off and on since before we got married, and we have a son together."

Sharelle gasped and became light-headed. It was like a nightmare that she couldn't wake up from. The pit of her stomach ached with an incredible gnawing sensation. She was completely devastated. The most demoralizing part of it was the manner in which he confessed. She kept her eyes glued to his, hoping to see some remorse and maybe some compassion—it wasn't there. All she saw in his eyes was a self-aggrandizing urge to purge. All she heard in his voice was a tone indicating that he was getting some sort of twisted pleasure out of watching her emotional demise.

She had so many questions that she didn't know what to ask first however, it didn't take her long to orchestrate a cross-examination.

"You have a son together? So, your mother and everybody knows about this?"

"No—no, but my mother did suspect that we were seeing each other and she told me to stay away from her. She never really liked her."

"Why didn't she like her?"

"She said she was a home wrecker."

"Well, she was right about that! Damn, I can't believe you've been living a dual life with another family throughout our entire marriage and the whole time it's just been one big sham."

The creamy dressing in her salad became diluted from the tears that ran down her face. They washed over the crispy tender leaves of baby herbs and lettuces like a flowing stream that purifies as it trickles over rocky falls, then comes to rest in a quiet pool of serenity. She quickly stopped her sobbing and blurted out,

"God help me, all this time I've been living a lie!"

"No, baby, no that's not true. You haven't been living a lie. I don't have another family. It was nothing serious it was just a booty call!"

"A booty call? A booty call? She protested. A booty call is when two people casually get together every now and then, with the main objective being sex with no strings attached. Having a relationship with someone for thirty years and producing a love child together while being married to someone else—that's not a booty call, it's an affair! Now you just sat here and confessed that you and Sheiba have a son together. What else is that, if it's not a family?"

"No Shar, he's not my son."

"Oh, here we go with the lies again, and you can't even do that right!"

"Shar, I've only seen the kid once, and he looks nothing like me. Besides, she was still married when he was conceived. He must be about 30 years old or so, and I've only seen him once."

"I don't believe this. This sounds like a segment of who's your baby daddy? From the Monty Covich show. Wouldn't you want to know for sure if that's your son? I mean, why didn't you insist on a DNA test?"

"Well, because she told me later that he wasn't mine. She only said that the baby was mine because I was about to marry you."

Sharelle had nothing but disdain for Eric at this point. He couldn't have had any compassion for the heartache that he put her through; otherwise, he wouldn't have prefaced his big confession with such devastating news. Instead of mitigating the damage that he caused, he only exacerbated it with the momma's baby, daddy's maybe drama. It was clear that his motives were embedded in narcissism. He simply threw in some extraneous information that served no purpose but to cause Sharelle more pain and to maximize the dramatic effect.

Chapter Thirty

He was different from the way she remembered him. He was tall, dark, handsome, and delightfully charming. She didn't remember the charming part from way back then and really, not so much even the tall and handsome parts. She only remembered the dark part, the only attractive thing about him.

A lot had changed since she last saw Blake Pearson, all those twenty-seven years ago back in Cali. He had been a long-time childhood into adulthood friend who once had a serious crush on her. They lived on the same street in an upscale neighborhood of Los Angeles. He had such a crush on Sharelle that he used to tell everybody that he would marry her when they grew up.

At one point, he became so annoying that she would turn around and go back in the house if Blake was there when she came out to play with the neighborhood kids. After a while, it became apparent that it wasn't just a coincidence that no matter what game the kids were playing, whenever she came outside, the game would change to R.C.K. (run, catch and kiss). She soon realized that it was all courtesy of Blake. To her relief, he eventually grew out of that.

As often happens, she never heard anything more about him. They sort of lost touch once they both went away to college. It was the extent of their relationship once they went their separate ways.

A couple of years after college, she remembers hearing mention of him landing a position as a producer of a popular television sitcom, but the source of information had the details so twisted that it was impossible to verify. And now, in a strange twist of fate, she bumped into him at the airport in Detroit while waiting in line to check her bag at the ticket counter. He, too, was flying out of Detroit but on a flight back to L.A.

She could feel the hairs on her neck stand up throughout the long, arduous schlep through the maze leading to the ticket counter. She had an eerie sense that someone was staring at her. She kept looking back to see if she recognized anyone, but no one looked familiar. A couple of times, she met the gaze of a guy she didn't recognize, but quickly dismissed the synchronous eye contact as simply embarrassingly lousy timing.

Just before her turn to approach the counter, she heard a voice call her name.

"Excuse me, is your name Sharelle?"

She looked him up and down, wondering how he could have possibly known her name, then replied.

"Yeah, how'd you know that?"

"Hey girl, I thought that was you, it's Blake!"

Her eyes lit up with excitement when she realized it was her old friend. Blake was so happy to see her that when they embraced, he lifted her straight up off the floor and swung her from side to side like a rag doll. She stared in awe at him and said,

"I can't believe it—Blake Pearson. It's so good to see you!"

Back in the day, she called him milk dud head. The name was indicative of his close-cut hairstyle that barely covered his bulbous, chocolate-colored noggin. Then, because he was so long and lanky, his head looked like a giant milk dud on a stick. Now, he was a hard-body of at least six-five, two-fifty. The only thing that hadn't changed was that rich, dark chocolate complexion.

"My God, how many years has it been? How are you?" asks Blake.

He definitely had changed for the better, but as gorgeous as he was on the outside, she could sense that there was something inside that was even more special about him.

After checking her bag, she looked back at him, smiled, and waved goodbye. Then, as she turned to walk away, she heard him call.

"Sharelle, wait. Do you have a minute?"

She nodded and stood at the end of the ticket counter and waited for him to check his bag. Then he approached and asked,

"I'll walk you to your gate. What time is your flight?"

"Oh, it's not until 8:55. I got here a little early 'cause I was delayed getting through security on the trip out here, so this time I didn't want to take any chances."

"Yeah, same here. Since we both have a little time before boarding, do you want to go and have some coffee?"

"Sure, that'll be nice."

She and Blake settled in one of the airport cafés and began catching up on old times. They each had at least an hour before either of their flights departed, so they decided to make the most of their time together. It was nice to have someone from her past to sit and laugh with. It was just the kind of diversion she needed to keep her mind off the recent discovery that had just shredded her heart into a thousand pieces.

It was refreshing to see that he was in no way pretentious. Not once did he try to put down any tired mack daddy lines on her. In fact, he seemed more interested in her life than trying to impress her with his own.

She eventually found out through their conversation he had established a pretty impressive career for himself. In fact, she was shocked to find out that their lives had actually crossed paths during the last twenty-seven years without either of them knowing it. Blake explained that after finishing college, coincidentally, he went to law school at Princeton in Princeton, New Jersey.

Upon completing his law degree and passing the state bar exam, Blake worked for a couple of years with the district attorney's office in Middlesex County. However, he soon decided he didn't want to practice law after all. He explained how he became disenfranchised by the court system and its unwillingness to fairly represent black youth.

His final straw came when a colleague of his within the D.A.'s office, a white attorney, misrepresented a young black male in his senior year of college. A prominent white business owner accused the young man of selling drugs.

The business owner was furious that his daughter, who attended the same college, had been dating this young black man. So, he concocted this story about the young man selling drugs and using his daughter's car to stash them. After learning the young man had been driving his daughter's car to go to work at a local fast-food restaurant, the father planted crack cocaine in the glove box.

One evening, after the girl's father notified police that the car had been stolen, the young man was arrested after being pulled over. A search was conducted, and as expected, drugs were found. The young man was charged with trafficking crack cocaine. Although there was evidence that showed that the father set the young man up, it somehow wasn't allowed as evidence in court.

Blake was appalled when he overheard a conversation between the court-appointed attorney assigned to represent the young man and another attorney discussing the case. The representing attorney asked the question of the other. "You know how these black kids from the ghetto afford college, don't you?" His pathetically bigoted answer was, "just sell crack if you're poor and black!"

The two attorneys laughed heartily while a young man's future hung in the balance. Because of racist views and apathy, another promising, innocent young black kid was sentenced to prison. Blake had seen it happen way too often while at the D.A.'s office and just couldn't bear to be affiliated with that type of injustice anymore.

After much soul-searching, he changed his career focus. He went into forensic investigations with the U.S. Attorney's office in New Jersey. He remained there another year until he was granted a transfer to the U.S. Attorney's office in Los Angeles. Of course, neither he nor Sharelle knew that the other lived in New Jersey during that time. Finding the irony hard to believe, she said,

"Blake, I lived in Jersey for over twenty years I, too, moved there right after college. So, how could we have both been living there at the same time, for years, and never even know? It's not like Jersey is that big!"

"Just wasn't in the cards, I guess," he replied.

She couldn't help but notice that he wasn't wearing a wedding band, nor did he once speak of a wife, but she's learned not to make any assumptions where that's concerned. As of late, she had been taking her own private survey. She had concluded that the absence or presence of a ring on the ring finger means nothing these days.

She noticed something else. She noticed a peace had fallen over her in the past half-hour while talking to Blake. She hadn't discussed anything about her marriage besides the fact that she was married. Still, somehow he brought her comfort without even realizing that she needed comfort. There was such sincerity in his soft, soothing voice. Yet, at the same time, he conveyed a robust masculine quality.

Although he steered clear of prying into her personal life, he was curious about what brought her to Detroit and why she was headed to Charlotte. He inquired,

"So, Sharelle, do you have relatives here in Detroit?"

"No—well yeah, I guess I do. My husband has been assigned to work here temporarily."

"Oh, so you were here visiting your husband?"

"Yeah—I don't know anyone here in Detroit."

"So, what's going on in Charlotte?"

"Oh, I live there now. We moved from New Jersey after living there for the last twenty-something years. Eric's company recently transferred us there."

"Really? How do you like living in Charlotte?"

"I really like it there, it's nice. It's a welcome change to those cold New Jersey winters, although North Carolina can get a little chilly sometimes too."

She looked at her watch and saw that it was already 8:30. She told Blake that she needed to get over to the gate to get ready to board her flight.

"Well, Blake, it was so good to see you. My flight should be about ready to board now, so I'd better get going. By the way, what time does your flight leave?"

"Oh, my flight doesn't leave until 10:15."

"Wow, do you think you got here early enough?"

"Actually, my flight was originally scheduled to leave at 8:35, but it's been delayed for some reason. You know, you just can't figure the airlines these days. But, before you go, I'd like to give you my numbers. I'd really love to hear from you sometime."

"Oh, okay, and I'll give you mine."

"Are you sure it'll be okay to call you?"

"It's my cell, by all means, feel free," she assured.

"Great! Listen, I really hope we can talk again, let's not let another thirty years go by, okay?"

"Okay, Blake. Have a safe flight. Bye."

He grabbed her around the waist and gently pulled her toward him. She was thrown off guard when he reached up and cradled her head in both of his hands, and then leaned down to place a kiss delicately on her forehead. It was a magical moment that would leave an indelible image in her mind. She walked away thinking, *"Who knew that Milk Dud head would've turned out to be such a charmer!"*

Chapter Thirty-One

Sharelle awoke the following morning to the sound of someone entering the front door. She quickly hopped out of bed to prepare to defend herself against the intruder. As the sound of footsteps grew closer, she remembered the gun Eric had purchased for their protection. After much hesitating, she decided that she would go and retrieve it, but her decision turned out to be too late. The intruder was already standing at the entrance of her bedroom. She stood there frightened, defenseless, and face to face with--*Eric*?

"Oh, you know what—you are so lucky you didn't get shot, bruh!" she shouted angrily.

Apparently, he had driven all night from Michigan back home on a mission to save his shattered marriage. She wished he had stayed where he was. He was the last person on earth that she wanted to see. Especially since his objective was to try to resurrect a marriage that she now realized they never had in the first place.

What if she hadn't been so indecisive about getting that gun? It could have been the perfect crime. She could have busted a cap dead in his cheatin' ass and been totally exonerated for the shooting on a self-defense plea. After all, she wasn't expecting Eric. As far as she knew, an intruder had breached her home's security and put her life in mortal danger.

The evil thought gave her a fleeting moment of morbid satisfaction on some pathetically small level. Granted—not her finest moment, but if it weren't for the fact that Eric was the father of her children, she might not have thought it such a bad idea.

Still, good thing her better judgment won out. It would've been devastating for her children to learn that their dad had befallen such a fate—even more devastating, at the hands of their own mother.

He looked as if he expected her to be glad to see him. He actually thought he had done a tremendous chivalrous deed by rushing to be by her side to comfort her. She wondered who he thought he was fooling. As of late, he didn't do anything where she was concerned without it benefitting himself in the process.

She didn't fall for it for one minute. *"Oh, Eric rushed home to do some damage control alright—if anything, it was to control damage to the bank account,"* she surmised.

He tested the waters by speaking to her, making sure to choose his words very carefully.

"Hey, baby I couldn't stand to see you leave like that. Can I have a hug?"

"No, I don't want to hug you, nor do I want you to hug me. In fact, I don't want you to touch me—period."

"Baby, I know you're hurt and angry, and you did nothing to deserve this. This is one hundred percent my fault, this is my problem."

She wondered if he actually thought that she blamed herself for his lack of integrity and inability to exercise self-control.

"You got that right! I know too well, it's not my fault," she insisted.

"Baby, what I'm trying to say is I have a problem, I'm sick, and I need help. I've tried to stop many times, but I just don't have the self-control. You have to believe me. I never wanted to hurt you."

"Face it, Eric, you're a liar and a cheat, and it's always been about you. No one else is important as long as you get what you want."

She marched out of the room, slamming the door behind her. She headed upstairs to her office and noticed an article on the desk she had found while researching An Exposé of Indiscretion. The article was written by Michael Herkov, Ph.D. He explains the biochemical model for sex addiction. She re-examines the article.

"The brain tells the sex addict that having illicit sex is good the same way it tells others that food is good when hungry. These brain changes translate into a sex addict's preoccupation with sex and exclusion of other interests. Compulsive sexual behavior despite negative consequences and failed attempts to limit or terminate sexual behavior…the addicted brain fools the body by producing intense biochemical rewards for this self-destructive behavior."

As she read further, she came across an online evaluation listing signs and symptoms identifying a sex-addicted personality. She selected each symptom that applied to Eric and then allowed the online test to evaluate them.

The test revealed that he was off the charts. At that point, she felt a slight bit of compassion for him. The emotion was in total conflict with what she thought she should feel. She thought she was justified in despising him. She felt that it should be her prerogative to hate him. After all, he's caused her great emotional pain. Hating him would've been so much easier. She could've simply packed up her life, sued him for divorce, and never looked back. But, in reality, she knew it wouldn't be that easy. She had a heart. She hated no one. Although he had caused grave destruction to their marriage, she thought about her vows. Just because he spat in the face of God by not holding true to the vows that he spoke when they married, she wasn't going out like that.

So, instead of making any major decisions about her future, treatment for his illness would have to take precedence.

She went back downstairs and into their bedroom to talk to him about what he planned to do concerning this great epiphany. She questioned him to gauge his level of sincerity about getting help.

"So, have you thought about getting some counseling?" she asks.

"Yes, I have. Before I left Michigan, I called Dr. Rollins, and he gave me a referral to a psychologist here in Charlotte. So I'm going to call him today to make an appointment."

"Okay. Well, look, I hope you're doing this for your own mental health and not just to make it look good for me. Right about now, I'm not even dealing with what should happen between us. I'll support you through your therapy, but beyond that, I'm not making any promises."

His eyes welled up, and he exhaled an audible sigh of relief. He was completely overwhelmed by her undaunting compassion and concern. He remembered it was those virtues, among others, which impressed him to the point of falling in love with her in the first place. He then went on to express deep regret.

"I understand. And no, Shar, I'm not just doing this for you. I'm first and foremost doing this for me 'cause I need help, and I'm tired of all the lyin' and duckin' and hidin' and totally screwin' up my life. When I look in the mirror, I see shame and guilt, and I'm tired of living like that—and I know all this drama will probably end our marriage, but I have to say, I feel so much better now that I put it all out there. Believe me, Shar, I want to change."

He spoke with such conviction that somehow she believed him. For the first time in years, he really sounded sincere. Maybe this was the turning point in his life, but she knew she had busted him before, and he was just as sorry then. However, there was something different this time. She still didn't fully trust him, but something was definitely different.

Chapter Thirty-Two

"Joy, I'm nearby and I was wondering, if you feel like some company?, said Sharelle

"Yeah, sure, come on over. I'm just chillin', that's all."

"Okay, I'll see you in a bit."

She hadn't spoken to Joy since she returned from Michigan, and she desperately needed to get out of her house of pain for a while. She needed some uplifting, and Joy was always good for a laugh.

She left Eric at home in what appeared to be a dazed state. She didn't know if he was in shock due to missing his daily dose of porn or what his problem was. In fact, if he needed his daily fix, she would be happy to leave so he could have all the privacy he wanted. At this point, she couldn't care less whether he succumbed to a fatal dose or not. She was on an emotional roller coaster—sometimes, she felt compassion, and sometimes, she just didn't care.

She arrived at Joy's house about half an hour later and rang the doorbell. By now, Joy was five months pregnant, so she knew she'd have to allow a little extra time for her to waddle to the door to let her in. She finally opens the door and says,

"Hey, girl. Come on in."

"My God, look at you, you're really starting to poke out there," Sharelle remarks.

"Yeah, and I feel it too. I'm starting to feel like a beached whale."

"Well, you look beautiful, Joy."

"Yeah, well, I don't feel so beautiful."

She was lying through her teeth about Joy looking beautiful. She looked a mess. However, seeing her friend having such a difficult time and feeling so down on herself broke her heart. The way she saw it was if a little white lie could give her friend some encouragement, then no harm, no foul. That was the least she could do.

Most women are simply radiant while pregnant, but there are some women that pregnancy just doesn't do any justice at all. Joy fell in the latter category. As much as she didn't want to admit it, she didn't have that pregnant glow. Instead, her complexion had become blotchy and blemished, and she was starting to get that "pregnant nose" look. Sharelle often wondered what caused that to happen, but more importantly, she was glad that she was one of the few that it didn't happen to.

"So, what's been going on? What do you have to tell me that you couldn't talk about over the phone?" Joy asks.

Sharelle was a little taken aback that she jumped right to the subject before at least offering her something to drink. She was usually on point with the social graces, so this was a little outside her character. But, as was the case here lately, she just chalked it up to hormones gone wild.

"Well, I just got back from Michigan."

"Oh yeah? You went to visit Eric?"

"Who else?"

"So, how was it there?"

"I was just there a couple of days. I didn't do much."

"Shar, you didn't come over here to tell me that you went to Michigan and didn't do anything, what'd you and Eric do?"

"Argued mostly."

"Really? What happened? Tell me."

She didn't really want to sail right into the subject. Instead, she came over to visit Joy in hopes of having a little light-hearted chit-chat with a friend, but Joy was determined to jump head-first into the drama, so she had little choice but to oblige her.

"Alright, I'll tell you. Let me see, where do I start? Okay, on one of Eric's visits home for the weekend, I sneaked and had copies of his keys made to his condo there in Michigan...."

"Oh girl, no, you didn't!"

"...Yeah, I did, and I'm not proud of it, but you know a sistah's gotta do what a sistah's gotta do. So anyway, I planned a trip there this past weekend unbeknownst to him. He had planned to work Saturday, so I made plans to arrive while he was at work."

"Yeah, and what'd you do?" Joy asked while perched on the edge of her seat.

"Calm down, I'm trying to tell you. I searched his condo, and I found some very incriminating evidence. I found a box of condoms, his secret phone I told you about, and...."

"Uh oh, you didn't cut him, did you?

"...No, I didn't cut him, but you haven't even heard the worst part."

She paused for a few seconds, and when she resumed speaking, her voice started to crack as she recounted the distressing details of her visit. The pain was still too fresh in her mind to talk about it so matter-of-factly.

"He has another secret phone, and I found it in his nightstand drawer. Some skank sent him some disgusting pictures and left him a voicemail message calling him sweetie."

"Oh, Shar, that's just one of those 900-number sex lines he called. I think there's a way he could have their pre-recorded messages sent to his voicemail. And the pictures girl, you know you can download those from the internet all day long. C'mon Shar, you said yourself he is a porn freak. I mean, I know you don't condone pornography, but isn't that better than him sleepin' around?"

"Actually, Joy, no, it isn't. That's a cop-out that porn addicts use. It's the same as with drugs. When someone's heavily into porn, they need to take it to the next level because the high that they get from the porn isn't enough after a while. Besides, you have it all wrong anyway. This was no 900 number. It was some chick's personal phone number. I know 'cause I called her, and if somebodys out there trying to promote those pictures on the internet for profit, they need to be shot 'cause homegirl looks a steamin' hot mess!"

Well, if she looks that bad, then you don't have a damn thing to worry about," Joy insisted.

She went on to tell Joy all of the sordid details of the phone conversation with Sheiba, the misguided minister, and then changed the subject.

"Oh hey, I talked to Blake the other day—you know my friend from L.A. that I hadn't seen in years?"

"Really? Are you two tryin' to hook up or somethin'?"

"No, no, it's nothing like that. We vowed to keep in touch, and I just found out that my agent is planning my book release party in L.A., and I just wanted to give him a head's up."

"Oh yeah? When is it?"

"I'm not sure of the exact date yet, but it'll be a few weeks from now. I told Blake I would e-mail him an invite when everything was finalized."

"Ooooh, I want to go!" Joy begged.

"Well, you know I want you to be there, but are you sure you can travel right now?"

"Girl puh-leeze, I ain't tryin' to let this baby stop me from doing what I want to do. Besides, it's your book release party, I wouldn't miss that for the world!"

"Alright, then, I guess it's on. Oh, and before I forget, I just want to thank you for suggesting I give Lee a call."

"Lee? Who's Lee?"

"Joy! The psychiatrist we met at the club? Dr. McCreamy, as you call him."

"Oh yeah! Dr. Feelgood. How's that going?"

"Oh, now he's Dr. Feelgood. I swear you have more names for

that man. Anyway, I'm glad I called him, and it's going well. As a matter of fact, he thinks I'm really making progress."

"See, I told you. So just stick with it, you'll get your memory back. I can't help but believe that."

At around 8:00 p.m., just as she was leaving Joy's house, she received a text message from Tracy. It was another cryptic message of a somewhat ominous nature. It read:

"BROKEN DREAMS AND SHATTERED WISHES,
SPAWNED A PLOT MOST CRUEL AND VICIOUS;
LOOK TO IRAM'S QUEST FOR RICHES,
THEREIN LIES A SWIM WITH FISHES."

The message may as well have been written in Greek because it made absolutely no sense to Sharelle. However, she understood fully that Tracy's Madame Cleo routine was starting to piss her off.

Chapter Thirty-Three

G reat! I'll meet you at the hotel around 2:00," said Sharelle's father, Paul, who still lives in L.A. He was looking forward to her coming to town the following Friday. The time had finally come. The book release party for An Exposé of Indiscretion was jumping off this weekend at the Four Seasons Hotel in Beverly Hills. Her publishing agent, Kirsten, was sparing no expense in organizing the event. This gave her some insight into the expectations on the part of Poole & Rofford about the profit potential of her book.

She had already approved her proof copy, complete with the enticing cover that her genius graphics artist designed, which looked beautiful. She felt an overwhelming sense of pride and accomplishment in knowing that her resolve and dedication to this work would somehow reach someone and potentially save them from themselves.

This was her baby. She had labored, given birth, and nurtured this wonderful creation, and now it was time to send the product of her labor of love off into the world. She had finally told her story, yet her story was far from the end. In her own real-life drama, there was still much work to be done. However, this was a happy time in her life. She wouldn't allow anyone or anything to put a damper on it. Therefore, Eric would not be at the release party. She had decided not to even mention it. Sharelle wanted only well-wishers and people who had inspired her to be there. She felt he hadn't supported her in her work all along, so why should he be a part of a celebration of something he had no interest in?

Besides, she would rather not have to wear a phony smile and appear to be happily married to him just to keep up appearances. For her, happiness and marriage had become two concepts in complete and total opposition. But, of course, she didn't always feel that way. Still, in light of the current events in her life, she no longer espoused that happily ever after ideal anymore.

Clearly, frontin' had never been something she was comfortable with, so she figured, why put herself through all the embarrassment? She decided the best thing to do was to tell him that she was simply going to L.A. to visit her dad.

While packing for the trip, she was reminded of Tracy's spooky text message and decided to give her a call. Tracy answers.

"Hello?"

"Hey Tracy, it's Shar."

"Hey girl, how're you doing?"

"I'm fine. Is everything okay with you?"

"Yeah, I'm fine. I've been trying to reach you for a few weeks now, but all I get is your voicemail. So, what on earth is going on with you?"

She tried not to sound perturbed with Tracy. Still, as much as she tried to keep the conversation cordial, she struggled to contain her agitation.

"Tracy, I've been meaning to call you since I got your last text message, but to be honest with you, it made no sense to me, so I just decided to ignore it. But seeing as I mentioned it, can you tell me what that message was all about, in God's name?"

"Oh yeah. Well, I know you think I lost my mind, but when these things come to me, I have to go with it."

"Tracy, I don't have the slightest idea what you're talking about. Just tell me, why do you keep sending me these ridiculous text messages?"

"Shar, you have to trust me. Occasionally I get these crazy messages from the universe, and I don't know what they mean, but believe me, these messages always have significance. It's just a matter of deciphering what the universe is trying to tell us."

"Okay, got it! Now, can we talk about something else? how's your boy, Marcus? Have you spoken to him lately?"

"No, but I e-mailed him, and I'm waiting for him to e-mail me back. Shar, don't try to change the subject."

"Look, Tracy, I've told you before, I get my direction from God, not from Orion, not from the little dipper, nor from Star Jones, okay?"

Tracy pleaded with her to try to make sense of the messages. Finally, at significant risk of losing her friendship with her, she forced the issue.

"C'mon Sharelle, think. Do you know anyone by the name of IRAM? That name keeps echoing in my brain."

"No I don't, Tracy! But I do know the name of a good psychiatrist! Do you need his number?"

"Okay, Shar, I see I've struck a nerve."

"Hmm, ya think?"

"Alright, alright!—I won't send you any more text messages. However, if you really want to regain your memory and learn the details of your accident, I strongly advise you not to dismiss what the messages are trying to tell you. This kind of revelation doesn't come to me that often, but when it does, I take heed because it's usually something serious."

After abruptly ending the conversation with Tracy, Sharelle went back to packing her clothes. For her life, she couldn't decide which dress she should wear on the night of the book release party. It was a toss-up between the basic black Valenciaga and the fuchsia Sue Fong. But, whatever she decided, it had to be perfect. This would be one of her biggest nights, and she wanted to shine.

Over the next few days, she would have a busy schedule—with her hair appointment, facial, mani/pedi, and on Thursday, her therapy session. She considered canceling her weekly appointment with Lee because so much had to be done. She knew she would miss her session next week because she would be in L.A. However, the mere thought of canceling for this week just didn't sit right with her. Since she promised Lee that she would be committed to her therapy sessions from now on, the one thing that she didn't want him to think of her was that she was not a woman of her word.

Around 3:15 that afternoon, Eric returned home from work. Ever since he cut short his assignment in Michigan, he had been trying his hardest to get back in Sharelle's good graces. But the betrayal still seared her heart just as a sirloin grilled over fiery hot coals. He entered the bedroom and greeted her in a presumptive manner, which was immediately met with an unmistakable air of rejection.

"Hey baby—how was your day?" he asked, approaching her with lips puckered.

She maneuvered her way around him, trying to make it appear as if she was unaware of his intentions, and replied,

"It was alright. How was yours?"

As the days went by, it became more and more obvious that as much as she tried to put his selfish, destructive behavior behind her, she would never trust him again. After twenty-five years of nothing but lies, how could she? How could anyone? Despite everything, she was pleased that he was seeking counseling for his addiction. Though she supported and encouraged him through his therapy, she knew she could never tell him about her own with Lee.

Chapter Thirty-Four

During her next therapy session, Dr. Alston listened intently as Sharelle described the text messages from Tracy. She was surprised that she even mentioned them, as that only made it appear that she validated them as having some real meaning. But to her, as much as she didn't want to admit it, they did have meaning. They either meant that someone was screwing around with her head, or maybe something was trying to get her to pay attention.

Lee started his probe of her psyche. He was hoping to unlock this mystery that now seemed to loom over her like a storm cloud.

"Sharelle, I find it particularly interesting that one of the messages mentions crimson visions, don't you?"

"No, not especially," she answered.

"Well, you've had nightmares about a red car chasing you, haven't you?"

"Well, yeah, I have."

"You've also had seizures after seeing images of a red car, right?'

"I have, once or twice."

"Have you ever told your friend Tracy about the nightmares?"

"No, no, I haven't. I did tell her about the seizures, though."

"Which is why she's obviously concerned about you. Still, that doesn't explain the reference to the color red in her text message."

"Okay."

She wasn't sure where he was going with this exchange, but she was hopeful that something positive would come out of it. He continued.

"You see, what I'm getting at is your friend Tracy may be on to something here. There is such a thing as mental telepathy. We all have the potential to be clairvoyant to some degree, but some people are more sensitive to it than others."

"So, Lee, what are you saying, that I should take stock in these messages?"

"I'm saying you should try to dissect them to see if there's anything you can learn from them."

He sat straight in his chair, startled by her sudden outburst of laughter. With a look of surprise, he asked,

"Did I say something funny?"

She covered her mouth, attempting to hide the rudeness of her mirth.

"No, Lee, I just didn't have you pegged as one of the Psychic Network's psychic friends, that's all."

Although he wasn't offended, he didn't find the remark quite as humorous as she did.

"Look, I'm not saying that I believe in horoscopes, tea leaves, or anything like that. I'm simply saying that there is data that substantiates the psychic phenomena known as E.S.P. or extra sensory perception but anyway, I digress.

Now, let's get back down to business. Do you remember anything about the day of the accident?"

"Some things," she answered.

"Can you tell me about some of those things?"

"Well, as a matter of fact, speaking of Tracy, I remember that I was headed to her house that day. She was having a cookout."

"You went alone?"

"Yes. Eric and I had been arguing, and he stormed out of the house and didn't come back in time, so I left without him."

"Okay, and what happened next?" Lee asked.

"I remember driving down the highway in South Jersey, and when I got off, I believe I took a back road."

"Did you see any other cars on that road?"

She scratched her head and looked toward the ceiling, searching for some recollection of the landscape surrounding her that day. She answered with uncertainty.

"Umm, I vaguely recall seeing one other car on the road, but I might be confusing real-life situations with the nightmares."

For a few seconds, Lee sat silently and pondered Sharelle's statement. He looked toward the large picture window of his office as he contemplated the ambiguity of her account of what she saw. The sun flooded the office and met his gaze, which illuminated the bronze hue of his eyes. Then, it came to him.

How Sharelle answered his next question would change the entire focus of his analysis. He chose his words deliberately yet challenged her to pull the details from the deepest depths of her psyche.

"Sharelle, let's assume that you saw another car on that dirt road, meaning that it happened in real life and not in a dream. If you can remember, what color was the car you thought you saw?"

"Oh God, I don't know."

"Just give it some thought. What color do you think it was?"

She nervously twirled a lock of hair between thumb and forefinger, then responded.

"Ummm, let me see. I believe there may have been another car, and I think it was, blue? No, no, it wasn't blue. Hmm, was it maybe a, reddish color?"

Her eyes stretched wide open at that moment, as though she'd just been hit with a thousand volts of electric current. Then she frantically exclaimed,

"Yeah, that's it! I remember! I'm almost sure there was another car, it was red!"

"Very good, Sharelle, do you realize what just happened? You just had a breakthrough!"

She sat there with her face in her hands and cried. She cried tears of joy, as this was confirmation that she was actually making progress. For the first time in years, she could see the real possibility of fully regaining her memory.

After her session was over, she remembered something else. She remembered that picture of her daughter Maya. She remembered placing a picture of Maya on the bulletin board in her office at home. She recalled the photo showing Maya standing in front of a red sports car. She also recalled getting a chill down her spine whenever she looked at it. Sharelle raced to get home to have another look at it. She was certain that the picture was trying to tell her something. There was something more to it than she had previously realized. She immediately called Tracy to apologize for blowing her off.

"Hello," answers Tracy.

"Tracy, it's Shar."

"Oh, hey, Shar. This is a pleasant surprise. I didn't think you would ever speak to me again."

C'mon Tracy, I wouldn't just kick you to the curb over something like that. Anyway, that's why I called. I just wanted to say I'm sorry for yelling at you."

"Eh, such is the life of a psychic, not everyone wants to hear what I have to say."

"Well, I'm starting to pay closer attention now. Some stuff in those messages is starting to make sense to me, and I need you to help me figure out what they're trying to tell me."

"Well, another one came to me last night, but I didn't want to piss you off by texting it to you."

"Really? What does this one say?"

"Well, I know I wrote it down and put it somewhere around here. Wait! Hold on a minute while I look around on my desk."

Tracy returned to the phone, sounding agitated.

"Hello, Shar?"

Sharelle responded.

"Yeah, I'm here."

"You know, I really have to clean my desk. I can't find a thing in that mess. Anyway, let's see if I still remember, I think it goes something like this." Tracy recited from memory.

> HAILED AS MISTRESS ONCE IN LIFE,
> IRAM CAUSED SUCH PAIN & STRIFE.
> RECALL DETAILS OF HER REIGN, AND
> MEMORY WILL COME BACK AGAIN.

"Okay, that's it! I've got to find out what the significance of this IRAM is," insisted Sharelle.

"Shar, you know I got your back. All I've been trying to do all along is help."

"I know Tracy, and believe me, I appreciate your help."

Once at home, she headed straight upstairs to her office and plucked the photo of Maya standing in front of the red car from the bulletin board. She strained to try to make out the reflected image of the plate on the car's front end. It was too distorted to see. Then, she remembered why she had tacked the picture there in the first place. It was such an adorable picture of a little toddler-sized Maya that she intended to have it enlarged. She would decide whether to have it matted and framed once she saw how well the enlargement worked out.

As what usually happens, she wasn't at home five minutes before the phone rang.

It was Eric calling. While still clinging to the picture of Maya, she answered.

"Hello?"

"Hey, baby, how're you doin' today?"

"I'm fine. How're you?"

"Good, good; where've you been? I haven't been able to reach you at home or by cell all day."

"Yeah, well, I went to the dentist today. On the way there, I was charging my phone, and when I went into the office, I guess I just forgot and left it in the car. I just got home."

"Oh, I see. Well, listen, I thought about picking up a pizza on my way home, and maybe we could watch a movie. What do you think?"

She had been dying for the release of the latest Teran Terry movie and hoped he would be interested as well.

"What movie were you thinking of watching?"

"Uh, that Teran Terry movie. You know, the one with Jana Smith and Moni Shaw in it?"

"You mean, "Why the Hell Did I Marry You?"

"Yeah—yeah, that's it!"

"Okay, that's fine."

"You want to see that one?"

"Yeah, that'll be fine."

"Okay, well, I'll see you in a bit."

"Okay, bye."

Chapter Thirty-Five

O ver one hundred people turned out for the book release party on Saturday night. Her girls Joy and Tracy even flew in for the occasion. Sharelle couldn't believe Joy took a flight to be there for her, especially since she hadn't been feeling very well lately. She was equally surprised that Tracy came, especially considering how she had recently treated her. But these were true friends of hers. If ever she could count on someone to be there for her, she knew that Joy and Tracy would always have her back.

Kirsten outdid herself with the party planning. Everything was decked out in black, silver, and white, from the balloons and confetti to the china and linen tablecloths. On each table was a centerpiece with white rosebuds and baby's breath. Emerging out of the center of each floral arrangement was a miniature replica of An Exposé of Indiscretion. All were bound in black, the title gleaming in embossed silver. The absolute pièce de résistance was the five-foot-tall ice sculpture carved in Sharelle's likeness. None of the beautiful surprises thoughtfully prepared on her behalf were as exciting as seeing an invited yet unexpected guest. That surprise guest was Blake Pearson, her childhood friend that she recently reacquainted with at the airport in Detroit. She e-mailed him an invitation, but didn't get a response from him. So the saying goes, no news is good news. However, as far as he was concerned, she was afraid that no news meant *hell no, I won't go news*. Since she didn't get a response from him, she simply assumed the latter. However, there he was, looking like a chocolate-covered Adonis. He looked like he should've been on the cover of People Magazine as the first eligible black man for the next season of The Bachelor. He was so handsome in his beautifully tailored black suit with a crisp white shirt and gold silk tie. What made him really fit the part was that he came bearing a bouquet of a dozen hot pink roses. Seeing him made her question, *"hmm, I wonder why there's only been one brotha selected to be The Bachelor? I'm sure plenty of brothas would enjoy having 20 women humiliate themselves by clawing each other's eyes out over him over eight or nine weeks! Besides, what Hollywood genius came up with the concept for that show anyway? It had to take a lot of guts to pitch a show about a bunch of desperate women throwing themselves at the same man to a major television network executive."*

Regardless, she was humbled that Blake thought enough of her to come out for her big night. Then there was her dad, Paul. He was beaming, just grinning from ear to ear. During the cocktail hour, he told stories to whoever would listen about seeing the potential in Sharelle long ago. While mingling, he caught her by the arm as she passed by and introduced her to one of his lawyer buddies. Although the guy seemed nice enough, she imagined him to be a lonely man. She knew it was probably an unfair assumption that the man didn't have anybody. Certainly, his rotund physique and Coke bottle bifocals don't make him completely undesirable. Besides, there's someone out there for everyone. But, indeed, if he had a woman, she would tell him that a form-fitting shirt that accentuates his man boobs is not a good look for him.

It didn't take long before her dad gave the poor man a whole dissertation about the family gene pool. He made it quite clear that he was the one who encouraged her to use her inherent gift for writing. She excused herself and moved on at the first sign of a pause in the conversation. And, of course, Arlene was there looking lovely as usual, posturing as only a proud mother could. She was in her glory telling people about Sharelle and Eric's fairy-tale marriage, which, of course, was just that, a big, fat fairy tale. When Arlene started with the embarrassing baby

Sharelle stories, she cut in.

"Hey, Mom, have you tried the cheese straws?"

Although, at times, embarrassing, she was happy to have her parents there to celebrate with her. Still, two very important people were missing from her special evening, Darius and Maya. They weren't there simply because she decided not to tell them about the event. It wasn't that she didn't want her children there to share in her night. In hindsight, she could have used them as bragging bait for Arlene and Paul and spared herself all the embarrassment. But telling Darius and Maya about tonight was as good as telling Eric. As sure as death and taxes, they would've slipped and mentioned it to their father, especially L'il Miss Maya. That child is like an old, broken down refrigerator...just can't keep nothin'.

While shaking hands and mingling with the crowd, everyone's attention was suddenly diverted to the loud thud of someone's hand beating on a microphone. Sharelle's agent, Kirsten, was attempting to make an introduction.

"Good evening, ladies and gentlemen. I'd like to take this opportunity to welcome you this evening to celebrate the release of what's sure to be a best-selling novel, "An Exposé of Indiscretion...."

A clinking of forks against water glasses and a rousing applause ensued.

"...and at this time, it is my pleasure to present to you the talented award-winning author, Sharelle Langford-Hughes."

She received a standing ovation that practically moved her to tears, which somehow she held back to avoid ruining her makeup. She approached the podium, thanked everyone for coming out, and gave a short speech about her writing career and how she came up with the idea for writing Exposé. She stated that she found the topic of pornography and sex addiction interesting and, after researching it, decided to write a novel based on the issue. She read aloud an excerpt from the book and, once again, thanked everyone for coming out in support of her.

After the formalities concluded, the party was on and poppin'. Blake came over to congratulate her and handed her the bouquet of roses, followed by a gentle hug. Then, she took her place at the table set up for her to sign copies of Exposé. After signing the first fifteen copies, she thought that back in the day, writers must have taken many years just to finish one book. It had to be grueling to handwrite a book with words numbering in the tens of thousands. For Sharelle, just signing her name fifteen times started her hand to cramping.

Chapter Thirty-Six

The view overlooking the twinkling lights of the L.A. basin was simply breath-taking. It always had been. The night sky was clear enough to see the Hollywood sign from the panoramic Baldwin Vista Hillcrest where Blake lived. He had taken Sharelle there after the book release party. It wasn't her plan to go there. She was supposed to be hanging out with Joy and Tracy, but Joy was exhausted from the festivities earlier in the evening. Tracy had an early flight out the following day and wanted to go back to her hotel room to get some sleep. Be it fate or luck, somehow, it just worked out for her to be able to spend the rest of the evening with Blake. A devilish grin fell over her face as she thought of her mother, Arlene. What would she say if she knew? She could just hear her saying,

Shar, you have a good husband, and the grass isn't necessarily greener on the other side, you know. Sharelle gazed at the city's twinkling lights while Blake poured her a glass of chardonnay. She imagined that her comeback to her mother would be, *"I'm not looking for a greener pasture; I just want one with no heifers grazin' in it!"*

Blake returned, trying not to spill wine from the glasses he held in each hand. He offered her a glass.

"Oh, thank you, Blake," she said.

"My pleasure. So Sharelle, do you miss L.A. at all?"

She took a sip while searching for something slick to say but then realized that the question really only required a yes or no answer.

"On occasion, but it's usually pretty short-lived."

"C'mon Shar, stop playin'. You know there's no other place you'd rather be than right here in beautiful Los Angeles," he chided.

"Oh, what do you mean, do I miss the whole Hollyweird scene? Not me. You can have it!"

He shot her a look that screamed liar!

"Okay, okay; maybe I do miss living in L.A. at times, but I really do like Charlotte."

She began to feel a slight chill from the constant breeze that whisked across her bare shoulders. Finally, after a couple of moments, he noticed her shivering and took the hint.

"Whew, it's getting a little chilly out here, I think we should go inside now," he suggests.

"Yeah, maybe so. I am starting to get goosebumps."

The interior of Blake's home had that lifetime bachelor "hood" look going on. It wasn't junky, but it was badly in need of a woman's touch. Judging from the lack of furnishings, he was obviously going for that minimalist look. Then again, a rare single man pays attention to details like decorative guest towels, wall sconces, or Murano glass accent pieces. For that matter, rarely do married men. However, some men think that hieroglyphics etched in the walls qualify as fine art.

But, a cave-like atmosphere wasn't what Sharelle saw at Blake's place. Instead, she saw a blank canvas. The architecture and modern design of the home definitely had that wow factor working—he just didn't know how to or didn't care to make the most of its potential. She was itching to help him with that, but she wanted to avoid overstepping her bounds. That kind of thing should be reserved for the lady in his life, if in fact, there was one.

He refreshed her glass of chardonnay. She happened to notice the label on the bottle as he poured. It was Kimball-Paxton, her favorite. Music began to play. It was Norman Brown, again, one of her favorites. Then, in a fleeting moment of paranoia, she thought, *"wow, what'd the brotha do—a Google search on the likes and dislikes of Sharelle Langford-*

Hughes? Hmm, it might not be a bad idea to Google myself to see just how much of my business is out there!"

He settled down in the chaise next to the sofa where Sharelle sat to talk.

"So, your son is in grad school, and your daughter is a freshman in college, huh? They sound like great young people."

"Yeah, all in all, they're good kids. I'm blessed 'cause they never really gave me any trouble. How 'bout you? Do you have any kids?"

"I have a six-year-old son. His name is Ryan."

Surprised at the news about Blake's son, she delved further.

"Wow, you have a son? That's great. Are you and his mom still together?"

"No, she wanted to get married, but I wasn't ready, so she broke it off."

"Do you love her?"

"I care for her, she's my kid's mother, but I'm not in love with her. But what about you? You've been married for a long time. Are you happy?"

She paused for a beat, and then answered after a long sigh.

"No, Blake, I'm not."

"You're not? Then why have you stayed in the marriage all this time?"

"Well, I thought we were happy at one time, but…."

"But he cheated on you, right?"

Rather than reveal information about the whole porn addiction thing, she decided to keep it simple.

"Yeah, how'd you guess?"

"I hear it all the time. That's probably why I won't get married. Marriages just don't seem to work!"

"Well, I wouldn't go quite that far as to say that marriage doesn't work. I just know that mine doesn't."

She leaned forward and picked up a photo album from the coffee table, hoping to change the subject. So, she leafed through the laminated pages and asked about the pictures in the book.

"Aw, what a cutie! Is this your son?"

"Yeah, that's Ryan when he was three."

"He's adorable," she comments.

"Yeah, but he's a bad little joker though. I constantly have to stay on his little butt!"

"Yeah, well, you better do it while he's still young 'cause a hard head makes a soft behind, you know."

She looked through the photo album and found an old, oxidized newspaper article. It was from a New Jersey publication—The Sun-Ledger. The picture corresponding to the article showed a tow truck pulling a car out of a swamp using a winch. The Associated Press article read:

Sunday, June 12, 2005, 3:15 P.M.

Woman rescued from swamp waters after suspicious car plunge.

She and Blake continued talking as she leafed through the photo album.

"So, how long are you in town for, Shar?" he asked.

"Oh—I'll be leaving on Thursday."

"Wow, that soon? Well, I better move fast, huh?"

She didn't quite know how to answer the somewhat solicitous question.

"Well, that depends on what you're talking about, Blake."

He ran a neatly manicured hand across his thinning head of wavy hair and clarified the question.

"Oh, sorry. I guess that didn't come out right, did it? What I meant was if I was going to take you out, I better do it soon, like tomorrow! So, how 'bout we get together and go out to dinner tomorrow night?"

"I really wish I could, Blake, but I haven't spent much time with my dad, and I plan to spend the rest of my time here with him."

The look of anticipation on his face changed drastically to one of disappointment. He regrouped quickly to reflect a more positive attitude.

"Oh, no doubt, no doubt you should spend time with your father.

I just hate to see you go, that's all."

She started to feel the strain of the fullness of her bladder. For some reason, chardonnay always ran right through her.

"Blake, where's your bathroom?" she asks with a slight sense of urgency.

"Go past the kitchen and down the hall. It's the first door on the left."

As she headed to the bathroom, she felt Blake's eyes sizing her up like a championship racehorse. She hoped he didn't notice the run in her pantyhose that she felt inching its way down her leg since earlier in the evening. On her trek down the hallway, she noticed that he had some décor on the walls—his diplomas. At least they were matted and framed and not just taped to the wall like you'd see after art period in a second-grade classroom. Besides, she didn't expect anything less. He was a classy guy, despite his minimalist bachelor crib.

Upon entering the bathroom, something immediately caught her attention. The toilet seat was down. For her, it indicated one of two possibilities. Either the last flush was initiated by a female, or his last visit involved copping a squat.

When she returned from the bathroom, Blake was searching through his CD cabinet. She sat back down on the sofa and picked up the photo album to look at the remaining pictures. Still curious about the newspaper article and its significance, she questioned him.

"Blake, why do you have this newspaper article in here?"

"Oh, that was the first big case I worked on with the U.S. Attorney's office in New Jersey. A woman was found in a remote area trapped in her car in a swamp. I was involved in the forensics investigation on the case."

"Oh yeah, I see your name mentioned here in the article. Do you know who the woman was?"

"No, I wasn't on the case long enough to find out. My team's job was to focus solely on the car, so all we were told was that we were to analyze the car involved in the South Jersey swamp water case. Not only that, I was told that the woman was in a coma during my part of the investigation. We were told that her family didn't want her identity revealed at that time."

"Really? Well, what happened? Did she try to commit suicide or something?"

"Actually, I don't believe so. However, there was evidence found at the scene."

She anxiously leaned in toward Blake to hear more details.

"What kind of evidence did they find?" she inquired.

"There was evidence of red car paint on the rear bumper of the woman's car. Her car was light blue. I had the paint chips analyzed from the bumper, and it was determined that the paint was manufactured by a Japanese paint company."

"Did they solve the case?"

"I don't think so. Forensic science wasn't heavily relied upon back then, and the investigators chose to lean toward more conventional methods. Basically, they saw no relevance to the paint chips having any connection with the accident. So shortly after that, I left the case and moved back here to L.A."

She sat momentarily, trying to envision the woman's horror as she plunged into the murky water. After shaking off the chill that ran down her spine, she commented,

"Wow, that poor woman. That had to be a hell of an experience, to be trapped in a car underwater."

Blake sensed a melancholy mood beginning to creep into the room and quickly tried to liven things up.

"Hey, why don't we have some more wine?"

"No thanks, Blake, it's getting late, and I think it's about time for me to go."

Again, he had that dejected look on his face but caught himself before she could notice.

"Well, I wish you could stay longer, but I know you've got a long day tomorrow, so I'll take you home."

Blake took Sharelle back to the hotel so that she could check out and pick up her rental car. Before saying goodbye, they sat in his car staring into each other's eyes for what seemed like an eternity. Each knew what the other was thinking. The temptation was tormenting. As difficult as it was, they resisted each other's beckoning lips. Finally, unable to withstand further torture, he broke their gaze and reached over to give her a hug and kiss on the cheek. They each reluctantly said their goodbyes and vowed to keep in touch. For Sharelle, this enchanted evening was one she would not forget.

An Explicit Nature

Chapter Thirty-Seven

Red paint on the bumper was all she could think about on the flight back to Charlotte. Then, she thought about the details Blake shared about the case. *"Red paint on the bumper? I would think that would have some significance."*

Back on North Carolina soil, she pulls into the driveway of her home and is greeted by Amber Randall from next door.

"Hello, Sharelle, how are you?" says Amber.

"Hi, Amber. I'm well, how're you?"

"I'm fine. Sharelle, I know you're busy, but I just wanted to show you really quick some jewelry that I made."

"Oh, I didn't know you made jewelry Amber. Let's see what you've got."

"It's a hobby of mine and, no pressure, of course, but I just figured if you knew someone that has a birthday coming up or something…."

"Oh, how cute, what are they made of?"

"I make them out of clay and then paint them."

"Well, thanks, Amber. I'll certainly keep you in mind when I'm looking for a unique gift for someone."

"Okay, thanks. I'll see you later."

Sharelle had been living in Allyson Heights for two years, and that was the most conversation she had ever had with her next-door neighbor. Well, there was that time when Amber came over to borrow some flour to bake cookies. But, other than that, this was the most that Amber ever had to say to her. But, of course, it was only because she was trying to sell her something.

The fact was that Amber's two-year-old daughter could have made better jewelry with Play-Doh than that crap she was trying to pass off. Sharelle went into the house thinking, *"She better not hold her breath waiting for me to buy any of that garbage!"*

Heading straight to her bedroom, she unpacked her bag and slipped into a pair of her most comfortable sweats and her favorite tee shirt. It was the one with the sentiment which said, Love is like a roller coaster; when it's over, you throw up. She had an entire collection of those kinds of novelty tee shirts. She owned at least ten which expressed every sentiment imaginable. Some people write poetry to express themselves. Sharelle not only writes, she wears expressive tees.

She used to have another favorite that said, Life's too short to dance with ugly men. It was only recently that she retired that one. She had been doing the Lambada with a reasonably good-looking man for the past twenty-five years, and look where that got her. She began to think that the possibility actually exists that she and an ugly man just might be able to dance to the same beat.

As a result, she stopped wearing the ugly man tee shirt. Instead, she found herself gravitating to the one about love being like a roller coaster instead. Maybe it's a way of expressing her feelings without verbalizing them. Perhaps it's a way of adding a little levity to her situation.

Whatever the reason, this tee shirt just seemed apropos. Just as a roller coaster has its ups and downs, so has her marriage. However, she was starting to feel the effects of the downhill ride. For her, this last plunge turned out to be way too steep.

After changing, she went upstairs to her office to check her e-mail. When she entered the room, she noticed the picture of Maya that was tacked to the bulletin board. She was reminded of her intention to have it enlarged and framed. Completely forgetting about her e-mail, she removed the picture and ran downstairs with it clutched in her hand. She tucked the photograph into an envelope and placed it in the new Dolce

& Giabbana handbag that she bought the other day from the hotel boutique while in L.A.

She noticed the pack of gum that she'd forgotten that she had tucked in the inner pocket. She opened the pack and popped a stick in her mouth.

While putting on her barely broken-in Jumpman sneakers, she heard her phone ring. She hurried to answer it. It was Joy.

"Hello?" she answers.

"Hey girl, you back home yet?"

"Yeah, I've been home for about 45 minutes or so, how're you feeling?"

"Heavy! But other than that, I feel alright. I just called to say that the book release party was really nice. I had such a good time."

"Oh good, I'm glad you enjoyed yourself. I was worried that it might be too much for you."

As usual, Joy was full of surprises. Sharelle thought that the evening might have been too tiring for her friend. However, Joy being the wild girl she is, was about to reveal that she had a private party of her own which, by far, outlasted Sharelle's. Joy continues.

"Oh, I had a ball! I met me a cute hunk of a hottie there."

"Hottie? Okay, Joy, what's the deal? You and I both know that hottie is not a part of a sistah's vocabulary when describing a brotha, so what's up?"

"Well, maybe he's not a brotha."

"Huh? Not a brotha? Well, what is he then?"

"Look, Shar, all my adult life, I've been living on a steady diet of dark meat, and I'm about burned out. Besides, variety is supposed to be the spice of life, so I just figured I would spice up my life and add in a little pork."

"Pork? Joy, what exactly are we talking about here?"

"Pork, you know, the other white meat? He's a white boy!"

Sharelle drew in a gasp with the suction of a Hoover. She sucked wind so hard that her gum shot back into her throat, causing her to choke until she could cough it back up again.

"Joy, are you serious? Do I know this guy?"

"I don't know, you might. He works for Poole and Rofford. He's one of their copy editors. Do you know a Chip that works there?"

"Chip? That's his name?"

"Yeah—Chip."

"Oh yeah, he's definitely a white boy, but I have no idea who he is."

She was perturbed by Sharelle's reaction. She had always known her to be open-minded regarding cultural and racial tolerance. Yet somehow, her reaction to her new man didn't get the reception that she was expecting. She challenges her sincerity.

"Okay, he's a white boy, so what?"

"Whoa, hold up, Joy. I don't have a problem with him being white. I'm just surprised because I've never known you to date white guys before. Besides, let's just keep it real—you were the one who referred to him as pork, remember? And what about your pregnancy? He doesn't have a problem with that?"

"Actually, he thinks I'm the most beautiful thing he's ever seen. At least, that's what he told me."

Sharelle offers a different theory.

"Or, maybe he's a freak and thinks, what the heck, she can't get pregnant!"

"Works for me! But, no, really, he's a nice guy, and besides, you know what they say, you ain't seen the light until you go white!"

Certain that she had never in life heard the phrase before, she counters,

"Uh—excuse me? That's one I'm sure I never heard anybody say but you! Last I heard, it was once you go black, you'll never go back!" But whatever, as long as he's a good guy, then more power to you, and I just hope he makes you happy; that's all I'm concerned about. But wait, I do have just one more question."

"What?"

"Whatever happened to Robert?"

"Oh, him?"

"Yeah, you know, that guy that impregnated you?

Joy sucks her teeth, then continues.

"Girl, I kicked his butt to the curb. He's trying to deny that this is his baby because he's afraid his wife will find out."

"Well, I can halfway understand him not wanting to tell his wife, but denying his own child, that's just...."

"You can say it, it's fucked up!"

"Yeah, that's exactly what it is. But, wait a minute, hold up, don't try to throw me off the subject. I wanna know what happened after the book release party. Just what did you and Mr. Hottie do?"

"Aw girl, get your mind out of the gutter. It wasn't even like that. He just took me sightseeing in Hollywood, then we stopped at a restaurant for coffee and dessert, and he took me back to the hotel."

"Annnd?"

"And—what?"

"And then I suppose Prince Charming kissed you on the hand at your hotel room door, and you both said goodnight, right?"

"Oh, we said goodnight alright, but it wasn't no hand kissin', and it sure wasn't standing in front of no hotel room door! So let's just say, what happens in L.A. stays in L.A., alright?"

"Okay, I feel you, but try getting at least one slogan right. It's "what happens in Vegas, stays in Vegas, jeez!"

Chapter Thirty-Eight

For some inexplicable reason, Eric had begun demonstrating an interest in or curiosity for Sharelle's writings. Maybe it was the reality of seeing the proof copy with its abstract graphics, which graced the glossy black cover. Then again, the name Sharelle Langford-Hughes printed in bold block lettering was a real attention-grabber all to itself. However, it was more likely the title. An Exposé of Indiscretion, that resonated most with him. During dinner, he questions her about the book's content.

"I see your book has gone to print, huh?"

Unsure of the intent behind the question, she hesitates for a beat.

"Uh yeah, it has. Why do you ask?"

"Oh, I can't be interested in what's going on with your book?"

"Sure you can. It's just that you've never shown any interest before."

"That's not true. Maybe if you had clued me in that you were writing a book, I would've had a reason to show some interest. So, what's the book about?"

Sensing that the discussion was about to get heated, she took a large gulp from her glass of pomegranate juice and then answered.

"It's about porn addiction, you should read it."

"Porn addiction, huh? Why should I read it, because it's about me?"

"No, Eric, it's not about you. It's about porn addiction in general and how it affects people who have the addiction."

"What are you supposed to be now, a psychiatrist?"

"O-o-kay, I can see where this is going."

"Shar, you knew exactly what you were doing. You know as well as I do that you wrote this book out of revenge. You wrote it to get back at me!"

"Eric, don't flatter yourself. Did your porn addiction inspire me to write about the subject? In part, yes. Is your name mentioned anywhere in the book? No. My book is a novel. It's a work of fiction. Perhaps if you tried reading some of my work, you would find some appreciation for it."

"Appreciation! Why would I appreciate you trying to make me look bad? It's just a bunch of bullshit, that's all it is!"

"Eric, believe me, I am not trying to make you look bad, you do a good job of that all by yourself." He storms out of the room. Then, it dawned on Sharelle when her gift for writing re-emerged, so did her sense of empowerment. She was proud of her work, and never again would she allow him to get in the way of it.

While there was a break in the action, she decided it would be an excellent time to take a trip to the copy store. Earlier, she had placed Maya's picture in her purse and was headed for the copy store, and then got side-tracked. Now, it would be a good excuse to escape the tense atmosphere at home.

Once at the store, she used the photo processor available for public use. She placed the photo onto the scanner and selected an 8 × 10 enlargement. After cropping out the background of trees and distant buildings, she zoomed in on Maya's image, hoping to get a clearer view of her adorable baby face. Satisfied with her amateur photo retouching, she printed out her resized copy.

When the photocopy emerged from the processor, she eagerly pulled it from the tray. She was pleased with the enlarged image of her baby girl, but something else about the picture disturbed her. The mirrored windows of the building in the background cast a bright glare. It was as though a ghostly image outlined Maya's small frame.

Behind her, just outside the left outer edge of the glare, was a mirror image of the red car. The reversed image of the personalized license plate was now clearly visible in the enhanced photo. As she read the license plate, she began to tremble. She tried as hard as possible to keep her composure, but there was no stopping it. There was no doubt in her mind that a seizure was inevitable. Thus far, she had never had a public episode and was determined to keep it that way.

She scurried out of the store to avoid embarrassment and public humiliation and jumped into her car. Once inside the car, her arm writhed and convulsed wildly. As the arm flailed up and down, its wild movements were impeded by the steering wheel's stationary resistance. She managed to control the convulsions by forcing the arm between her legs.

Once the seizure subsided, she sat for a moment, trying to catch her breath. She expected that at any moment, one of the store's employees would come after her for leaving the store without paying for the photocopy. After checking her rear-view mirror for any signs of police presence, she got out of the car, adjusted her clothes, and re-entered the store. She was relieved that her brief shoplifting excursion seemed to have gone unnoticed.

She stood at the checkout counter for at least two minutes waiting to pay for the photocopy when she realized why she wasn't apprehended when she ran out of the store. She thought, *"no wonder no one came after me; these employees are a bunch of slackers."* Then, annoyed with the lack of service, she called out in a firm voice to get an employee's attention.

"Excuse me, is there anyone that can help me here?"

After making the purchase, she couldn't get back into her car fast enough. She had to get another hard look at the newly printed photo. She turned on her car's interior lights and examined it again. Though she didn't want to believe her own eyes, she knew the picture couldn't lie.

The reflected image of the license plate on the front of the car in the background revealed the letters I, a backward R, an A, and M. Her mouth fell open as she stared at the letters. With shaking hands, she immediately fished her cell out of her purse to call Tracy to inform her of the discovery. Before Tracy could finish saying hello, she began blurting out what she had learned.

"Tracy, IRAM! You were right! I'm looking at it! I'm looking at it right now!"

"Shar, what are you talking about? What do you mean you're looking at it? You're looking at what?"

"Tracy, remember that word IRAM that keeps appearing in your dreams? Well, IRAM is on somebody's license plate. I'm looking right at it!"

"Where are you? Where is the car?"

"No, no! I'm at the copy store. I came here to enlarge an old picture of Maya from when she was little. In the photo is a red car in the background, and after I enlarged it, I could see the front license plate, which says IRAM on it!"

"Okay, Shar, what are you about to do? Can you get over here right now? We have to figure this out."

"I'm on my way. I'll be there in about an hour."

Along the drive to Tracy's house, she wracked her brain, trying to put the pieces of the puzzle together. She had no idea who or what IRAM was, and even more confusing, why the letter R was backward. Sharelle wondered,

"could it be something of a company trademark, like Toys Я Us or is it just somebody's less than creative way of making their name distinguishable by using a hallmark?" Regardless, the plate had to have been custommade. Even though DMV issues personalized plates, I'm pretty sure they draw the line at backward letters."

She made it to Tracy's house in less than an hour. She did 80 mph (ca. 129 km/h) practically the whole way, slowing down long enough to show respect for suspected speed traps. Immediately upon letting her in the house, Tracy hustled her into the home office. Without an ounce of patience, she prompts her to show the photo.

"Alright, c'mon, break out the picture."

She removes the photo from a manila folder and points out the license plate image in the background. Still puzzled about its meaning, she comments on the backward letter R.

"This definitely says IRAM, but what do you think the backward R represents?" she asks Tracy.

She first ponders the question and then examines the photo. Finally, after a few seconds of intense inspection, it hit Tracy why the letter R was backward.

"D-uuh! What are we thinking? Of course, the R is backward. It's a reflected image from the mirrored windows! The other letters aren't backward because the view will always be the same any way you look at them. A mirror image of the capital letter M will still appear as an M. The same goes for the letters A and I."

"Oh my God, you're absolutely right! I didn't even think about that. So, that means that the entire image is actually reversed."

Sharelle grabs a pen, writes the letters in reverse order, and is shocked at what appears before her eyes.

"Mari! Oh my God, I don't believe this! I just can't believe this!"

"What, Shar? Who is Mari? Is it somebody you know?"

"Tracy, unless it's a different person, Mari is this psycho chick with whom Eric was having an affair, maybe fifteen or so years ago. Let me tell you, this chick has issues. I mean, she was stalking us and the whole nine. I cannot believe Eric had the audacity to take my baby around that psycho!"

"Okay, Shar, calm down. We're not a hundred percent sure yet. Let's just backtrack a little. I think we might be on to something here. Luckily, I saved every one of those messages that came to me in my dreams, and I still have them in my phone. So, now that there's a possibility that we know who IRAM is let's see if we can decipher what the messages mean."

For the next two hours, the ladies delved deep into the cryptic messages that had come to Tracy during her sleep. Sharelle was more eager than ever to figure out what the messages were persistently trying to convey.

Chapter Thirty-Nine

"What more do you want me to tell you, Shar? We've been over this a thousand times—it was just an accident," said Eric. More than ever, Sharelle pressed Eric for details about her accident from so long ago. For years, whenever she asked him to tell her exactly what happened, he would give her some vague details about her skidding off the road and slamming into a tree. Then he would abruptly end the conversation.

He didn't want to tell her much more in detail because he didn't want her to have to relive the horrible event repeatedly. He told her that the doctors advised him to help her stay calm by avoiding discussions about the accident and discussing pleasant things. The irony is that not knowing is what was extremely unpleasant.

So, this time around, she wasn't going for the bull. Eric was hiding something, and she knew it. She was determined to find out just what happened on that fateful day in the summer of 2005. And if he wouldn't tell her, then she would just have to find somebody that will.

He had wormed his way out of the conversation using the excuse of wanting to take a shower. After he left the room, she took advantage of his absence and made a discreet phone call to Joy. Joy answers,

"Hello?"

"Hey Joy, what's up?"

"Hey Shar, nothing really, what's up with you?"

"I got some news to tell you, girl."

"What?"

"I have a book signing tomorrow at Binder's Bookstore in the Northlake Mall. Can you meet me there?

Joy believing that Sharelle is being insensitive to her extremely pregnant condition, retorts.

"Are you serious?! Shar, I'm on leave from work now because my ankles swell when I do a lot of walking and you want me to go to the mall? Besides, I already have a signed copy of your book."

No Joy, it has nothing to do with the book and, believe me, you won't have to do much walking, you can sit the entire time. Just come to the bookstore. I have something really important to talk to you about."

Still resisting the trip to the mall, Joy presses.

"Would you just tell me what this is about?"

"I can't go into it right now. Can you meet me or not?" Sharelle demands.

"Aww, Shar, I hate when you do that. Alright, alright, I'll be there, what time?"

"Meet me at about eleven o'clock."

"Alright, eleven, it is."

"Good, I'll see you tomorrow then."

"You better not be late."

"Joy, it's my book signing, of course, I'll be on time. I'll talk to you later. Bye."

Sharelle woke up earlier than usual the next morning. Her mind raced all night due to a hellish nightmare. This one was about the woman found in her car in the swamp. She couldn't stop thinking about her. *"Who could do such a vile thing? Did she survive? If so, how is she doing now?"* These were all questions that raced through her mind all night long. She felt compelled to write about the woman, though she knew nothing about her.

After making herself a cup of coffee, she went upstairs to her office to check her e-mail. She noticed an e-mail from Tracy. The subject line read: BLAKE CAN HELP U. When she opened the e-mail, it contained a brief message which said,

"Hey Shar, didn't you say that your friend in California (Blake) was in law enforcement in New Jersey at one time? So he may be able to research that car in the picture for you."—Tracy.

She sat there momentarily, wondering why Tracy would assume Blake knew anything about the car in the picture. Then it dawned on her that she was right.

"Of course, Blake should be able to help, he once worked with the U.S. Attorney's office in New Jersey. He should be able to find out if the car in the picture belonged to the same Mari I think it is," she thought.

She immediately ran to get her phone and located Blake's number in her contacts. She called and got his voicemail, then it dawned on her that it was only 6:30 in the morning in L.A. Having no other alternative, she simply left a message.

"Hi Blake, this is Sharelle. I just wanted to say thanks for attending my book release party. I hope you had a good time. I know I did. Oh, and thanks for showing me a good time afterward, too. But what I really called to talk to you about is…well, I sort of need a favor. Can you call me back when you get this message? We'll talk about it then, alright? Well, I look forward to hearing from you soon, and I'll talk to you later. Okay, bye-bye."

By now, it was after 9:30, and she decided that she'd better start getting dressed. The last thing she wanted was to be late for her own book signing event and to have to hear Joy's mouth. So she quickly showered, threw on her navy blue pin-striped Markell Nors pantsuit, and was headed on her way.

It was a glorious day of bright sunshine and clear blue skies. She couldn't ask for a more perfect day for her book signing. *"On a day like this, there should be no excuse for a poor turnout,"* she thought.

The morning rush on I-485 had long been over, but she came upon a pocket of heavy traffic after sailing along for a good stretch.

"Hmm, must've been an accident," she thought.

238

As she weaved in and out of the slowing traffic, she heard her phone ring. She secured her earbuds in her ears and plucked the phone from her handbag to check the caller I.D.—it was Blake.

"Hey, Blake."

"Hey Sharelle, how you doin'?" he responds.

"I'm good. How 'bout yourself?"

"Oh, everything is everything. I got your message, what's up?"

She pauses briefly as she searches for the right way to introduce her request for information.

"Well, I apologize for calling so early but remember when I told you I was in an accident some years ago back in Jersey?"

"Yeah, I remember."

"Well, there are some things that I need answers to regarding that accident Blake, and I was hoping that you might be able to help me."

"Really? I'm not sure what I can do, Sharelle, but I'll help you any way I can. What do you need?"

Again, she hesitates while twirling her hair around her finger, hoping that what comes out of her mouth next won't make her sound like a head case. Blake prompts.

"Sharelle, are you still there?"

"Yeah, yeah, I'm still here. Listen, I found this picture of my daughter when she was around three years old, and I don't know where it was taken. I'm sure it was somewhere in Jersey, but there's a car in the background, and I need an I.D. on it."

"An I.D.? Okay, but that sounds like something you could get from the DMV, don't you think?"

"Possibly, I mean, I haven't checked, but this picture is at least fifteen years old. That information is more than likely archived somewhere. It would probably take them forever to find it and to get back to me with it."

Suspicious about her intentions, Blake carefully prods for more information.

"So, are you saying that you think the car in the picture had something to do with the accident?"

"I don't know, I know it's a long shot, but something just doesn't sit right with me pertaining to that car. For one thing, the license plate seems familiar."

"Why is that? What's familiar about it?"

"Actually, it's only the front plate. The plate is personalized with the name Mari on it."

"Wait, let me get a pen and jot this down."

He returns after locating a pen and asks for the details.

Okay, now, what is it? A New Jersey plate with the letters M-A-R-I-E?"

"No, leave off the E. It's just M-A-R-I."

"Really? That's an odd way of spelling it."

"Yeah, that's what caught my attention."

"Okay, now what about the rear plate?"

"There was no rear plate. The car was new and only had a temporary plate in the back window with the expiration date."

"Temporary plate in the rear window, okay, got that. Do you know what type of car it was or the model year?"

"No, I just know it's a red sports car. So, I'm thinking it had to be a 2005 model."

"Well, it's not a lot to go on, but let me ask you—do you know this Mari?"

"That's what I'm trying to find out, if it's one and the same."

"What do you mean, one and the same, the same as what?"

Sharelle was hoping that the line of questioning wouldn't come down to this, but she knew that she had to be forthcoming if she wanted his help." She answers,

"Hmm, well, do you remember me telling you that I left my husband because he had an affair some years ago?"

"Yeah, I do."

"Well, that woman he had an affair with was named Mari, spelled

240

the same as on that license plate."

"Ahhh, I see, and you think this could be her car. But wait. Why would your daughter be in a picture with a car that belonged to some woman your husband was cheating on you with?"

"Go figure! That's exactly what I'm trying to figure out."

"Well, if it does turn out to be her car, then that dude is about as low down and dirty as they come!"

Chapter Forty

"Whoa! You weren't kidding when you said your feet swell. They look like two loaves of rising bread dough," Sharelle jokes insultingly while enjoying a robust laugh. Joy stood not at all amused and rolling her eyes. Meanwhile, Sharelle tries, unsuccessfully, to switch gears over to that of concern. Despite her efforts, an unintentional roar of laughter came bellowing out of her mouth. Again, she fails miserably in her attempt to show compassion.

"I don't mean to be funny, Joy, but it looks like you're baking bread in your shoes!"

"Okay, Shar, enough already! I don't see what's so damn funny! I came here because you asked me to come to support you, and now you're just gonna sit there and make jokes?"

Sharelle gathers her composure, realizing how inconsiderate she has been. She apologizes and then takes on a more sympathetic tone.

"Joy, I'm having a little fun, that's all. I'm sorry if I hurt your feelings. I didn't mean it that way."

She then extends open arms to offer a conciliatory hug.

"C'mon girl, gimme a hug. You know I was just playin' with you," she assures.

Joy cozies into one of the cushy reading chairs while Sharelle sets things up for her book signing. She proceeds to tell her about the latest developments in her quest for information surrounding her accident. Joy sits, hanging on to every word. Obviously, she's put the teasing she received just ten minutes earlier far behind her.

After about fifteen minutes of giving Joy the details, Sharelle reveals something that startled even herself. She comments.

"Joy, I don't know why I feel this way, but I have this strange feeling that someone may have plotted to kill me years ago."

"What! Who do you think tried to have you killed?"

"I'm not sure. I just have this funny feeling."

"Okay, Shar, I think you might be taking things a little too far. I mean, I'm glad to see that things are gradually coming back to you, but how much of what you're recalling is really what happened?"

"Maybe you're right, Joy. On the other hand, maybe I'm just paranoid."

Joy pauses momentarily, tilting her head slightly skyward. She senses a ripe opportunity for major payback. She responds, verbalizing each and every word with cunning deliberateness.

"Paranoid? Nah, I don't think you're paranoid. Now, if you had said schizoid, I would've definitely agreed with you on that, 'cause your ass is crazy as hell!"

Sharelle stood motionless with a stunned look on her face. Joy braces her pregnant belly to keep it steady while she enjoys a good belly laugh while Sharelle stares blankly. Once the initial shock of the off-color joke passed, she joined Joy in the seemingly endless laugh marathon.

"Okay, Joy, I deserved that. You got that off, girl. You got me." She concedes.

By now, patrons were filing into the store and coming over to the table where Sharelle was to sign books. Joy gave her a hug and wished her well as she left to go home to put her twice than normal-sized feet up. Sharelle was surprised to meet a few fans that already owned a copy of Exposé and came just to meet her in person and congratulate her on the book's success. All in all, it turned out to be quite a productive day.

When she returned home after the book signing, she found Eric had come home early from work. He was in the backyard cooking steaks on the grill. That was a welcome sight to her—not so much Eric, as it was him cooking. She peeked her head out the back door to greet him.

"Hello, Eric."

"Oh hey. Where've you been?"

"I was at the mall. I had a book signing at Binder's bookstore to-day."

"Ah, a book signing, eh?"

It was apparent that his tone suddenly became less than cheerful. Actually, it was anything but—cheerful. Simply to avoid conflict, she immediately turned around and came back inside. She found it interesting that the mere mention of anything concerning her book could negatively affect him.

She went into her bedroom to change into shorts and a tee shirt. She decided to wear the one which said—SOMEBODY PUT A STOP PAYMENT ON MY REALITY CHECK. The sentiment seemed to fit how she was feeling at the time. After all, she keeps bumping her head against the same brick wall. She's still expecting Eric to be happy over the success of her book when, by now, it should be evident that it ain't gonna happen.

During dinner, they each ate in separate rooms. There was still a distinct air of tension looming throughout the house. On trips back and forth to the kitchen, for one thing, or another, they would occasionally cross paths. Still, neither would allow themselves to set eyes upon the other. She always hated the futile exercise. It was such a juvenile way of dealing with issues. It was like playing the opposite of the staring game, where the first to blink loses. In their silly test of wills game, the first to look into the eyes of the other loses. As much as she hated it, she would rather play along than risk having a domestic incident occur in her own home.

She went to bed early that evening. She was exhausted from the book signing event from earlier in the day. Stirring in her sleep, she was disturbed by that familiarly annoying light. She attributed it to Eric falling asleep again with the T.V. on, yet she couldn't hear any sound. Curious about what was going on, she lifted her head and slightly opened one eye. Suddenly, the images on the screen changed, and the sound instantly became audible. She knew immediately what was going on. By now, it was clear, if not predictable. Eric was watching porn again. Although it was brief, she was able to catch a glimpse of two intertwined naked bodies on the screen before he could change the channel. Of course, he thought he was both slick and fast enough that she could not have caught him. So, she let him believe that his surreptitious maneuver went utterly undetected. She then went right back to sleep without saying a word.

Eric had stopped going to therapy for his porn addiction. He hadn't had a session in over a month now. He felt he was strong enough to abstain from porn on his own and that four therapy sessions had cured him of his obsessive behavior. Sharelle knew differently. She knew that in four sessions, he could not possibly rid himself of the demons that had plagued him for most of his lifetime.

But, she wasn't relying solely on psychiatric counseling as a methodology for rehabilitation anyway. Instead, she had incorporated a spiritual course of treatment into the mix. With both weapons, she was confident that he would recover. However, what she didn't count on was his lack of sincerity and lack of commitment to his own recovery.

She had noticed the gradual return of his short temper and reclusive behavior—classic signs of addiction. However, just as in the past, she dismissed the signs or excused them as temporary lapses. Though her faith in God's ability to overcome anything was strong, her faith in her husband was all but gone.

Chapter Forty-One

Almost forgetting her appointment, Sharelle rushed to get dressed, hoping to make it to Lee's office on time. She arrived at the office with only minutes to spare and signed in at the receptionist's desk. She had barely sat down when Lee called her in.

"Hello, Sharelle, come on back."

"Hi, Lee," she said while still catching her breath.

As if he realized she needed a moment to settle down, he excused himself while he dictated some last-minute notes on his pocket-sized tape recorder. He then turned his attention to her.

"So, Sharelle, it's been a couple of weeks since we last met. How did your book release party in L.A. go?"

"Oh, it was perfect. I wish you could have been there."

"I bet it was nice. Well, I might not have been there, but...."

Lee suddenly stood up from his chair and walked over to his desk. To her surprise, he lifted a copy of An Exposé of Indiscretion from his desk and smiled. She gasped with delight. She couldn't believe her eyes. He commented,

"I bought it on Amazon."

"Wow, thanks for supporting me, Lee."

"Well, I was a little curious, and I thought it might give me some insight into your mental state. Besides, it's just good reading. I'm really enjoying it."

"Well, thank you, I really appreciate that."

"It was my pleasure. However, you can show your appreciation by autographing it for me," Lee quips.

"Oh, by all means. I most certainly will."

"Good deal. Now, let's get down to business. What's been going on with you over the past couple of weeks? Any new developments?"

"Actually, there are a few new developments."

"Yeah? Care to share?"

"Well, as a matter of fact, I solved the IRAM mystery, at least partially."

Lee hesitated for a beat. Then, with a confused look, he asked for clarification.

"The IRAM mystery? What's the IRAM mystery?"

"Remember I told you about my girlfriend's text messages—you know, Tracy, the psychic?"

"Ah, yes. I do remember."

"Well, I have this picture of my daughter as a little girl standing in front of a red car, which I don't recognize. And, on the front plate of that car is the name, Mari."

"Okay, go on," he urges.

"IRAM is Mari spelled backward."

"Well, that's good, Sharelle. That shows good deductive reasoning skills."

It became apparent to her that Lee didn't see the significance of her revelation. She became frustrated and was determined to have him understand the correlation between Mari and the red car.

"Lee, don't you see? I realized that what appeared as IRAM in a reflected image in a mirror was actually Mari in reverse. If you recall, Mari is the woman with whom Eric had an affair years ago."

"Okay, that makes sense. However, how does this relate to your recollection of events from your accident Sharelle? I'm not following you."

"That's the part I haven't fully figured out yet. But, in my heart, I feel that my nightmares of being chased by a red car probably have something to do with Mari, I just can't prove it."

"Do I hear you saying that you suspect foul play concerning your accident?"

"I know it probably sounds crazy, but yes, I do."

Lee suddenly became silent and started writing feverishly on his notepad. It was as if he had so many thoughts running through his mind at once that he couldn't get them down on paper fast enough to capture each of them. His seemingly incessant writing made her somewhat uncomfortable. She kept trying to read his face to get a sense of what was going through his mind. Yet, he was writing with an absolute expressionless sense of determination. To break the monotony, she searched for a mint inside her handbag. Then, while staring out the window, she made a mental list of what she needed to get from the grocery store. After all of that, he was still writing. Sitting there, not knowing what all the writing was about was excruciating for her. She felt she had to interject something into the deafening silence. She hoped that if she said something, anything, it might make him stop all that annoying writing.

"Uhh, Lee, did I mention that I had another seizure since I last saw you?"

Her plan seemed to do the trick. Lee looked up from his notepad, peering over the top of his wire-rimmed glasses, and then responded,

"No, Sharelle, you didn't mention that. So what were the circumstances surrounding this latest episode?"

"It was when I went to have the picture I found of my daughter in front of the red car enlarged. So, I went to a copy store to have it enlarged, and that's when I could make out the name on the license plate and saw that it read IRAM. I don't know, I guess it was just too much of a shock for me."

"Well, what that suggests to me, Sharelle, is that you realize that your memory is slowly returning. It's a little scary not knowing what those lost memories will have in store for you. Sometimes we feel more secure just burying our heads in the sand and subconsciously choosing not to remember things.

For you, that red car and the name Mari are triggers. In other words, we now know that those two stimuli evoke a response within you. We just need to work on learning what it is about these triggers that disturb you. Nevertheless, I'm encouraged about your progress thus far, and you should be too."

It was such a relief for her to hear Lee say something positive, especially after doing all that writing. She was beginning to wonder if he was making a recommendation to have her committed. Or, maybe, writing a dissertation about paranoid schizophrenia, declaring her as the disorder's poster child. Now she could continue confidently in her mission of finding the rest of the pieces to the most complicated puzzle of her life. Still, she's anxious about the seizures and looks to Lee for assurance.

"So, Lee, are you saying I will continue to have these seizures until my memory fully returns?"

"Well, Sharelle, let's put it this way. Until you reconcile whatever it is that you're suppressing and allow it to surface, you will probably still have seizures. However, the more suppressed pain you confront head-on, the less suffering you will eventually experience.

As I said, you know what your triggers are. Once you acknowledge the pain these triggers represent, you'll get stronger, and the seizures will cease. It's like they say in the world of physical fitness—no pain, no gain. The only difference is that we're talking about mental fitness instead of physical fitness. So, don't be afraid of the pain. It's a means to an end, and the results are worth all of it."

"Let me ask you, how is your husband handling all of this? Is he supportive?" Lee asks.

"You mean my seizures or my writing?"

"Well—both, actually."

She hesitated while tears started to pool in her eyes. After a few seconds, she gathers herself and replies,

"He doesn't know about my seizures."

"He doesn't know? How is that possible, you haven't told him about them?"

"No, I don't want him to know."

"Why not?"

"Because I don't want him to think I'm crazy."

"Sharelle, that's your husband. I would think he'd be concerned, wouldn't you?"

"No, Lee. He would use it against me to make me feel bad about myself. That's what he does. Whenever I confide in him about something troubling me, he turns it back on me to make me the problem. So I stopped confiding in him a long time ago."

"That's really unfortunate. You do realize that there is a bigger problem at work here, don't you?"

"Oh, most definitely."

"Do you know what it could be?"

"Yes, I do. My husband is a porn addict. I believe he puts me down to deflect attention away from his own problem. I think he feels that as long as he can find fault with me, he won't feel so bad about himself."

"You're very perceptive, Sharelle. I know that I haven't met your husband, but from what you're telling me and what I know about sex addicts, that's exactly how they cope. They make those closest to them and those who can see through them to be the ones with the problem. Then, they will say and do anything to keep the focus off of themselves. So, I would venture to say that you've also been taking a lot of emotional and verbal abuse through the years."

"Yes, as much as I hate to admit it, I have."

"Well, believe it or not, that explains many things you're struggling with right now. Just understand—he can't destroy you unless you allow him to."

"Oh, I realize that, Lee, and I assure you I'm not going to let that happen!"

"Good for you. Well, that's about all we have time for today. So just remain encouraged, and I'll see you next week, okay?"

"Okay, Lee, thank you. I'll see you next week."

An Explicit Nature

Chapter Forty-Two

F our days have passed since she called and asked Blake if he could help her with information about the red car. She was beginning to wonder if he had just blown her off, or if maybe he simply forgot. She picked up the phone with intentions of calling him again but then got cold feet. Then, her phone rang as if through some sort of telepathic communication. It was Blake. Before the phone could barely complete the second ring, she answered.

"Hello?"

"Hey, Sharelle, it's Blake."

She tried to appear surprised that it was him calling. She didn't want to give him the impression that she was too overly anxious to hear from him. She apparently forgot that caller I.D. is standard issue with all cell phone service these days. She'd have to answer the phone blindfolded not to know who was calling. Still, she responds as if taken by surprise.

"Oh, hi, Blake. I didn't catch your voice at first. How're you?"

"I can't complain. How 'bout you?"

"Everything's good, so what's up?"

"Well, I just wanted to get back to you with some information I found."

"Oh great! You did find something?"

"Yeah, I did. Your suspicion may be correct, Sharelle. That plate was a vanity plate issued by the Middlesex county DMV back in 2005. The car registered with that plate was a 2-door Nissan 300ZX2+2 in red. The owner's name is Mari, but I'm unsure how to pronounce the last name. It's H-O-W-E-N.

Sharelle burst out in such hysterical laughter that tears came to her eyes. She laughed for a good ten seconds before collecting herself and then replied,

"You are kidding! I never knew the skank's last name, but I'm going to go with "Ho-in" because that fits her to a tee."

Blake tried to keep from laughing, but he couldn't resist the opportunity to comment.

"You know, centuries ago, people got their surnames from the types of trades that they were skilled in. You know, like a sheep herder was named Shepherd or a bread maker was named Baker. Family names were derived from the way that they earned a living. If that holds true, this poor girl didn't stand a chance. I mean, it was already pre-determined what her skills would be from birth. So all I can say is she better be very careful when pronouncing her name…."

They both share a hearty belly laugh together when Blake attempts to steer the conversation back on track.

"Anyway, don't get me started. What about the car, was the car in the picture a Nissan 300ZX?"

"I can't tell if the car is a Nissan 300ZX because where my daughter is standing in the picture, she's blocking the nameplate. But it's definitely a sports car."

"Well, Blake, thanks for all your help. At least that answers my question. Now, I know my husband would stoop low enough to take my children around a woman he was cheating on me with. It all makes sense now.

My son actually told me once that he didn't want to ride with the lady with the red car anymore. When I asked who the lady was that he was speaking about, he told me that it was his daddy's cousin—whose name he couldn't remember, of course. So, it proves that Eric was obviously lying to the kids so that the only thing they could possibly tell me was a lie."

"Wow, Sharelle, I'm really sorry about that."

"No, Blake, it's okay because the more I learn about this person I've been living with all these years, the stronger I become in my decision to leave him. So once again, thank you, and I'll talk with you soon, okay?"

"Okay, Sharelle, just let me know if there's anything more I can do to help, alright?"

"Okay, Blake, thanks again. Bye-bye."

She sat thinking about her conversation with Blake. She felt sorry for her two children. She thought about how confused they must have been, having been placed in a situation where they knew something wasn't right concerning their father and this other woman. They were both too young to question the lies their father was feeding them, yet their young instincts told them that something didn't feel right.

"Maybe that's why Darius asked me if I knew his daddy's cousin with the red car. In his own juvenile way, he was trying to see if I could confirm his dad's story. A story which he was, obviously, thoroughly unconvinced of," thought Sharelle.

In the middle of daydreaming, she suddenly saw an image quickly race through her mind. She shook her head as if to shake the image out of her consciousness, but it returned with even greater frequency and vivid clarity. It was an image of her driving a car while being chased by another. The vehicle that chased her was, predictably, a red sports car, a red sports car that looked a lot like Mari Howen's.

As the image repeatedly played in her mind, she got a cold chill and started to tremble. She strained as she shut her eyes, trying to think of other things, but the image kept creeping back into her thoughts. It was as though it was taunting her, demanding that it become the focus of her attention.

As the image became sharper in detail, she started breaking out in a cold sweat and the trembling intensified. Within seconds, her right arm started to quiver. The quivering began in her shoulder and continued until it worked its way down the entire length of her arm. Her fingers clenched into a tightly balled fist until her nails dug painfully into the palm of her hand. She could feel her throat getting dry as she hyperventilated rapidly through her mouth.

Just as she feared, the arm started to jerk out of control and knocked over a vase of fresh-cut flowers that sat on the nightstand. Her intention was to clean up the mess, but the unruly arm was so out of control that she couldn't do anything except ride it out. Desperate to regain control, she catapulted herself onto her bed, pinning the arm beneath her.

Unrelenting was the image of the red sports car that continued to fire over and over through her mind. The arm continued to writhe violently under the weight of her body as if it had a mind of its own and longed to be free. With it now restricted in its movement, the mental image of the car chase started to slow down.

Rather than racing through her mind repetitively, the image began moving in slow motion. The same image scrolled through her mind like a broken reel-to-reel filmstrip. Instead of a smooth transition from one scene to another, the image skipped erratically from beginning to end, then back to the beginning again.

It was as though a remote control gave commands to her brain, and somehow, buttons were repeatedly being pressed, alternating between pause and play. Approximately three minutes had passed when she noticed that the arm had calmed down considerably, and the mental images faded. She remained still. She lay on the bed until a sense of peace shrouded her exhausted body and released the grip from her anguished mind.

With the threat of the seizure finally over, she remembered something that Tracy had communicated to her in one of her crazy text messages. She remembered something was in it about 2+2, but she wasn't exactly sure how it read. So, she decided to call Tracy to refresh her memory.

"Hello?" Tracy answers.

"Hey girl, whatcha doin'?"

"I'm trying to find these stupid receipts that Darryl put, who knows where so that he can file our taxes. Why, what's up, girl?"

"Oh, I'm sorry, looks like this is a bad time."

"No, no, it's okay. I need a break anyway. What's up?"

"Tracy, I talked to Blake like you suggested, and he identified the car in the picture."

"Really? So, who's the owner of it?"

"Well, it did belong to that woman, just like I thought. Her name is Mari Howen."

"See, I told you he could help, what else did he say?"

"He told me what type of car it was, which is why I'm calling. In one of your text messages, there was something mentioned about IRAM's reign, wrath, or something like that. I'm trying to find out if there's any relevance to some of the information that Blake gave me.

Of course, when you first read the message, I wasn't trying to hear all that, but for some reason, now it stands out in my mind. I don't know why, but I think that text message might contain a clue about that car. Do you know which one I'm talking about?"

"Let me see, I think I remember seeing it just the other day saved in my phone. Hold on a minute while I look through my saved text messages...."

She waited anxiously while Tracy scrolled through her many saved texts. The fascination with texting was something that she would never understand. She was convinced that texting would be the eventual downfall of interpersonal relationships as they had traditionally been known. After a few seconds, Tracy returns and says,

"Okay, I found it. Tell me if this is the one:

"TWENTY-SIX LETTERS FROM A TO Z; IN TWO OF THEM, THERE WILL IRAM BE. TRUST THE MIND'S EYE TO HELP YOU SEE HOW DANGEROUSLY CLOSE DEATH CAME TO THEE."

"Is that the one you're talking about?"

Frustration was becoming evident in Sharelle's voice. She sucked her teeth and replied,

"No, it's definitely not that one. That one makes no sense whatsoever!"

"Wait a minute, Shar. We figured out who IRAM is through these premonitions, so don't be so quick to discount their meaning. Let's look at this one for a minute and see if we can figure it out."

"Be for real, Tracy. Mari is four letters, not two. Besides, these aren't premonitions; they're freakin' riddles, okay?"

"Shar, just calm down and listen a minute. I don't think this is referring to her name at all."

"Well, what else could it be? It says that IRAM will be in two letters between A and Z. IRAM has four letters. It's nothing but nonsense!"

"Shar, it says that IRAM, now known as Mari, is in two letters of the alphabet, right?"

"Right."

"Well, generally speaking, if you're in something, then you're probably surrounded or enclosed by it, right?"

"Okay, I hear you."

"Okay, so we need to think along those terms. We just need to go through the alphabet to see which letters make sense, that's all."

Sharelle becomes flustered and asks Tracy to move on to something else.

"Oh boy! This is way too much like work for me. Can we return to this one later and look into the one I called you about?"

"Okay, well, I think I have the one you're talking about written here in my journal. How about this one?

CRIMSON VISIONS YOU WILL HAVE RESULTING OUT OF IRAM'S WRATH…"

Sharelle interrupts.

"Yep, that's it! Hold up a minute. I'm writing this down. Visions you will have…out of IRAM's wrath. Okay, now what else?"

"…IT ALL COMES DOWN TO SIMPLE MATH;

LET 2+2 DIRECT YOUR PATH," recites Tracy.

She finishes writing down the passage, thinking initially that she was on to something. After taking a second look, she realizes that she didn't understand the message after all.

"Okay, I got it! Hmm, nah, that one doesn't make any sense to me either."

"What doesn't make sense about this one, Shar?"

"You know, the part about 2+2 directing your path.

Obviously, 2 + 2 equals four, and I think it has something to do with a car, but four? Four what? Tires? Is it saying to follow the path of four tires? That tells me absolutely nothing. That could be anybody!"

Totally not phased by Sharelle's ranting, Tracy interjects.

"Shar, what type of car did Blake say that it was?"

"He said it was a 2005 Nissan 300ZX, why? Wait a minute, that's it! The two letters of the alphabet are Z and X! That must be it. She drove a 300ZX!"

Suddenly Tracy got a brainstorm and told her to hang on while she logged onto the internet. When she returned, she announced that she found some not-so-trivial trivia that would interest her.

"Well, check this out. Did you know there's such a thing as a Nissan 300ZX, 2+ 2?"

"Oh my God! You're kidding! Okay, so now I'm convinced. So those are the two letters Z and X, and then if you tack on 2+2, that's exactly the kind of car Blake said it was, a 300ZX 2+2!"

Chapter Forty-Three

Saturday morning, Eric awoke much earlier than his usual pre-dawn waking hour. It was somewhere between 3:15 and 3:30. Sharelle wasn't exactly sure because it took her a few minutes to reach a level of consciousness to look at the clock.

She was being jostled around by Eric's persistent attempts at repositioning her. It seemed to her that she had only been asleep for maybe two hours. That seemed to be the only time he wanted intimacy—when she had been completely exhausted and had been up late. She had been up writing until around 1:00 a.m. She had been working on her most recent project, entitled *So Distant Lover*.

It was to be a story about a man who was emotionally handicapped and had difficulty in relationships due to his inability to express love for a woman. Although the story had nothing to do with Eric, she saw many parallels that could be drawn from him.

As Eric persistently tried to arouse her from her state of sleep, she became cognizant that she was being tossed around and snapped angrily at him.

"Would you stop it!" she protested.

Angry that she would not oblige him in his cave-man attempt at love-making, he fired back, saying,

"What the hell is wrong with you?"

"Eric, I just got to sleep, and I'm tired!" she replied.

"You're tired? You're always tired. I'm the tired one. I'm tired of your tired ass!"

The abuse was getting to be more and more frequent and just plain intolerable. Sharelle never could understand how a person could go from having intimate feelings toward someone to, in an instant, despising them. It only served to infuriate her that much more.

It seemed that Lee hit the nail right on the head. Eric was unhappy with himself and was determined to dehumanize her because of it. It wasn't her fault. She tried to tell him about the consequences of overindulgence in pornography. She showed him literature on the subject, which clearly outlined the gradual destructive effects on one's psyche. He's heard countless sermons by the pastor of their church, cautioning against inviting that evil spirit into one's life. Yet, he always knew more than any psychologist, any pastor, and, certainly, more than she could ever know.

Like so many times before, she got up and left the room. She went upstairs to the guest bedroom and attempted to go back to sleep, but tossed and turned instead. The vile words he directed at her echoed through her mind like a broken record. The more she tried to ignore the demeaning comments, the louder they resonated. Then, to further torment her consciousness, the images of the red car chasing her returned.

Before long, she found herself in a battle, and the battle was being fought all within her mind. She imagined the unimaginable suffering of the prisoners of war. On a much smaller scale, she, too, was being subjected to torment. Hers was the propagandizing tactics of mind control courtesy of her spouse coupled with sleep deprivation.

The words kept getting louder and louder, and the images became more and more graphic. Then, as the battle raged in her mind, a strange thing happened. The words became muted, and the visions of the car chase became more vivid and more telling.

Instead of the same chase scene being played repetitively, scenes that had never appeared before were suddenly revealed. Now the red car was ramming her car bumper. There was no longer any doubt. This was the same car as the one in the picture with Maya. She began to recognize the surrounding landscape in the images. She saw herself driving down a dirt road that ran through an area densely populated with trees.

Her body became rigid as she saw her car race down the darkened path. Then, unexpectedly, she felt a sensation that made her sit straight up and grip the sheets on the bed tightly. It was the sensation of falling. All of her senses seemed to engage at once as she experienced this harrowing event.

Suddenly, there was a brief moment of total darkness out of the blue. Then, as a bolt of lightning, more frightening images flashed through her mind. The sensory information fired wildly throughout her brain—one intense image after another.

Her heart pounded as she saw images of her head slamming into the steering wheel, causing her skull to fracture and the flesh on her forehead to rip open. She saw images of blood gushing from the gaping wound on her head. The blood rushed from her head profusely. The bleeding mimicked the ebb and flow of the rhythmic beat of her pulsating heart.

As tears rolled down her cheeks, she sat trembling in horror due to the graphic nature of the nightmarish visions. They had become too explicit, and she wanted them to stop. Then, the cerebral rampage started to wane just as she felt she couldn't take anymore.

The images played out with such realism that she knew they couldn't have been figments of her imagination. Then, as her brain activity subsided, one final image appeared before it all faded to black. It was the painful vision of herself—slumped unconscious over the steering wheel of her own car.

This was her day of reckoning. It had finally happened. Her memory had returned—all at once. She had prayed for this day to come, yet she didn't feel, in the least, like celebrating. Although she never in her wildest dreams thought it would happen this way, she would take it any way she could.

As frightening as it was, she finally had the answers she was looking for. Just as she had thought—her accident was no accident. Instead, it was a carefully orchestrated plot—with the intent to kill.

After settling down, her thoughts immediately turned to Blake's newspaper article about the woman in the swamp. She thought to herself,

"Could that have been me? Was I the woman in the swamp?"

She was anxious to call him to get more details about the accident, but it was too late to call. So instead, she decided to get some sleep and reach out to him in the morning.

Chapter Forty-Four

It was 7:00 a.m. when she woke up. She felt different somehow. She felt light and liberated. She didn't understand why, but she felt alive for the first time in years. Although it was early, she just had to call Tracy to tell her about her visions during the night.

"Tracy, are you awake? It's Shar. Wake up. I have something to tell you."

Tracy tried to sound as if she were already awake, but it was evident from her voice's raspiness that she had awakened her out of deep sleep.

"Yeah, I was just turning over. What time is it?" Tracy asked while still in a daze.

"It's about ten after seven. Are you awake?"

Yawning, Tracy answers.

"Yeah, yeah, I'm awake. What's up?"

"Tracy, I had a seizure last night."

"You had a what? A seizure!! Are you okay?"

"Yeah, yeah, I'm fine. Actually, I don't know if you can call it a seizure, but it was weird. I kept seeing all these visions in my head. They were visions of Mari chasing me in my car, ramming her car into mine, and then forcing me over an embankment into a swamp. It was like I was watching a movie, and I was the starring role."

"Wait a minute, wait a minute. Was this a dream?"

"No, it wasn't a dream. I was fully awake, but my mind was racing, and these images were vividly running through my head. Tracy, I'm certain of it, Mari tried to kill me. She forced my car off the road into a swamp, and I was knocked unconscious. That's how my accident happened and how I lost my memory. I just know it!"

"Okay, Shar, calm down. How do you know for sure?"

"Because I remember now, I was coming to your house that day. It was the day of your housewarming. You were having a cookout, and I was supposed to be there a little early to help. I remember I was running late because Eric and I had an argument, and he left in a huff. I was trying to wait for him to return, but when he didn't return after so long, I just left. You know, your housewarming was around the same time Mari called my house, threatening me and telling me that I'd better leave town."

"Shar, you better be careful. Those are serious allegations. You have to be absolutely, positively sure about this before you go making claims like that."

"I know Tracy, but I feel strongly about this. I know I'm right. I just can't prove it."

"Well, doesn't Eric know how the accident happened?"

"Of course he does, but he's hiding something. Whenever I ask him about my accident, he gets upset and tells me I skidded off the road and ran into a tree. Then he just blows me off by saying that the doctors advised him to help me keep my mind off of it. He says it's for my own good."

"Well, we both know that's a bunch of crap," replies Tracy.

"You see what I'm saying? I refuse to let this go. I have got to get to the bottom of it. So, I'm going to call Blake to see if he can get the investigation reopened."

"Well, the universe did send me messages that urged you to investigate. However, you said there was no evidence of foul play in the original investigation, isn't that right?"

"That's what I was told, but there's more to this than what Eric has told me, so I'm just gonna pursue it myself."

"Well, one thing I know about you is when you decide to go after something, wild horses can't stop you. So, I hope I won't regret getting you all fired up about this. You know I got your back, right? Just promise me you'll be careful, okay?"

"Girl, I got this covered now that I have my memory back."

After Sharelle's conversation with Tracy, she waited another couple hours before calling Blake. She was surprised to reach him directly on the first try. She made her case for a new investigation of the accident.

"Blake, I have some good news!"

"Hey, I always like to hear good news, what's up?"

"I have my memory back. Isn't that great?"

"Wow, Sharelle, that is great. I'm really happy for you. How'd it happen? Did you just wake up and remember stuff all of a sudden?"

"Well, it's a little more complicated than that, but I did remember a lot about my accident, which is why I called you."

"Well, I'm not sure where I fit into all this, but okay, let's hear it."

"Well, I need you to help me get the investigation of my accident reopened."

"After all these years, Sharelle? I don't know. I mean…"

"Blake, I know, without a doubt, that Mari Howen tried to kill me."

"Hold up! How can you be so sure?"

"You know that article in your photo album about the woman in the swamp?"

"Yeah, but…"

"Blake—that was me!"

"Whoa, whoa! Wait a minute, wait a minute, hold it. Why on God's green earth would you think that woman who ended up in the swamp was you, Sharelle?"

"Well, let's start with the fact that my accident occurred on the same day and in the same general area."

"Yes—coincidentally."

"And how 'bout the car pulled from the swamp, It was light blue. It just so happens that I owned a light blue BMW that was totaled when

I had my accident."

"Sharelle, do you know how many light blue Beamers there were, and still are, out there?"

"Well, my guess is only one that was found in a swamp in the New Jersey Pine Barrens. But, c'mon, Blake, there are just too many similarities to ignore this. I truly believe that the car that was in the swamp 15 years ago was my car, and Mari Howen was the one that was responsible for it being there."

Blake defends. "Look, the police conducted an investigation and found no evidence of foul play in that case. It was simply ruled an accident, Sharelle."

"Okay, that's true, but do you remember telling me that you found red paint chips on the bumper of the woman's car that was pulled out of the swamp?"

"Yeah, I lead the forensic investigation in that case, but they disregarded the forensic evidence, again, because there was no sign of foul play."

"Blake, I beg you to request that the detectives look at the forensic evidence. I'm certain it will show that Mari Howen's car impacted mine and forced it into the water."

"Sharelle, you know I'll do anything for you, but this is monumental. I mean, what happens if you're wrong? My reputation is at stake here."

She pleads with Blake, confident that she can't be wrong in her assessment of the details.

"I swear, I wouldn't ask if I weren't sure about this. Please—this will haunt me for the rest of my life if I don't find out the truth."

"Alright, I'll make a few calls and get back to you."

"Thank you, thank you! You have no idea how much this means to me, and I know I owe you big time!"

"Oh yeah, and you better believe that!"

A few days passed, and no word from Blake. Sharelle started becoming anxious, but hesitated to call him again for fear of being a nuisance.

So, she waited. To keep her mind off of things, she decided to engage in one of her favorite pastimes, shopping. Joy's baby shower would be coming up in a couple of weeks, and she didn't have a clue about what to buy. After all, she hadn't been baby shopping in almost twenty years. Outside of diapers, formula, and bibs, she was at a loss about what else babies needed. All she knew was that the baby would be a girl, which didn't help all that much.

Anyway, she thought shopping for a baby again might be fun, if nothing else, for the nostalgia of it all. On the way to the mall, she called Joy to gather some pointers. Joy answers,

"Hello?"

"Hey, Mommy, whatcha doin'?"

"I'm nesting."

"You're nesting what?"

"You know, I have all this pent-up energy, and I'm organizing and cleaning like crazy. I'm getting ready, you know, nesting."

"Ohhh, nesting! Okay, I almost forgot about that. Well, I won't keep you. I'm out shopping, and I just wanted some ideas about what to get for the baby, any ideas?"

"I don't know, anything, I guess."

"C'mon Joy, that does me no good. I don't know what to get, and I need your help."

"Okay, I tell you what, I'm on the baby registry with Talget. You can choose something from the items I selected there."

"Oh great! That makes things so much easier."

Out of nowhere, Joy throws her a curve. Not being the sentimental type, she hinted that she expects Sharelle to play a huge role in her baby's life. Joy replies,

"Yeah, I thought it would be more convenient for everyone. Even though, I was kind of expecting something a little more special from the baby's—*godmother*."

"Godmother? Oh my God, Joy, are you asking me to be the baby's godmother?"

"Well, of course, who else would I ask?"

"Ah, Joy, you're gonna make me cry now. That's so sweet."

"So, is that a yes?"

"Yes, are you kidding? I'd be honored to be the godmother of your baby. Thank you."

"Don't thank me, I'm just glad you said you'll do it 'cause I'm gonna need some help!"

"Oh please, girl, I'm excited about it! Besides, they say it takes a village to raise a child, and I'm more than happy to do my part. By the way, speaking of villages, will Prince Charming be playing any role in the baby's upbringing?"

"Who, Chip? Of course! As a matter of fact, he already is. You know, he insisted on buying the baby's furniture."

"Are you serious?"

"Yeah, and he says he wants to be a father figure to the baby too."

"Wow, now that's a switch, a single white guy who wants to play daddy to someone else's black baby!"

"Don't laugh. It's not as uncommon as you think. It's en vogue for white people to adopt black babies these days, you know. Look at Angelina and Madonna."

"Yeah, well, I guess you've got a point there. However, you can't deny that it's a very commendable thing that they're doing. Oh hey, I have some good news to tell you."

"Oh yeah? What is it?"

"I'm getting my memory back."

"Really? That's great, Shar! What happened?"

"Things just started coming back to me, and now I remember how my accident happened."

"Wow, well, it's about time. So, tell me, what do you remember?"

"Well, I've had these nightmares about this red car chasing me, and I just recently found out why. Remember I told you about Eric's little fling with some chick 15 years ago?"

"Yeah, what about it?"

"Well, that hussy threatened me back then, telling me that I'd better leave town, and when Eric dumped her so that we could reconcile, she tried to take me out."

"What do you mean she tried to take you out?"

"Remember, I told you that I thought that someone tried to have me killed, and you laughed at me? Well, I was right. She tried to kill me, Joy. She forced my car off the road into a swamp, and when my car hit the water, I hit my head on the steering wheel. That's how I got a head injury which caused my memory loss."

"Get the hell outta here! You mean that trick actually tried to kill you?"

"Yeah, sounds like something out of a movie, huh?"

"That chick is straight crazy! Please tell me you're going to press charges and have that psycho bitch locked up, Shar?"

"Well, that's my hope, but I have to prove it first, and it has been 15 years since the accident."

"I don't give a damn if it's been since the beginning of time, that bitch needs to go down!"

"Don't worry, I'm workin' on it. I've got Blake looking into it for me."

"Shar, you can't tell me that Eric didn't know something about this."

"I'm not sure, but I remember seeing a passenger in that car with her, and it looked like a guy, but the windows were tinted, and I couldn't tell who it was."

"It was probably Eric."

"I really don't know, Joy."

"You know, I always thought there was something fishy about that story Eric told me about you running into some damn tree!"

"Yeah, well, your instincts were right. I definitely didn't hit any tree. Anyway, girl, I'm at the mall now, so let me go and find the perfect gift for my goddaughter-to-be."

"Okay, I'll talk to you later."

"Okay, happy nesting!"

Chapter Forty-Five

She had gotten the news from Blake, which was precisely what she expected. A new investigation of her accident uncovered previously overlooked evidence of foul play. Although it would take a few weeks for the D.A.'s office to convene a grand jury, the inclusion of the forensic evidence would prove invaluable in bringing charges against Mari Howen and, subsequently, taking the case to trial.

Sharelle was ecstatic about the news. She would finally have a chance to look her adversary in the face and know her true identity. Finally, this woman who caused such pain and anguish would pay a hefty price, and deservedly so. This stalker, who once stalked vindictively, would now be stalked judicially. Her stalkers would be a jury of twelve strangers. She found incredible irony in the whole situation. She wondered what it was about a man that could drive a woman to such desperation. She was confident that in all her years on the face of the earth, she hadn't found any man worth killing over and most definitely not worth going to prison over.

Apparently, Ms. Howen felt differently, at least she did back then. Chances are she'll have second thoughts now, but remorse won't get her very far. Miss Thing will be looking at fifteen to twenty on lockdown, all over a sex-addicted man, whose only motive from Jump Street was to feed his addiction. Sharelle imagined that the humiliation alone had to be eating her up inside. Now, to add insult to injury, her freedom will be snatched right from under her.

Yet, to Sharelle, somehow, it didn't really seem fair. This woman was lied to, deceived, and sold a bad bill of goods by a man who didn't care about his impact on another person's life. Eric didn't care that this woman he cheated with would fall hopelessly in love with him and stop at nothing to have him. He didn't care that this woman might be mentally fragile and easily driven to the point of insanity. Not that Sharelle felt pity for the woman, still she wondered,

"Isn't he, on some level, responsible for the destruction of this woman's life? Or, at the very least, isn't he responsible for her losing the ability to freely live it?"

In essence, he committed an act of war. He recklessly ascribed to a fundamental strategy known as destroy and conquer. The objective is to destroy the infrastructure and military might of a territory so that it can be conquered and, ultimately, possessed. That was precisely the strategy he used to get women, except to him, this was a tool for making love, not war.

Yet, while playing his little game, he got the strategy all wrong. He conquered women using deceit, but when caught in his own web of lies, he threw them away like garbage, leaving them emotionally destroyed. Sharelle knew there had been other lives that he had conquered and destroyed as well, fragile, desperate lives, all for the sake of playing the game.

From the time Sharelle was a young child, it had been her nature. She always had compassion for the underdog. For sure, Mari Howen was dead ass wrong, but she felt that the onus shouldn't be entirely upon her shoulders either. Her opinion was that he acted as an instigator in the matter. If not for his lies and deceit, Mari Howen would never have seen her as the enemy.

Now, Sharelle would have to confront Eric with this new development. She thought long and hard about how she would approach the subject with him. She didn't want an argument, but it was inevitable that the dialogue wouldn't be pleasant. Finally, she decided the best way to handle it was not to tip-toe around it but to just do it!"

She went upstairs where he was playing a video game. She entered the room with a sense of purpose and addressed him in a tone that indicated that this was something serious.

"Eric, we have to talk," she exclaimed.

"Uh oh, what'd I do now?"

"I know how my accident happened, Eric. I didn't crash into any tree."

"Oh, c'mon Shar, not again with the accident! Can't you just give it a rest?"

"No, I couldn't, Eric! Not at least, until I got the truth. I have my memory back, and now I know what really happened, and I think you do too."

"Okay, what supposedly really happened, Shar?"

"That trick, Mari Howen, tried to kill me. She intentionally ran me off the road into the swamp and then left me for dead."

Eric nervously began running his hand back and forth across his forehead and asked,

"Where are you getting all this from?"

"I remember it! It all came back to me, and I remember it like it happened yesterday! Besides, I've checked it out, and it's been confirmed that I'm right."

"What do you mean it's been confirmed? Confirmed how?"

"I appealed for a new investigation, and when they reopened the case, they found new evidence. As a result, Mari Howen is being charged with attempted murder, and I need to know if you were involved."

He choked on his saliva, and his eyes stretched as wide as half-dollars. He sat straight up in his chair, placed the video game controller down on the ottoman, and asked,

"Shar, are you suggesting that I tried to kill you?"

"I'm suggesting someone was in that car with Mari Howen, and I need to know if that someone was you, Eric."

"Look, I might be a lot of things, but I'm not a murderer. Besides, do you actually think that I would try to kill you over a piece of ass?!"

274

"I'm simply trying to get to the truth, and if you were involved, I'd like to find out from you instead of from a detective. Either way, the truth is going to come out."

He leaned forward in his chair, shook his head, and buried his face in his hands. He sat silently for a good minute or so. Perspiration began forming along his hairline, indicating that he was starting to feel the heat. He gradually lifted his head, looked at her with tears in his eyes, and confessed,

"I told her not to do it, I begged her not to, but she wouldn't listen to me. After you and I argued that morning I went to her house. I went there to break it off with her. I didn't want anything to do with her anymore, so I told her that. She was just leaving to go somewhere and asked me to take a ride with her to talk.

I told her I was leaving and that I had to get back home because I was going to Darryl and Tracy's cookout in South Jersey. She started crying and pleaded with me to get into the car, so we could talk."

"So, you got in the car with her?" she inquired.

"Yeah, I thought we would just sit in the car or go somewhere to talk, but she jumped on the parkway and started heading south. I told her to let me out, but she kept driving."

Still doubting his sincerity, she questions,

"I'm sure she had to stop at some point. So, why didn't you just bail out?"

"Her car had child protection door locks where only the driver controls all of the doors. She had me locked in so that I couldn't bail out."

"Well, what made her stop in the Pine Barrens?"

"After we went so far down the parkway, I told her what exit to get off. I told her that she might as well drop me off at Darryl and Tracy's house. She wanted to go with me to the cookout, but I told her you were coming. I told her I would be there with my wife and that she and I were through.

After she got off at the exit, she turned down a dirt road because a tree had fallen, blocking the road. So she started down the detour, and the fool pulled the car over to the side of the road and went ballistic on me. When she stopped the car, she just started screaming and hitting me. I tried to calm her down, but she was out of her mind."

"So, then, what did you do?"

"I grabbed her by the arm and shook her a couple of times, and she finally stopped and just sat there crying. I told her to get herself together and to take me to Darryl and Tracy's, and that's when I saw a car coming down the road in the side view mirror. At first, all I could see was a cloud of dust, but as the car got closer, I recognized that it was you."

"What did you do when you realized it was me?"

"I panicked, I guess—then I told her to sit there and wait until you passed by." But the dumb bitch decided to pull off right behind you. I told her not to do anything stupid, but she said if she couldn't have me, then you wouldn't either, and then she put her foot in the gas."

As Eric revealed more of the sordid details of Sharelle's accident, guilt pierced his soul to the core. Tears started to roll down his face as he told what happened next. His bottom lip trembled with each word he spoke about that terrible day in the Pine Barrens. She prods for more details.

"What happened next, Eric?"

"I asked her what the hell she was doing, and she didn't say a word. She just stepped on the gas even harder. I grabbed the steering wheel, and we fought back and forth for control of it, and then before I knew it, she rammed into the back of you. Shar, I swear I tried to prevent her from forcing you over that embankment, but nothing worked. She was hell-bent on forcing you over, and if I interfered, we were going to crash. At that point, she didn't care about anything."

"After my car went over, what did you do?"

Eric began bawling like a baby. He was so remorseful that he could hardly speak, but she wasn't moved by his tears. When she thought about all the years she suffered because of his selfish behavior, his tears only made her more unyielding in her quest for the truth. Completely un-moved by his meltdown, she presses him to continue.

"What did you do? Tell me what you did!"

He responds almost unintelligibly.

"I—I tried to help you. I tried! I swear I tried!

"How did you try to help me, Eric?"

"I told her—I said to her, I'll slap the shit outta you if you don't let me out this car right now! I didn't care if I was killed in the process. I would try to save you even if I had to die trying! After you went into the water, she didn't even look back; she just sped off. I just thank God we came to a gas station about 3 miles away, just before the highway, and that's when she finally let me out. I ran over to the guy who worked there and told him to call for an ambulance because a car went into the swamp. So, the guy got his tow truck, and he and I hurried back to the site to rescue you."

"Who got me out, you and the tow truck driver or the paramedics?"

"Actually, it was the fire department rescue squad that pulled the car out and then got you out of the car. Then the paramedics started administering medical treatment right away, but it was me and the tow truck driver that kept the car from becoming totally submerged so that you didn't drown. We were able to get the hook onto the nose of the car to keep the water out of the front passenger area until the rescue squad took over."

"How did you get home?"

"I rode with you to the hospital in the ambulance."

"Didn't you have to talk to the police about what happened?"

"Yeah, I did."

"What did you tell them?"

"Shar, what does it matter? I helped save your life."

"I want to know, Eric. What did you tell them?"

"Shar, please."

"Tell me!"

"Okay, okay! I told them that I…Shar, please don't make me do this. I mean, haven't you heard enough already?"

"Dammit, Eric! For once in your life, stop thinking about yourself and take responsibility for what you've done!"

Covering his face with his hands, he sobbed uncontrollably from humiliation. He couldn't admit to her how he lied to the police to cover his infidelity. Yet, she insisted that he tell her how he handled the accident. He took a few seconds to gather himself and recounted to her the story he had given to the police.

"Okay, Shar, I'll tell you."

After a long pause and a deep sigh, he confesses,

"I told them I had a friend give me a ride to the cookout because you had already left me. When they asked me why I didn't drive our other car, I said I had planned for us to ride home together and didn't want to drive home in separate cars. I told them that as we were driving down the dirt road, I noticed your car floating in the water and had my friend rush me back to the nearest gas station for help. I didn't tell them who it was I was with. And I didn't tell them that you were forced off the road and into the swamp. Now, are you happy?"

"Happy? Am I happy? I should be happy that you lied to me, the police, and everybody else about how my accident happened? I should be happy that my own husband almost got me killed over a stinkin' piece of tail? You want to know if I'm happy, Eric? I'll show you just how happy I am, watch me!"

An Explicit Nature

Chapter Forty-Six

P arting is such sweet sorrow, as the saying goes. Unfortunately, Sharelle knew that to be all too true. As a result, she would begin making significant personal and professional life changes and disassociations.

One of the more bittersweet disassociations on the professional front would be with Lee. Today would be her last session. The two had formed a bond that each would sorely miss. Although this would be her farewell visit, she was delighted to leave him with a glowing report. She outlines the details of the past few weeks.

"Lee, it was the weirdest thing. I can't believe how my memory just came back all at once. It's really amazing."

"Sharelle, that's wonderful! I'm so happy for you. Now, what about the seizures? Have you had any lately?"

"No, that's what's so amazing to me. When my memory started returning, I thought maybe I would have a seizure, but I didn't then and haven't had one since. To top things off, I just became a godmother three days ago! Isn't that great?"

"That's all good news, Sharelle, excellent news. That's what I like to hear. So, it sounds like everything is going well then, huh?"

"Well, I wouldn't say that, but things are looking up."

"What else could be better? You're seizure-free, you have your memory back, and you're a new godmother."

"Yeah, and I'm so grateful, believe me, but with the return of my memory came some disturbing insight into the accident I had years ago."

"Really, what's that?"

"Well, my husband lied to me about how the accident occurred and, well, to make a long story short, it was a murder attempt by his ex-lover."

"What? A murder attempt?"

"Yeah, I didn't crash into a tree after all. You know, all those night-mares about the red car?"

"Of course."

"Well, I guess my mind was trying to piece the details of the acci-dent together. As I discovered in my sessions with you, the red car was a significant part. The woman he had an affair with drove a red sports car, and she ran me off the road into a swamp.

When I hit the water, my head hit the steering wheel, and I was knocked unconscious. That's how I lost my memory. The authorities in New Jersey reopened the case, and new evidence was examined, and that's how they found out it was an attempted murder."

"Well, I hope they caught the woman."

"Oh yeah, I believe she's going away for a very long time."

"I bet your husband feels pretty bad about all the trouble he's caused, huh?"

"Well, I guess, but that's another thing. I don't know if I'll ever forgive him for lying about it all these years. So, we're separating, at least, until I can figure out what I want to do. In the meantime, he's going back to therapy for his addiction. It's a step in the right direction. At least he can now admit that his porn addiction spiraled out of control. So, we'll just have to wait and see."

"Will you be staying in the area or are you moving elsewhere."

"No, I'm going to stay right here. He's moving into an apartment."

"Well, you're probably both doing the best thing for each of you. I hope it all works out for you, Sharelle, whatever you decide to do."

"Thanks, Lee."

"Well, this has been quite an experience for you. Do you have any questions or thoughts?"

"Yeah, as a matter of fact, I do. First, I want to thank you for helping me through all of this. I really couldn't have done it without you.

Secondly, I want to tell you that I've learned a lot about myself throughout this entire experience. However, the main thing that I learned is it's the painful things that we're forced to remember, that ultimately, help us to move on and forget."—Vivian Mason-Hunt

ABOUT THE AUTHOR

Mason-Hunt was born in Gary, Indiana and was raised in Los Angeles, California. As a Psychology major and alumna of Howard University, Washington, D.C. she developed a passion for the science. After college, she relocated to New Jersey where she married her husband of 41 years. They produced two amazing children, a son and a daughter, now adults. Currently, Vivian serves as a federal agent within the Department of the Treasury. An Explicit Nature, her first novel, illustrates her interest in the human psyche and is the prelude to future works relative to the subject. Vivian currently resides in suburban Nashville, Tennessee.

An Explicit Nature

www.ingramcontent.com/pod-product-compliance
Lightning Source LLC
Chambersburg PA
CBHW021505240626
47154CB00002B/514